CARNIVAL

firefly

Big Damn Hero by James Lovegrove (original concept by Nancy Holder)
The Magnificent Nine by James Lovegrove
The Ghost Machine by James Lovegrove
Generations by Tim Lebbon
Life Signs by James Lovegrove
Carnival by Una McCormack
What Makes Us Mighty by M.K. England

CARNIVAL

firefly

BY UNA McCORMACK

TITAN BOOKS

Firefly: Carnival
Hardback edition ISBN: 9781789095098
Paperback edition ISBN: 9781789095111
E-book edition ISBN: 9781789095104

Published by Titan Books
A division of Titan Publishing Group Ltd
144 Southwark Street, London, SE1 0UP.

First paperback edition: January 2023
1 3 5 7 9 10 8 6 4 2

A CIP catalogue record for this title is available from the British Library.

Printed and bound by CPI Group (UK) Ltd, Croydon, CR0 4YY.

Did you enjoy this book?
We love to hear from our readers. Please email us at readerfeedback@
titanemail.com or write to us at Reader Feedback at the above address.

To receive advance information, news, competitions, and exclusive offers
online, please sign up for the Titan newsletter on our website

TITANBOOKS.COM

DEDICATED TO

the Whitecrow crew, the very best band of rebels

AUTHOR'S NOTE

The events in this novel take place during the
Firefly TV series, before the episode "Heart of Gold".

E lsewhere in the city of Neapolis, people were getting ready for the party. Not here. Here, in a narrow back street, underneath the bright bunting and the red-and-yellow hanging flowers, Ava Jones was running for her life.

Ava was fourteen years old and very frightened. She'd arrived in the city from the sticks less than two hours ago. This was not the exciting adventure she'd dreamed of, but a terrifying encounter with people who meant her harm. People who were chasing after her.

Big tenement blocks loomed up on either side. Dashing past, Ava had seen gateways leading into little courtyards. She'd rattled a few gates, but they were locked. No entry. Nowhere to hide. Breathless, she ran on, shoving past a group of people, laden with bags, on their way back from the market.

"Zao gao!" one shouted after her. "Watch where you're going!"

Ava didn't stop; she didn't dare. Behind her the two men were gaining on her. She gulped and pushed on.

The alley led to a busy market square, full of noise and

smells, and people weaving their way through. Ava heard their chatter, the squawk and grunts of livestock. Kids running round, wearing bright masks shaped to look like sharp-eyed birds and fierce beasts. The rich scent of street food cooking on open grills, infused with unfamiliar spices. Covered stalls hawking everything: food, drink, leather goods and chintzy jewelry, tiny plaster Buddhas in many colors, and intricately carved wooden crosses. All manner of folks (Neapolis had something of everything, after all); buyers and sellers (you could buy anything here, after all); happy people, sad people, people with purpose, people who were lost, people who were trying to make themselves lost. Surely there was somewhere to hide in the middle of all this confusion? Surely one frightened girl could lose herself here in all of this?

Dodging into the first line of stalls, between a man selling brightly colored shirts and a woman selling a potent poteen, Ava felt a glimmer of hope at last. She dived under the cover of a little stall selling knitted and woven goods. Turning her back, Ava began to rummage through the wares. Another customer arrived, and the stallholder became busy. Furtively, ashamed of what she'd come to, Ava selected a silver and purple shawl, rolled it up, and tucked it under her arm. She left her own old orange scarf by way of an apology.

Leaving the stall, she saw a tray of *papier mâché* masks, and she grabbed one that looked like an owl. Quick as she could, she melted into the crowd, wrapping the shawl around her head and slipping on the mask. She was small for her age and would look like one of the other kids. She came out at the far side of the square. There she was caught up, for a moment, by a wavering line of monks passing through the street—chanting, dancing, shaking bells. By the time she untangled herself, she had been pulled to the far side of the market square.

Ava found herself beside a group of six or seven people, standing in front of a shrine to Buddha. She inched forward to take a better look. She'd never seen anything like this before. Nobody from Ava's town prayed to the little fat god. They were all good God-fearing Christians, with a preacher of their own who every week stood before them in the dark little wooden chapel and told them to work hard and not complain and that way the company would provide. Sisters, obey your brothers. Daughters, obey your fathers. Wives, obey your husbands. Ava used to see Aunty Eve's eyes rolling at this point. This shrine was a little house—almost like the nativity stable— with a pointed roof that was painted red, much brighter than anything from home. Young lime trees stood on either side, each one garlanded with little flickering white lights. The shrine itself was festooned with offerings: melted candles, drooping yellow flowers that released a heavy perfume, vivid little flags and ribbons. The little fellow himself sat on a plinth to the left-hand side. He was plaster, covered in gold paint, although rather chipped and weatherworn. Ava thought she knew how he felt.

She attached herself to the group and moved closer. Behind her, right up close, she heard a man speaking. "Well, I'm damned if I find her in all this ruttin' crush and I'm thinkin' we ain't gonna find her."

"We'd better, else there'll be hell to pay, *dǒng ma?*"

"Weren't my fault she got away—"

"You were the one holdin' her!"

"Gorram piece of *niú fèn* sunk her teeth in!"

Ava risked a look over her shoulder. They were here. The two men who, only half an hour ago, had grabbed her and tried to stick a needle in her arm. Ava, with more luck than perhaps she realized, had indeed bitten one, kicked the other, and made a run for it. She'd been running ever since. She turned back round quickly to face the shrine. Moving closer to the group, trying to make herself part of them, she accidentally knocked the elbow of the fellow next to her. She steeled herself for a blow, but instead he smiled, and offered her a burning taper.

"Do you want to light a candle?" he said.

"Can I?" she said.

"Sure." He pressed the taper into her hand.

"Do I say a prayer?" she said.

"If you like." He took a good look at her. "Remember— everything changes. Nothing stays the same. Good and bad."

Ava felt tears in her eyes. Well, she knew that already. A little awkwardly, she knelt down and reached forward to touch the taper against the wick of an unlit candle. The fire caught, and the little flame bounced up and into life. After a moment or two, Ava looked round. The men were gone. She could see no sign of them in the crowd.

"Be strong," she whispered. "Be brave." She clutched her stolen shawl tight and slipped away into the hinterland of the city.

* * *

Elsewhere, people were getting ready for the party. *Serenity*, moving purposely through the black, drew closer. In the hammock set up in the engine room, River Tam was sleeping at last, curled up like a child, her face turned to the lights sparkling on the wall. Her brother Simon—top three percent in his cohort across the Core worlds and gifted trauma surgeon (semi-retired)—began the slow process of extricating his hand from hers.

This was as delicate an operation as any Simon performed. Even the slightest movement might wake her. Sometimes he could settle her down again. Sometimes she woke screaming, and then… Well, that was not so much fun. That might mean another few hours holding her, talking to her, trying to reason with her… Simon Tam was a very tired man. In the couple of weeks since their sad visit to St. Albans, to take home the body of Private Tracey, River's sleep had been badly disturbed. Simon had been sitting beside her for hours on end, trying to persuade her that everything was okay. You couldn't always tell with River what the cause was, but this time, sifting through her angry, anxious words, Simon was sure that the idea of Tracey, sealed alive in his coffin, had triggered hazy recollections of River's own cryogenic confinement. No wonder she loved the sight of the vast and endless black.

Finger by finger, his breath held, Simon detached his hand from River's. She murmured a little, something incomprehensible (so much of what she said these days was

11

incomprehensible), but she did not wake. When he was free, Simon stood looking at her for a little longer, heart thumping with a particularly fierce combination of love, pride, fear, grief, loyalty, and anger. He watched the quakes and tremors and twitches as whatever horrors River had seen passed through her. Slowly, these fears dissipated, and her breathing softened, and her whole body settled into peace. Silently, he blew her a kiss. She wasn't going to wake, not for a while, and perhaps that meant that he could grab some rest now too. He left the engine room and found Kaylee hovering in the corridor outside.

"She sleepin'?"

"Mm," said Simon, rubbing his face. Looking after River was like a never-ending night shift on an emergency ward during the party season. "Let's hope it holds for a while."

Kaylee smiled. She was so nice, Simon thought; so pretty… "Thank you for the loan of your hammock," he said, hoping he sounded gallant.

Kaylee sparkled back at him, like the lights hanging up on the wall. She really was so pretty… "*Fang xin*," she said. "You're welcome."

"River loves the sound of the engine."

Her sweet smile faded ever so slightly. Frantically, Simon tried to work out what he'd done. Had he got it wrong again? He was grateful too, very grateful, beyond grateful, *stratospherically* grateful—should he have said that? He'd wanted to say something nice about her ship, because for some reason she loved this decrepit old deathtrap, but it looked like he'd gotten even that wrong…

Kaylee rallied. "Hey," she said, taking his arm, pulling him away into the corridor, "sounds like we're going to land on Bethel after all. You think you'll come down this time?"

"Bethel?" Simon tried to place the name. His memory used to be so good. "I... Do I know where that is? Why are we going there?"

"Inara has an appointment over the big weekend. And there's a new job. Came up on the Cortex as we entered local space."

"Oh good," said Simon, without enthusiasm. Usually, the jobs ended with him taking bullets out of people. "More exciting criminal fun times rounded off with two hours of emergency surgery. I can't wait."

"It's a *nice* world," insisted Kaylee. "It's *fancy*."

Simon, who had spent almost all of his life so far on one of the richest worlds in the Alliance, sincerely doubted that. He had a strong suspicion that Bethel was going to be yet another mud-splattered, cow-infested dung heap, but he knew better now than to voice such misgivings out loud. Kaylee got hurt when he said things like that, and Simon didn't want to hurt Kaylee.

"Well, maybe not *nice*," Kaylee amended, "but *fun*, you know? We should go and have some fun! You know how to have fun, don't you, Simon?"

Should he say yes? Should he go? He didn't want to be rude to her, not again, but all he wanted right now was some sleep... "I... I... Well, River..."

"River. Sure," she said, too brightly. "Of course. Yep." She headed off down the corridor to the dining room. Wearily, acutely aware that once again he'd disappointed, Simon followed. Shepherd Book was there already, and—*tā mā de*—so was Jayne, and Mal, all at one end of the table. Simon made himself a cup of chamomile tea and went to take the seat next to the Shepherd.

"Stinkin' flowers," Jayne muttered, as he went past with his cup, and then he seemed to recall that Simon could paralyze him and River could do whatever it was that River could now do. "Takes all sorts, I 'spose."

Simon, drinking his tea, listened half-heartedly to their conversation.

"In the Bible," said the Shepherd, looking dead straight at the captain, but with a twinkle in his eye, "Bethel is the place where Jacob had a vision of a ladder reaching up to heaven, with angels ascending and descending."

"Well, I ain't intendin' to have no visions, Shepherd," Mal replied, apparently unwilling to rise to the Shepherd's bait, "heaven-sent or otherwise, neither today nor tomorrow. We're here to do a job of work, nothing more—"

"The meaning of the name 'Bethel'," Shepherd Book went on, sonorously, "is the House of God—"

It was easy to be snide about chamomile tea, but it was soothing, good for relaxation, and it also helped you sleep. If Jayne Cobb cared, which Simon doubted…

"And there was I thinkin' Bethel was the party planet," said Kaylee, taking the seat across from Simon.

"Whores," agreed Jayne. Yes, that would be his idea of a party. "Hundreds of 'em. That's what I heard." He nudged the Shepherd, hard. "That what you mean by angels?"

"Not precisely," said the Shepherd. "There are many interpretations of the ladder, but I myself like the one where it represents a bridge between Heaven and Earth. I believe it signifies how God is always present in our lives. Or some kind of grace, at any rate."

Simon had taken up drinking chamomile tea during his residency. Some of the other students had laughed at him too, but they'd all been drinking it by the end, including those who were already halfway to being alcoholics. Now that had been a long year. Nothing compared to this one, mind you…

"I know there's all the gamblin'," said Kaylee, "but ain't there other stuff to do too this weekend?"

Simon thought he'd known back then what tired felt like. He'd been wrong, so very wrong. He was wrong about a lot of things, these days… Anyway, chamomile tea smelled *nice*. Made him think of being back home…

"*This stone that I have set up as a pillar will be God's house,*" intoned the Shepherd, "*and of all that you give me I will give you a tenth.*"

"I ain't givin' nobody a tenth of nothing," muttered Jayne.

"And for once I entirely agree with you," said the captain. Simon, closing his eyes, let the conversation wash over him. Perhaps some part of his brain would be able to sort through the noise and determine whether there was any useful information to be gleaned…

"Like, ain't there live music, and dancin', and that kind of thing?" said Kaylee. "It ain't all whorin' and gamblin'—"

"It ain't?" said Jayne, disappointed.

"We're here to work, Kaylee," said Mal, "not to party."

"Don't be so grouchy, Captain. It's Carnival! Hey, maybe I'll get to wear my dress again—"

"It's a very beautiful passage," said Book. "God's promise to us that even in our direst need we can consider ourselves not alone—"

"I'm sure it's a fine piece of fiction," said the captain, exasperation rising, "and you're more'n welcome to read it to yourself in the privacy of your own quarters, Shepherd, where you'll not be botherin' anyone else, but I'll thank you to keep all holy talk away from my dining table—"

"You like live music, Simon?"

Though the tea would certainly be nicer with a spoonful of honey stirred in... Was there any honey on *Serenity*? On Bethel? Were there bees on Bethel...?

"Simon?"

Simon, jerking awake, was suddenly aware of an expectant silence. He opened his eyes to see four people staring straight at him, with looks ranging on a scale from fond indulgence to violent dislike.

"I'm... I'm sorry," said Simon. "I... I... I think I must have dozed off. What were you saying, Kaylee?"

Jayne laughed. The Shepherd smiled. Kaylee looked hurt. "Don't worry. It don't matter." *Wrong again*, thought Simon. He grasped around for something to say. "Um, is there something special about this weekend?"

Kaylee brightened. "It's Carnival!"

"Ah." Simon didn't have a clue what that meant, and he didn't want to risk hurting Kaylee again by asking. "Carnival."

"If Captain Misery there will only let us off the ship—"

"Maybe when we're done with the job, Kaylee—"

Carnival, thought Simon. Was this something he needed to be worrying about? He sighed, and the Shepherd leaned in for a quiet word. "Shut your eyes again, son," he murmured. "We'll call you when we need you."

The Shepherd, Simon thought, was a very wise man. *Bethel*, he thought, *another dung heap*. But one that Kaylee wanted to see. Simon couldn't square this circle, not now. Instead, obeying his preacher, Simon closed his eyes again. His mind drifted back to Osiris, where the world had made perfect sense, before everything turned upside down and he found himself here, amongst strangers, trying to make a broken girl better. *Gǒu shǐ*, thought Simon, *I really am very tired...*

Before Ava Jones left her home up in Evansville to catch the big train down here to Neapolis, she'd been so excited, telling all her friends about the job at the hotel that Uncle Nate had fixed up for her, and how she was looking forward to seeing the city at last, and imagining the good times she'd have when she got there. The day before she left, a friend of her late aunt came up to her, and, quietly, pressed a card into her hand. "You find yourself in any trouble, honey," she said, "take this to a vidphone and call the number there. They'll help you out, best they can."

"Trouble?" said Ava. She wasn't anticipating trouble. She was heading off to the big city, like she'd always wanted to since Momma and Poppa had died. Free at last! Money in her pocket and all the big wide 'verse to explore. "I'm a good girl! I ain't plannin' on gettin' into trouble."

"Honey," said Aunty Eve's friend, "sometimes trouble comes lookin' for us. Take the card and make the call—if you have to."

So Ava took the card, and, showing some of the very good sense that her Aunty Eve had tried hard to instill in her while Ava was in her care, she had kept the card with a handful of other small treasures wrapped on her person, rather than stored in her little case. She wondered where that little case was now. All her clothes (including her best dress and best hat) had been in that little blue plastic case. She figured she wasn't seeing them ever again, and good hats and dresses don't fall out of the sky. But the card was safe (along with Momma's ring and the holo-images of Momma and Poppa's wedding day and a little squishy toy bear called Patches), and it turned out she had cause to use this card after all.

On a side street near the open market, Ava found a public vidphone and tried to work out what to do. Ava had never used anything like this in her life. She'd seen one, of course—she might be from the sticks, but she wasn't stupid, which more people ought to remember, particularly those trying to stick needles into arms. There was an old vidphone in the bar where Uncle Nate and his pals went drinking after their shift, but Ava doubted Uncle Nate had ever had reason to use such a thing either. Who was there to call? Everyone they knew was right there in Evansville.

The street was quiet. Ava took off the owl mask and stared at the smooth blank screen. Well, really, how hard could it be?

She reached a finger out to tap the cool plastic, and the screen sprang into life, all bright colors and flashing lights. A little cartoon rabbit bounced past and made her laugh; first thing about this place to do so. The rabbit hopped down a hole and pulled a cover over its head, but before instructing Ava in no uncertain terms to eat Joozy Frooty Treets. Maybe she would. The screen flickered and a soft voice said: *Insert card... Insert card...* over and over, until Ava obeyed, jamming the card into the only slot she could see.

The display on the screen changed again. Some numbers—that was her credit, she guessed—and a list named 'CONTACTS'. There was only one name there: *P.R. Quigley's Cleaning Services*, two Chinese characters, but nobody had ever bothered to teach Ava how to read them. Was this really somebody who could help? She hoped so. She touched the characters, and a green light flashed. *Connecting...* said the soft voice. *Connecting...*

It said this over and over for a while, then said: *Disconnecting... Disconnecting...* Ava tried again, and a third time, with the same unhappy results. So much for help. She looked down the street. The afternoon was wearing on and a breeze picking up. Ava shivered. She was glad of the shawl, although she still felt bad about how she'd got it. "*Thou shalt not steal,*" said the preacher, every weekend, although he did say some dumb things. Desperate times, she thought, perhaps she'd be forgiven. She gave the number one last try.

Connecting... Connecting...

The green light stopped flashing and held still. A voice came through—no face—and sounding a little distorted.

"Who's this?"

"M'name's Ava, ma'am."

"How did you get this number?"

"Missus Freeman, back in Evansville, where I'm from, she gave me it, ma'am. Said to call, if I needed help."

There was a pause. "You need help?"

Ava couldn't reply at first. Couldn't put into words all that had happened...

"Are you still there, honey?"

Missus Freeman had called her that. So had Aunty Eve. Maybe Momma had too. Anyway, it helped. "Two men..." Ava whispered. "Came at me... One of 'em had a needle... Please," she said. "Help me." She began to cry.

"Okay. It's okay, honey. Listen. Wait where you are. I'll call you back in twenty minutes. You hear? Don't move, and don't miss the call. I'll call you back. I promise."

The line went dead. Ava felt a cautious hope rise up. She stood by the vidphone, shawl covering her face, hoping that nobody else would come past wanting to use it and take up the line. She watched the time tick past slowly on the screen. Fifteen minutes, sixteen, seventeen. Twenty-one, twenty-two... Twenty-five... She was starting to think she'd been taken for a ride, when the light on the screen started flashing green.

Incoming... Incoming...

Ava touched the screen and the voice came through again: "Is your card in the slot?"

"Yes, ma'am."

"There's another number on there now. You need to call that number tomorrow morning. You need to call at the right time. Not before ten, and not after ten thirty. Got that?"

"Yes, ma'am. Tomorrow morning. Not before ten, not after ten thirty."

"They'll give you an address to go to. Tomorrow morning—not before ten, not after ten thirty."

The call ended, before Ava could say: But what should I do for the rest of today, ma'am? What should I do for tonight?

Ava looked round. All she could see was those big stone tenement buildings, turned inwards. No help there. She wandered down the street, away from the market, and found herself walking through a little park. She sat down on a bench and watched a group of children flying their kites: dragons and hawks and spaceships. Ava had never flown a kite; there hadn't been much time for that kind of thing back home, but something about the children's laughter made her think of Momma and Poppa, long gone, and Aunty Eve, who had always been kind, and she felt tears welling up. She shook herself. She was fourteen, grown-up, she wasn't a kid any more.

The kites caught in the breeze. The kids laughed when they lifted higher, shrieked when they swooped, groaned when they took a tumble down to the ground. After a while, they stopped, and opened up a picnic. Ava watched, trying to ignore her own hunger. She hadn't eaten since early this morning, just before the train arrived in Neapolis, and she didn't have any money. When the kids finished eating, they played a running game for a while, but the day was growing colder, the sun was getting cooler, and at last their grown-ups rounded them up to head home. The park was emptying. Ada got up and found a huge tree, its branches coming down to the ground, like a tent, and snuck underneath.

After about twenty minutes, one of the security staff lifted the branches. "Bad luck, sweetheart," he said. "We're wise to this spot."

"I just need a place to sleep for the night," Ava said. "Just one night."

"You ain't got a home?"

"I'm here for Carnival. Workin'."

"You ain't found a bed?"

"The boarding house got mixed up." Funny how quick the lies came, once you started. Stealin', lyin'... Preacher Wiley, if ever he found out, would tell Uncle Nate to use his strap on her. "Someone else has the bed tonight—"

"Well, I'm sorry, sweetheart, but if I let you stay here, I'll be the one lookin' for work in the morning."

"But where should I—?"

He shrugged. She could see he wasn't going to let her make herself his problem, so she gave up, and let him lead her to the gate. She watched him set the security codes, and the force barriers went up. She wouldn't get back in there so she turned and walked away.

Cities have a twilight time between the late afternoon and the evening, when the daytime businesses have wound down, but the nighttime pleasures have barely begun. Those who have finished for the day have gone home and are settling down comfortably to supper and bed; those who are going back out again are not yet ready to hit the town. There's an hour or two when a city is neither one thing nor the other, where a girl wandering stands out. Someone without a destination. Someone without a place. As Ava walked, she felt more and more conspicuous, easier and easier to find. She needed somewhere to hide for the night…

Be strong, she thought. *Be brave.*

She turned a corner and found herself back in the market square. The place was very different now; empty and disheveled. All the buyers long gone; whoever remained of the vendors packing up their wares ready to be on their way. Ava wandered past the grubby stalls, the canopies flapping in the breeze. This wasn't what the city was supposed to be like. The city was supposed to be her big chance, her way out of the grind of poverty that was life out in Evansville. Ava wasn't afraid of work; she'd worked most of her life and she'd come here ready and willing to do what was needed. But she wasn't willing to be hurt, and Aunty Eve had always said to her, "*You don't let anyone take advantage, honey…*"

All I have to do, thought Ava, *is get through tonight. Tomorrow—someone'll come. Someone'll help me, surely…*

Across the square, lights were twinkling. Ava followed their lead back to the shrine, where her candle was still burning, the small flame dancing in the breeze. It turned out that the shrine stood a little in front of the wall, and there was a small space there, sheltered by the trees that stood on either side. Ava slipped into the gap. Hardly comfortable, but maybe she could spend the night here unnoticed. That was all she wanted: to lie low, be quiet, make it through the next day without being found. She curled up, resting her head upon her hands. She listened to the wind and stared up through the leaves. The lights on the boughs of the trees were twinkling, like stars, like hope or freedom.

* * *

Elsewhere, the party was about to start, and the staff at St. Freda's Hospital, Neapolis, were preparing for another grueling few days. They approached the whole period with the kind of grim fatalism more commonly found during lengthy sieges. Carnival was exhausting: a non-stop parade of injuries arising from too much drink, too few inhibitions, and the unfortunate combination of both. Their own small sweepstake included categories such as: *Most embarrassing injury. Most preventable emergency. Most ludicrous chain of events.*

This was one way to pass the weekend. Dr. Katarina Neilsen, who was responsible for emergency care at the hospital, had plenty of other things to keep her busy. Yesterday, for example, one of her best people, deciding he was unable to face another excessively stressful few days, had quit. Now she was short-staffed. She sat in her office staring at the staff roster, trying to stretch not enough people across too many hours in need of cover. There were limits to what she could expect: at some point, people got too tired and started to make mistakes. And each year, her people told her, Carnival seemed to get a little wilder, a little more violent, a little more out-of-hand. She had come to Bethel a few months ago from the Core worlds, hoping for something less tedious and predictable. Sometimes she wasn't sure she had made the right decision.

There was a knock at her office door. Katarina put aside her notes and called out, "Enter…" A sweet odor of perfume made her look up; the sight of her visitor made her rise from her chair. "Ms. Becker," she said, "I wasn't expecting you…"

Hilde Becker, richly dressed and ornamented, poised and utterly beautiful, moved smoothly into the room and gestured to Katarina to sit down. Permission to sit, in her own office. Only Hilde Becker could pull rank like this. She was head of the local Guild House, and one of the most influential people on Bethel. She also happened to be Katarina's employer. The Guild owned St. Freda's, as they owned large chunks of Neapolis. Only Jacob Roberts was more powerful, and Jacob Roberts and Hilde Becker were known to be good friends.

"Forgive me the interruption," said Hilde. "I know this is a very busy time. I wanted to check that you had everything you needed."

Katarina fell back in her chair. "Well, I'm critically short of staff."

"Short of staff?"

"One of my best people quit yesterday. Couldn't face another weekend of Carnival—"

"If you need extra funds, you can have them."

"It's not so much funds as the quality of the people available. I need specialists—"

"You've advertised on the Cortex?"

"Yes, but people come here to enjoy Carnival," Katarina said, "not to find themselves up to their elbows in blood, bone, gore—"

A wave of the hand made it quite clear that Hilde did not want to hear more details, gory or otherwise. "Spend whatever you need. Pay whatever it costs. The hospital plays an important part in maintaining the Guild's reputation on Bethel. I want the weekend to go smoothly." She looked impassively at her employee. "I'm sure you'll do everything to make sure that happens."

Katarina herself was less convinced about her ability to work that kind of miracle but she knew that Hilde wasn't interested in those kinds of detail either. When she started at St. Freda's, she'd quickly worked out what the working relationship would be. Katarina would present Hilde with problems; Hilde gave her the money to make them go away. In many ways, it was a satisfactory arrangement: St. Freda's had some state-of-the-art equipment these days. In other ways, it was not a good arrangement. Katarina hadn't yet had to present Hilde with a failure, but she wasn't looking forward to doing this when one inevitably arose.

"You should keep a little time free over the weekend," said Hilde. "To enjoy some of what's on offer."

Rich people, Katarina had noticed, had an amazing ability not to hear what was being said to them. She was not unused to wealthy people—she had grown up and done her medical training on Osiris, after all, and while her family had comparatively modest means, she had studied alongside some scions of the fabulously rich. She was not unused to companions either—had even engaged one herself on one sweetly memorable occasion—but the combination of wealth, power, poise, and beauty that came together in Hilde was particularly intimidating. Also, Hilde could fire her on the spot. Hilde scared the life out of Katarina, and she didn't know how to tell her 'no'.

"I'll try to catch a concert or two," Katarina said. "It would definitely be a shame to miss the whole party."

Hilde smiled. "You're not one for gambling?"

"Not really," said Katarina, whose day-to-day life already carried with it enough risk and stress.

"What a pity. Myself, I enjoy taking risks."

The console on Katarina's desk gently chimed. *Incoming... Incoming...*

"I'm so sorry," Katarina said, reaching to cut it off. "They can call back later—"

"Please," said Hilde, "feel free to take it."

That carried the weight of an order rather than a suggestion, so Katarina let the call come through. Her heart sank when she saw a familiar face appear on screen. Anna Liu—twenty years younger than Hilde, but with that same deadly combination of wealth, power, poise, and beauty. One of those scions of the fabulously rich that Katarina had met back on Osiris. Her friend, Katarina supposed she should call her, if the very rich do in fact have friends. Katarina lifted her hand, hoping to signal to Anna that someone else was present, and that she should rein herself in.

"Anna," she said, with a note of warning. "I'm pretty busy right now—"

Her friend's eyes sharpened. But her voice stayed light. "Kay, you're looking so solemn!" Anna raised a cocktail glass (How late was it, exactly? Katarina checked the time. Mid-afternoon. Not late enough.). "Smile!" she said. "It's Carnival!"

"Not until tomorrow evening, Anna."

"Anyone who's anyone started drinking yesterday—"

"I'll have to resign myself to being no one."

"Kay, you're my favorite someone. Can you talk? I have a favor to ask—"

"Can it wait? I have Hilde Becker here…" She left the implications of that hanging meaningfully and heavily in the air between them.

"Really?" Anna craned her neck forward, as if to try to catch a glimpse. "You do have such grand friends—"

"Ms. Becker is my employer, Anna, as you know."

Anna looked back mischievously. "I didn't mean to interrupt an important meeting."

"You're not interrupting. Yet."

"Don't worry, I won't keep you."

"You said a favor?"

"Mm. I wanted to know what your plans were for the weekend."

"I'll be working, I imagine," said Katarina, allowing a little irritation to creep into her voice. "It's not a great time for the hospital—"

"Oh, but they have to let you out to play at some point?"

"Well, I'll see how I feel at the end of the weekend."

"All right, Kay. Enjoy your *tête-à-tête* with Mzzz Becker. I'll speak to you later."

The call ended. Hilde, rather coolly, said, "I didn't know that you knew Anna Liu."

She didn't seem very happy about it either. Perhaps she didn't like the idea of Katarina having other friends in high places. Anna and her brother had inherited several of the casinos on and around the Platinum Mile. Only Jacob Roberts owned more on Bethel. Not that Anna appeared to take any interest in family affairs. She presented herself to the world as someone careless with her time and her money, someone who preferred partying to business.

"How did you meet?" asked Hilde.

"We studied together," Katarina said. "I was at the med school while she was at the business school. We room shared." In fact, Katarina had lived in the house that Anna's parents had bought for her to use while she was away studying. Katarina had been astonished by that; her first real encounter with real wealth. She remembered going shopping with Anna once. On the spur of the moment, Anna bought a vastly expensive pair of shoes. When she'd seen Katarina's expression, she asked what the matter was. "That's what I pay you in rent every month," said Katarina. An important moment, for both of them.

"Of course," Hilde said. "I forget your central planet connections. You seem so much one of us these days."

"I thought Bethel considered itself a central planet."

Hilde smiled, opaquely. "It's getting there," she said. "Though anyone who knows anything can see that it's rather rough around the edges. Still, I understand that's part of the attraction, for many of our visitors."

"A bit too rough sometimes, perhaps."

"It's only for a couple of days," Hilde said.

"A lot of damage can be done in a couple of days." Particularly when you were short-staffed.

"Not at the kind of event that I host. Which brings me to my reason for coming today. I have a small party happening on Last Night, you know."

Of course Katarina knew. A small party? The Guild's last night party was one of the most exclusive events on Bethel. People were desperate for an invite.

"And you're invited," said Hilde. "Do bring a guest, if you like." She considered this. "Not Anna Liu. She can be chaotic."

Oh, thought Katarina. *I wasn't expecting that...* "I... I don't know what to say. I'm very gratified, obviously, but it's going to be so busy here over the weekend, and I should be available—"

"I told you that money would be no object." A little steel had entered Hilde's voice now. "Hire whoever you need. Spend whatever's required. But come to the party."

Was it worth trying to explain again that you couldn't conjure the right people with the right skills out of the air? Hilde didn't look like she was ready to hear that.

"I'll do my best."

"I'm sure you'll manage," said Hilde, as she rose from her chair. "That's what I pay you for, after all." She smiled. "I'll see you at the party."

This was the problem with accepting patronage, Katarina thought, watching Hilde go; you were not permitted to say 'no'. One could spend whatever one liked, as long as you obeyed whims, did what you were told, and somehow achieved the impossible. *Money no object, eh? I wonder what would happen if I put that out on the Cortex...*

Joseph Liu didn't, in general, eavesdrop on his sister's calls, but there was something about the urgency in her voice that made him stop outside the door of her sitting room and listen.

"...No, listen to what I'm saying. I want a room, and I want a room tomorrow. Whatever you have to do to make that happen, do it. I'll pay a hundred platinum... Yes, you did hear that right. And if I have to, I'll buy the damn motel and make all the rooms available... Oh, good, I'm glad to hear that. Yes. Tomorrow. Thank you."

The call ended. Joseph waited a moment or two in case there was a follow-up, and then tapped on the door and went inside. Anna, his brilliant little sister, was lying on the couch, eyes closed. Joseph looked at her sadly. Anna, as a girl, always had so much *promise*... She'd shone at school, gone off to the central worlds at sixteen to study, went to college on Osiris, went into finance... And then their parents died, and she came home, and since then her whole life seemed to have been knocked off course. Gone was the ambition, the drive. All she seemed to want to do these days was stay out, drink, sleep until the afternoon. He tried to be patient, but he wished she would set herself straight.

"That sounded angry," he said.

She cracked open an eye. "Are you listening to my calls now?"

"They could probably hear you on the Mile. Are you moving into the hospitality business?"

"What?" she said.

"Buying a motel."

"Oh," she said. "No. Nothing like that. A friend arrived this morning and her room had been double-booked. I was undouble-booking it."

"For a hundred platinum?"

"I can do what I like with my own money, Joe."

That was true. Half of the estate had been settled on her by their mother and father, and it was none of his damn business what she did with the money. She could drink away the whole pile, and it wouldn't, technically, be even remotely his business. Except that he loved her, and he didn't think this life of hers made her happy.

"Must be a good friend," he said, still fishing. "Do I get to meet her?"

"When I say friend," Anna replied, "she's more a friend of Kay Neilsen's really. So no, probably not."

Kay Neilsen was one of Anna's old friends from her time on Osiris, who for some reason had followed Anna back here. Joseph had met Kay once or twice: a doctor, serious and intelligent. Why she'd come to Bethel he had no idea. He'd thought once or twice that there might be something between them, but when he'd broached the topic with Anna (he wouldn't have *minded*, he just wanted to *know*), she'd laughed in his face. "Kay? Oh, Joe, no! Absolutely not!"

"I like Kay," Joseph said. "I wish you saw more of her."

"Prefer her to my current gang, you mean?"

Anna's current group of hangers-on were the worst of Bethel's elite, in Joseph's opinion. Five or six years younger than her, and not a single intelligent thought between them. "I don't know what you see in them, Anna, that's all. You used to enjoy good conversation. That lot... they're dull. They have no opinions. It's all gossip."

"Nothing wrong with gossip," said Anna. "You can learn a great deal from gossip."

Joseph poured himself a drink and took the seat opposite her. "So what are your plans for Carnival?"

"I'm going to enjoy myself," she said.

"No change there," he said, lightly, although he wasn't entirely convinced that she enjoyed this life of hers. Mostly, she seemed to be doing nothing more than filling the hours.

"I see no reason to change," she replied. Then she seemed to decide to want to make an effort. She sat up, curling her legs beneath her, and smiled at him. "What are your plans, Joe?" she asked. "For First Night?"

A few years back, at this time of year, this big house up in the hills would be bustling with life, as they made ready for Mother and Father's First Night party. That was where everyone wanted to be on the first night of Carnival. Planning for one of these parties was one of Joseph's earliest memories: choosing the theme; sending out the invitations; picking out the masks and costumes. And then, on the night, Mother beautiful and funny; Father charming and expansive. All these happy memories brought to an end when their new flyer plunged out of the sky just short of the north-east perimeter road. The year after their death, Joseph had considered hosting a party of his own but knew he couldn't face it. Four years later, and he still couldn't. "I guess I'll go over to the casino," he said.

"You'll miss out on all the fun," she said.

"You've seen one parade, you've seen them all," he said.

"You won't be there all the time?"

He shook his head. "There's the party at the Guild House," he said. He didn't want to go to that. Jacob Roberts would be there, satisfied how things had turned out on Bethel, and there was the head of the House too, Hilde Becker. Joseph found her cold and calculating. But these days you had to be seen at the Guild House party. So Joseph would be seen, although he'd taken the precaution of engaging a companion for the night, to do the small talk for him.

"Maybe I'll come by the casino later," Anna said. "Waste a little money."

She wouldn't. She never came near any of their casinos. She preferred to waste her money elsewhere. "You know, Anna," he said, "at some point you're going to have to decide what you're going to do with the rest of your life." *You have to put what happened to them behind you...*

She raised her glass. "I've already decided."

"I mean something serious."

"I'm very serious about what I do."

"You weren't like this before..."

"Before, Joe?"

"Before you went to the Core. You used to work so hard. We all thought you were going to do great things—"

"I didn't like the Core worlds," she said. "I thought they were dull."

"Dull?"

"The people—all the same. Their conversations—all the same. I know we think those worlds are so beautiful, so shiny, but..." Anna shook her head. "Bethel is so much more *interesting*, don't you think?"

"That's a long way round of saying that you got homesick, Anna."

"Perhaps I did get a little homesick. There's nothing like this in the Core worlds. Everything is so smooth. Here…"

"You like the rough edges, hey?"

He couldn't read this expression. Sometimes she slipped away from him, and he didn't know what she was thinking, couldn't begin to guess.

"I wouldn't say that I *like* them," she said.

"I'm sorry you didn't like Osiris." Joseph had loved his time in the Core worlds. The order and regularity of life had suited him. He'd planned to open a restaurant on Sihnon. He loved to cook, and he loved the restaurant business. "I'd happily go back there if it wasn't for all this…" He held his hands out, rather helplessly. He'd been home on Bethel when their parents were killed and he hadn't left since. Someone had to keep everything running, and Anna wasn't going to do it.

"Poor Joe," said Anna. "Trapped by inheritance, while I have all the fun."

"You know," he said, "Father intended for you to take a full part in the business." Maybe he could persuade her to do more. Maybe he might still get to leave here…

"Maybe one day," she said. "Right now—I worked so hard for so many years. I intend to enjoy myself."

Or maybe not. Joseph looked down into the glass. "Do you remember," he said, "the parties Mother and Father used to have?"

"Not really," she said, but of course he knew she did.

"Maybe we should start them up again."

"Joe," she said. "Those days are over. They're not coming back."

She was right. Joseph finished his drink and stood up. "Don't get hurt, Anna."

"Hurt?" She was looking at him in real surprise. "What makes you say that?"

"Those friends of yours… They're not that nice."

"Oh." She relaxed back into her seat. "I see. I won't, Joe. Not that way."

"And the preacher said to the companion, 'Those ain't potaters!'"

A raucous burst of laughter jerked Simon awake. He had a cold cup of chamomile tea in front of him and a crick in his neck. The dining room had become much busier: Zoë and Wash were at the other end of the table, holding hands. Inara was leaning against the doorframe, cool, distant, smiling that quiet smile that always seemed full of secrets. Everyone was there. Almost everyone. Simon said the first thing that came into his head; said what was always on his mind.

"Where's River?"

Kaylee, opposite, said, "She's still sleepin', Simon."

"Okay. And… what's happening?"

"What else?" said Kaylee. "Schemin'."

"Now that you're back with us, Doc," said the captain, "we can go through the plan."

"Oh, yes, the plan," said Simon, pulling himself more or less upright. "I'm glad to hear there is one at least."

"I'd hold fire on that, son," said Book. "We ain't heard the details yet."

"No need to be anticipatin' trouble, Shepherd, it'll come lookin' for us by itself," said Mal. "But it's a fine plan, as you'll know when I've had my chance to tell you—"

"Stop fussin' and get on with it," muttered Jayne. He was flipping a pocketknife open and shut, open and shut.

"Far from bein' a house of God," said Mal, "Bethel is more what you'd call a den of vice."

"That's my kinda house of God," leered Jayne.

"My apologies in advance, Shepherd," said Mal, "for putting you in the way of maybe seeing all manner of unseemliness—"

"Accepted," said Book, with a gracious nod of his head.

"So," said Mal, "the planet upon which we'll shortly be coming to land is called Bethel. Now, small world like this, more or less out on the Rim, people most usually come for one thing. Might be farmin', might be minin'."

"Me, I'm here for the whorin'," said Jayne.

"We ain't here for the whorin'," said Mal.

"Well, I am," said Jayne. He reached across the table to spear his knife into an apple and bit down hard. *Was it too much to hope he'd break a tooth*, wondered Simon. *Apparently so.*

"Now, a man on this den of vice, name of Jacob Roberts, put out a call on the Cortex for some people needed for a job. Seems Roberts owns a lot of businesses down here—"

"You mean whorehouses," said Jayne, mouth full.

"I don't," said Mal, and Simon, who had attended one of the best medical schools in the central worlds, taught by some of the most inspirational professors in their field, began to despair of ever learning anything from this conversation. He caught Inara's eye. She didn't do anything as broad as wink back at him, but he saw the slight twist of her lips. *Patience*, she seemed to be saying. *All will be revealed.*

"Mal," said Inara. "Don't rise to the bait. Just tell us what the job involves."

"I'm coming to that," said Mal. "First thing you got to understand—Bethel got settled back in the day because of the minerals under the surface. Whatever it is that they dig up out there in the desert, people in the Core worlds want a great deal of it."

"It's called verterium," said Wash. "It goes in components for calibrating navigation systems." He looked around. "What? Why are you all looking at me like that? You think I don't *know* things?"

"I'm impressed, sugar," said Zoë, taking possession of both his hands.

"That," said Wash, leaning in for a kiss, "is pretty much all I care about."

"I'll take your word on the components and the calibrating," said Mal.

"When I think of Bethel I think of the casinos," said Kaylee. "You know, all those fancy people dressed up and spendin' their money like it's goin' out of fashion—"

"A lot of people made a lot of money out of vertenium," said Mal.

"Verterium," said Wash.

"Whatever it's called they made a fortune. And they wanted to live somewhere a mite fancier than a dustbowl minin' planet. And that's where the casinos came in. The idea was to bring a little glamour to their world."

Jayne, finishing the apple, threw the core onto the table. "I ain't followin'. What's fancy about diggin' rocks up from the ground?"

"With the casinos came the hotels," said Inara. "Some of them are very expensive. They attracted wealthy people from the central worlds. The more people who came, the more they wanted to do. There's the restaurants, the nightclubs, the shows and entertainments. Not to mention the exclusive resorts out along the coast."

"Money brought money," said Mal. "Walk round parts of Neapolis these days, you might think you were in the Core." He didn't sound very happy about that, Simon thought.

"So what's the job, Captain?" said Zoë.

"More to the point," said Book, "which side of the law is it?"

"Strictly legal this time, Shepherd, as I'm sure you'll be glad to hear."

"That I am," said Book.

"I hope it takes us somewhere fancy," said Kaylee, longingly.

"It's a security job," said Mal. "Shipment of erbonium being transferred off world." He looked at Wash. "Anything you'd like to share about erbonium, Wash?"

"We've hit the outer limits of my expertise," said Wash. "I only minored in minerals." He shrugged. "More of a hobby than a specialty. Not even a hobby, really. More of a near-total lack of interest."

Sometimes, Simon thought, sitting round this table was like watching an elementary class at show and tell. Reaching into his pocket, he pulled out his encyclopedia.

He held it under the table and began to read. *BETHEL*, he read. *LOCATION: Red Sun system. POPULATION: 530,000. MAIN SETTLEMENTS: Neapolis (capital); Evansville, Nashton, Lauriston, Mount Greyling.* (Simon shuddered slightly at the thought of what these crappy townships would be like, but perhaps he was being unfair and none of them burned passing strangers at the stake…) *CULTURE*…

"Erbonium," said Book, "comes in mighty useful in the manufacture of lasers."

"Geologist and man of God," said Mal. "No end to your talents."

"I dabble," replied Book.

"Well, today we're dabbling in providing a security detail for that shipment of erbonium. This shipment has to be off world before the party really starts, which, so I'm told, is this evening."

Kaylee sighed. "So nothing fancy, then."

"Not today, Kaylee," said Mal.

ECONOMY (read Simon)*: Mining; hospitality. Bethel's wealth derives from two main sources, the chief of these being the extraction of various rare minerals necessary for interstellar navigations. The mining operations are chiefly situated in the desert regions located upriver from the capital. [See entries on: verterium, erbonium, malefinium.] In the past two decades, however, a rising proportion of the world's income has derived from the dozens of resorts and entertainments clustered in and around Bethel's main settlement, Neapolis. This, with the looser gambling laws on Bethel, has made the city an increasingly popular destination for tourists across the central worlds…*

"At least it's not criminal," remarked Book. "I gather that the casinos are only the tip of the iceberg when it comes to the local economy."

"Just the very upper tip of that iceberg of interest to us today, preacher," said Zoë.

"Still," said Book, "might be wise to bear in mind that there will be others in Neapolis with designs very different from our own."

"Hence the job," said Mal. "Watch that shipment when it arrives at the train depot; make sure it gets over to the docks before the party starts. Nobody else to get near it; nobody else to get their hands on it."

"Why us?" said Wash. "Is there no one else in the whole of Neapolis willing to take on a job like this? Why's it come up on the Cortex?"

"Good question," said Mal. "Right now, as I suspect you all know, that fine city is the cusp of its busiest few days of the year. Big party happenin' in Neapolis this week. Everyone who could do this job is either workin' already or plannin' on misbehavin'."

CULTURE: Bethel is chiefly known for the celebrations that take place in Neapolis over the weekend of the spring equinox. These events, which are centered on the part of the city known as the 'Platinum Mile'...

"Oh," said Simon, as several things clicked into place. "Carnival."

His colleagues gave a small and not remotely complimentary round of applause.

"You're catchin' up, Doc," said Mal.

"Sounds fun, don't it?" said Kaylee, hopefully.

Simon, picturing the alcohol-related injuries that inevitably ensued, thought that it sounded like hell. "For some definitions of fun," he said, before he could stop himself. Kaylee's sweet smile faded away and, from the doorway, Inara frowned at him and shook her head. *Why am I such a jerk? Was I always such a jerk and nobody told me?*

"Ain't no fun to be had by anyone on board this ship until the job's been done," Mal said sternly. "Me and Zoë—you too, Jayne—we're to get this cargo safely from the rail depot over to the space port, on board the freighter, and make sure that nobody with differing designs for the shipment gets near it."

"Sounds easy enough," said Jayne. He was digging pieces of apple out from between his teeth with the tip of the knife.

"Ain't ever easy," said Mal. "You know, I could do with a fourth body on this ride… Wash?"

"Um," said Wash, "when you say 'body'…"

"Wasn't meant to be taken literally," said Mal.

"But it's out there now," said Wash. "The idea of it. Literally and very unappealingly out there—"

"Maybe the doc'll come along," said Jayne, wiping the knife clean on his shirt. "Show us what he's made of."

"Maybe I won't," Simon snapped back.

The room went very quiet.

"Is it me," said Wash, "or has it gone chilly in here?"

"Whatever." Jayne snapped his knife closed and put it away. "Not like you'd be any ruttin' use anyways."

No, he wasn't forgetting that Simon could paralyze him. That River could… well, who knew, really, what River could do? And all of that meant that the balance of power between them had shifted significantly. Did anyone else on *Serenity* know why? Did anyone else know that Jayne had called the Feds on them on Ariel? What would Mal do, if he knew? Simon had worked out pretty quickly that there was no point running to Mal with his troubles. This was something he had to learn to deal with himself; it was part of what his life was now. This sullen ceasefire with Jayne would hold, for a while, but Simon wasn't banking on it lasting, and he wasn't sure yet what he was supposed do should the violence break out again. Just hope it wasn't fatal—for him, and for River.

Shepherd Book was looking at him thoughtfully. Simon stuffed the encyclopedia back into his pocket, pulled out a pen and paper, and began to make a list of what he needed for the infirmary. Listing things was soothing. *I just need the 'verse to stop throwing curveballs at me for a while*, he thought. *Let me get my bearings...* They were short of bandages. They were *always* short of bandages. Simon half suspected Jayne of eating them.

"You know," said Mal, "the doc's not so useless these days. He might well come in handy—"

Book leaned forward in his seat, putting himself between Simon and Mal's sights. Simon kept his eyes down on his list. "I think I'll come along too if you're willing, Captain."

"You sure about that, Shepherd?" said Mal. "There'll be guns."

"But no need to be firing them as I see it," said Book. "Always happy to lend a hand if necessary."

"Den of vice, huh, Shepherd?" said Jayne.

"House of God," said Book, unperturbed.

"And there's my fourth man," said Mal, cheerfully. "Wash, you and the doc are off the hook."

Book leaned back in his seat. "Thank you," murmured Simon, who appreciated the small kindnesses even more these days.

"You're welcome," said Book. "Might be a good idea to get some sleep while we're gone, though."

I plan to, thought Simon, and carried on writing. *And maybe, when I wake up, I'll be back on Osiris and this long and truly appalling nightmare will finally be over...*

On the other side of the table, Kaylee sighed.

"All right," said Mal. "Me, Zoë, Jayne, Book—we got a meeting with this man Roberts in a few hours. Everyone else, once we're down, you're to stay on board *Serenity*—"

"Oh, *Captain*," said Kaylee.

"The job should be done by the mid-afternoon," said Mal, "after which—"

"Whorin'," said Jayne, a man confident in his predictive abilities.

"After *which*—" Mal ignored the interruption, "I might consider the possibility of a little recreation time."

Kaylee's smile lit up. "Shiny," she said, much mollified.

"Come to my shuttle, Kaylee," said Inara. "We'll take a look at your nails before you go out."

"And while you're busy with such life-and-death activities," said Mal (*I'm not*, thought Simon, seeing Inara's expression, *the only jerk round here*), "we'll be off to make an honest livin'."

"I suppose honest makes a change," shot back Inara.

"Good enough for me," said Mal.

As the captain walked past, Simon reached back and handed him his list. "That's what I need," he said. "When you're paid. If you're paid."

"Huh." Mal stared down at what he'd written. "Anyone ever told you, Doc, that your sarcasm is your least appealin' trait?"

"Oh, it's the sarcasm, is it?" said Simon. "I was under the impression that it was everything in combination."

Mal patted him on the shoulder. He beamed across the table. "Don't frown, Kaylee," he said. "Party later."

He went on his way, whistling, leaving Kaylee and Simon in the now blissfully quiet dining room. "How I miss the grown-ups," said Simon, "when they go out to play."

Kaylee smiled at him. Simon managed a smile back.

"Bed?" said Kaylee.

I can't cope with much more of this, thought Simon. "Kaylee... I..."

"Simon," she said, "I mean—you should probably go to bed. Alone. To sleep."

"Oh. Yes. Of course. Bed."

He stood up. From along the corridor, a voice called out, a girl's voice, with a rising note of terror. "*Siiiimonnn...? Simon!*"

"Oh Simon!" said Kaylee. "I'm sorry!"

"Of course," said Simon, heading off at pace toward the engine room. "Of course this happens now."

* * *

Ava woke to the clatter of the market coming back to life. She sat up, cold and stiff, rubbing life back into her hands, trying to ignore the sharp pangs of hunger in her belly. She fumbled around for the owl mask, only to find she'd rolled onto it during the night, and it was broken into pieces. Tears sprang to her eyes. Sure, it was a piece of market stall junk, but she'd liked it and it had helped take care of her. She shook herself, hard, 'cause tears weren't gonna help her, and shoved the broken pieces into her pocket. She wriggled out of her hiding place and came round to look at the shrine. Her candle was still burning, more or less, but the flame and the lights hanging in the trees looked washed out and sickly. Reaching out, she touched the little statue of the Buddha and thanked him for keeping watch over her all night. Even as she did so, she laughed at herself. Silly of her. Aunty Eve had tried to warn her about having a sentimental streak. *Wishin's all very well, Ava, but wishin' won't help in need. You got to be doin'.*

"All right, Aunty Eve," she mumbled. "Better get doin'."

Ava took stock of her situation. Early morning. Dawn light trickling between the buildings. Later, when the sun was higher, it would be warmer, a nice spring day, but right now there was a chill to the air. Ava could cope. Evansville was freezin' in the winter months, and Uncle Nate wasn't so good at makin' sure there was wood or coal for the fire. Yes, she'd cope, and now all she had to do was make it to mid-morning, make the call, and surely then these people, whoever they were, would help her, somehow?

46

There was a baker's stall across from the shrine, opening up for breakfast. The smell of fresh bread was tantalizing. Ava walked over and, catching the stallholder's eye, said, "Excuse me, ma'am, can you tell me the time, please?"

"It's little after six thirty, honey."

Ava sighed. Hours to kill. "Thank you," she said, and turned away.

"You don't want anything, honey? It's all freshly baked."

Ava held out her hands. *No money.*

"No cash, hey?" The woman looked round. "Who's you with, honey? You seem a little young to be out on your own at this time of day. Where's your ma and pa?"

Ava shrugged. She shoved her hands in her pockets and moved on, trying to think where she could go. Maybe back to the park? Would they mind if she sat there until it was time to make the call? Found out whether there really was someone out there who could help…

"Hey, wait!"

Ava turned to see the baker running toward her. She stopped to shove a pastry into Ava's hands. "That should keep you goin' a while," she said. "You in town by yourself, honey?"

Ava nodded.

"You got a place to go?"

Ava half-shrugged, half-nodded. "Maybe."

"Well, you keep your head down till you're fixed, d'you understand? And listen," she leaned in. "Keep away from the sheriff's men. Some of them—they ain't good, and they're particularly no good for girls like you. You got that? Don't ask for help from anyone like that, because you can't tell

47

the good ones from bad, and the bad ones won't be helpin'. They'll be hurtin'. Got that?"

Don't ask for help...

Ava nodded and went on her way. She walked slowly down the street, past the vidphone, and to the park. When the security guard arrived to open up, he recognized her at once. "Back again, huh? You're keen."

"I like it here."

"Seems so. Band'll be comin' on at nine," he said. Then, seeing her face, went on, "Cheer up! It's the first day of Carnival!"

Ava tried to follow his instructions, but there wasn't much fun to be had watching other people enjoy themselves, and the band were playing songs that reminded her of Aunty Eve, and that made her feel worse. She was glad when the time came to make the call. She left the park and went back to the vidphone. She watched the Joozy Frooty Bunny and even started to hum along with the tune. When that finished, and the display came up, she put the card into the slot, like she'd done the day before, and touched the screen to call the new contact. *Connecting... Connecting...*

"It's Ava," she said, when the lights stopped flashing. "I was told to call, after ten—"

A voice came through. No face, again. "There's an address put on your card. Look it up on the map when we're done. You need to get there by three this afternoon, and no later than three-thirty. Got that?"

"Yes, ma'am, I got—"

The call disconnected. Ava found the new contact. *Mag Coirc Motel and Bar, Celestial Way*. She touched the words and a map popped up on screen. Right by Roby Docks, where the spaceships berthed. Looked like a long walk… She took the card out of the slot and walked back to the market. The baker, seeing her approach, gave her a warm smile.

"Hello again, honey!" she said. "You all right? How was that pastry?"

"It was grand, ma'am, thank you. Much appreciated."

"You need something else?"

"I need to ask my way, if you can help. I'm to meet a friend over by the docks—"

"The docks?"

"Where the spaceships come in."

"I know the docks, honey. But are you sure? It's not very nice over there."

"I'll be okay," said Ava. "How quick can I get there?"

"Quickest way's by tram, but…"

But Ava didn't have money for the tram. "And walkin'?"

"Walkin'?" The woman sighed. "You sure this is a good idea, honey?"

"I'm sure. She's a family friend. Friend of my Aunty Eve." Which wasn't quite a lie, when you thought about it, and mentioning family seemed to make the baker happier about sending this girl off by herself.

"Walkin'll take you a couple of hours, maybe a little more. It's a long way!"

Ava nodded. That was enough time. "It'll be fine," she said. "Thank you very much, ma'am, for all your help."

"Wait a moment," said the woman. She went round the stall and then came back with a paper bag, which she shoved into Ava's hands. "Something for the journey," she said. "You take care, now."

Ava, a lump in her throat, couldn't reply. She went on her way. From the bag rose up the warm scent of bread.

Neapolis stood at the mouth of a mean little river that crawled north through almost the whole of Bethel's main continent. Dotted along that river like junk stones on a cheap necklace lay the mining towns. Mal could see those places in his mind's eye: poor old dusty places; everyone there with a hacking cough, right down to the smallest kids. Kind of place you ran a mile from, should the chance ever arise. No life for anyone there, just hard work, company rules, and most likely a preacher man telling you that you should be glad for the little you got. Not that Jacob Roberts would be spending much of his time in towns like that. No sir, Jacob Roberts was a rich man—fancy, as Kaylee might say—who clearly liked the best of everything.

Look at this room now, Jacob Roberts' office. Six stories up on a big steel building that lay at one end of the Platinum Mile. A corner room with two walls made completely of reinforced glass. Mal would bet the last of his own platinum that Jacob Roberts often stood here to look out across his kingdom and think about what a mighty fine man he was, with the best of everything, top of the world. But out of the corner of your eye, you could still see the desert, hard and red and unforgiving.

"Not the prettiest of planets, is it, sir?" said Zoë, her voice low.

"What makes you say that?" said Mal.

"Surface all painted, but when you look closer, you see the chips and marks. All done on the cheap."

"Yes, well, we're not here to admire the architecture, Zoë—"

"I know I'm not," said Jayne.

"Close your jaws, Jayne," said Mal. "And keep 'em closed."

Zoë wasn't wrong though. Mal had noticed the same, coming through the city. Bethel's location had, by good fortune, put it safely away from the war between the Alliance and the Independents. The residents had used this position, far away enough to avoid the main fighting, but close enough to play both sides to their advantage. Made promises to everyone; even kept some of them. There were many here that made a lot of platinum during the war. Could you fault them for making the best of a bad situation? Mal Reynolds did. Now those fine upstanding citizens of Bethel wanted to enjoy the benefits of being a Core world: comfort, security, shiny offices, and not much thought for any suffering that might have been caused along the way.

Take a look at this room now. Great big desk, made of chrome and steel. Empty, except for a state-of-the-art console. Mal didn't meet too many men as fancy as this one, but when he did, he was always struck by how empty their desks were. They had people to fret the details, of course. Just had to sit around—look at that black leather chair. You could sink right into that and shout out a few orders and people would jump and do whatever you told 'em. There was a lot of leather in

FIREFLY

this room, Mal thought. The Shepherd was standing over by an ostentatious bookcase next to the door, stuffed full of volumes bound in the stuff. A lot of cows had given up their lives so that Jacob Roberts could look like a learned man.

"Hmm," said the Shepherd, closing the book he was holding, slotting it carefully back into place. He came to stand with Mal and Zoë, admiring the view, taking in everything around him. Whatever this man had been in the past, Mal thought, he weren't always a preacher. He moved like a soldier, but smooth, like a well-kept machine. Still, Mal was glad he'd offered to come along for this ride. No way he would have dragged the doc along on this jaunt, for all Jayne's goading. For one thing, the boy was dead on his feet. For another, he would have been less use than a paper hat in a foxhole. Still no harm in tweaking him; keep him on his toes. Boy had to learn to live in this world he'd chose. Worse people than Jayne after him... Mal's eyes flicked over to Jayne, prowling around near a flashy display of whisky bottles. Had the doc worked out yet what Jayne had done back there on Ariel? Mal wasn't tellin', that was for sure; it was all over and done with as far as he was concerned. Maybe the doc would have his own opinions on that, should matters ever come to light. Yet another complication from bringin' those two on board.

"Interesting planet," remarked Book.

"Jayne would say so," said Mal.

"You know, if we'd come fifty years ago, there'd be nothing here but desert. A few wooden shacks. You know the kind of place."

Mal knew the kind of place intimately. "I surely do."

52

"Now look at it," went on Book. He rested his hand against the glass and they both stared out along the Platinum Mile. "Babylon the Great."

Mal did not always appreciate how the Shepherd's mind turned inevitably Biblewards, but he had to admit that the comparison was apt. The Mile was a long boulevard that sliced through the heart of Neapolis, two long strips of grand and gaudy buildings: casinos, hotels, clubs, venues for all manner of entertainments, fine and not so fine. These buildings glittered in the morning sun; come the evening, the view from this spot would be of sparkling lights, the glitzy fronts and facades of the big casinos. On the main night of Carnival there was the parade, and on the last night, in Grand Green Park, at the far end of the Mile, there was a huge fireworks display. Yes, thought Mal, if you stood here in this office long enough, you might make the mistake of thinking you were king of the 'verse.

"*Come out of her, my people,*" the Shepherd intoned, softly, "*so that you will not share in her sins, so that you will not receive any of her plagues; for her sins are piled up to heaven, and God has remembered her crimes.* Revelation 18," he finished, in a cheerful voice. "One of my favorite verses."

"You're a brave man, preacher," said Zoë, "quoting from the Good Book in present company."

Book smiled. "An apt quotation, though, wouldn't you say?"

"Babylon fell in an hour, if I recall rightly," said Mal. "I don't see Neapolis and her people fallin' anywhere but upwards."

"God's plans," said Book, "are not always clear to us."

"As long as he got nothin' planned for me today other than smooth sailin' toward a profit, God and I'll rub along just fine."

Mal turned away, signaling in the firmest way possible that this particular line of conversation was now at an end. The door opened, and their employer, Jacob Roberts, entered. Behind him came another man in a sheriff's uniform. Mal stiffened; so did Zoë.

Gorram sheriffs! Is there a warrant out on me that I knew nothing about? Hard to keep track of the things, sometimes.

"Captain Reynolds, yes?" said Roberts. He strode across the room as if he owned the place—which, Mal thought, was fair enough, on account of the fact that he *did* own the place—and came to a halt next to Zoë. He was a big man, had an inch or two at least on Mal, maybe even on Jayne, and he was broad too—not carryin' weight so much as bulk. Mal would hesitate before throwin' a punch on him—not that he thought it would come to that. Mal had his eye on the sheriff, who stayed over by the door, and did not proceed toward arrestin' any person present.

"Admiring the view?" said Roberts. "I do it all the time. When my grandfather came to Bethel as a boy, he had nothing. And he built this," he waved his hand to encompass the Mile, "all this, out of nothing."

Well, thought Mal, sharing a look with the Shepherd, there would have been more to the whole business than that. Some shady dealing, certainly a great deal of violence, and no doubt a fair amount of other people's labor, slave or otherwise. Mighty towers didn't raise up in the desert all by themselves. Roberts turned his back to his inheritance and took his place in the big leather chair. "Take a seat. All of you."

The four of them did as instructed and Mal, sinking back into his seat, could see now how carefully the desk and chair had been positioned. Roberts was lined up so that the big boulevard, the whole empire, was stretching behind him. Looked fine, but Mal had something else preying on his mind.

"Forgive me for statin' the obvious," he said, "but there's a sheriff in this room and—hard-workin' and law-abidin' though I am—I'd still like to ask whether or not this is a prelude to some kind of unpleasant officialdom."

"Sheriff Zhao," said Roberts, by way of introduction, and Mal, twisting his neck to try to take a good look, saw the sheriff touch the brim of his hat by way of greeting. "He wanted to meet you."

"Pleased to make your acquaintance," said Mal.

"Huh," said Zhao.

"Any particular reason you wanted to meet us?" Mal tried.

"I wanted a good look at you," said Zhao. "I don't have the people to cover this job, not during Carnival, so I suppose you'll have to do."

"Thank you for those kind words, Sheriff."

"I know your type, Reynolds," Zhao said, with a sigh. "And if there's even the slightest spot of trouble, I'll lock you up, and I'll take your ship. I've neither the time nor the inclination for anything out of the ordinary this weekend."

"Then you can sleep easy tonight knowing we are of the same mind, Sheriff," said Mal, words as smooth as he could make them. "I've neither the time nor the inclination neither. Straightforward job, straight in and straight out. Might take a day or two after to enjoy what the world has to offer, but then we'll be on our way."

"Happy now, Marcus?" said Roberts.

"Guess I'll have to be," said Zhao. He nodded at Zoë and the Shepherd. "Miss," he said. "Preacher." He eyed Jayne, snorted, and then went on his way, closing the door behind him.

Roberts, leaning back in his mighty fine big leather chair behind his mighty fine desk, looked at Mal and his crew like they were something he might not be pleased to find stuck on the heel of his boot. "I heard that you were a maverick, but is there any particular reason you've brought a Shepherd along with you?"

"Always nice to have someone who can put in a word with the Almighty," said Mal.

"In the unlikely event I want a sermon, I'll know who to ask," said Roberts. "Let's talk business."

Roberts pressed his hand against the console and the surface of the desk came suddenly to life: a map of the city of Neapolis. Mal leaned forward. Easy to spot the Platinum Mile, and the red dot to one corner marked their current location, seemingly.

"In about two hours, the upcountry train from Nashton will arrive at Great Northern station," said Roberts. "Comes in at that time twice weekly. And today, a very special shipment arrives. Ten crates' worth."

"That'll be the erbonium," said Jayne, as if for all the world he knew what the hell he was talking about.

"A man who knows his minerals," said Roberts.

"Lasers," said Jayne. "I like 'em."

"Usually, this shipment comes through the week before Carnival," said Roberts. "There have been some delays this year, for reasons with which you need not concern yourselves. Your concern is no more and no less than seeing that these ten crates are brought safely from the train depot to the space port and put on board the *Millicent*, which is due to take them off world later today."

"*Millicent*, huh?" said Jayne, and snickered. "Sounds girly."

"Shut up, Jayne," said Mal. "You were sayin', Mr. Roberts?"

"Yes, you're to escort the shipment safely from here," as he sketched the route, a red line lit the way on the map, "to here."

So, all they had to do was move these crates round the north-west edge of the city. "All the clearances?" Mal checked.

"Automated. At the depot, you shouldn't have to speak to another living soul. There'll be folks at Roby Docks to help you load and move the shipment to the *Millicent*."

"Huh," said Mal. "That'll take—"

"About two hours, yes," said Roberts.

"For which you're payin' us—"

"Two hundred platinum, yes."

There was a pause while everyone did the sums. What they'd earned haulin' those energy bars to Patience, Mal thought. A job which had come with all manner of trouble, not to mention many unkind words about his character.

"Two *hundred*?" said Jayne, incredulously. "What's the catch?"

"No catch," said Roberts. "It's a straightforward job and it's easy money."

"Ain't no such thing," said Jayne—fairly, Mal had to admit.

"All I want is for this to be done quickly and quietly," said Roberts. "I want no trouble—not at all, certainly none from you and your people. If trouble comes your way, I want you to do what's necessary. Zhao won't press charges if there's any shooting."

"Shiny," muttered Jayne.

"Any *unnecessary* shooting," clarified Roberts. "And I want no shooting at all, if that can be helped. I want this shipment off of Bethel before the party starts tonight. Now, I'm sure I don't need to tell you—"

Whatever it was, thought Mal, looked like he was about to tell 'em anyway…

"—that I'm a powerful man on Bethel. If anything goes wrong, I'll be holding you people fully accountable."

The Shepherd inserted himself back into the conversation. "No reason to think anything should go wrong," said Book. "Unless there's something we don't know."

"Nothing to know you don't know already," said Roberts.

Book, with a frown, said, "That's not quite the same thing—"

"Leave it, Shepherd," cut in Mal. "Man's said all he wants to say, and I don't see us needin' to know more about his business. Job's clear to me—clear to you too, I'd say."

"Good," said Roberts. "Then we're done here, and you can be on your way. The train arrives at Great Northern in a couple of hours and you're not being paid to sit around here. There are two trucks downstairs for your use throughout the job. Get yourself and your people and your preacher over to the depot, Captain, and see this business done. I want this off my mind before Carnival starts."

Roberts stood up. Mal, standing across from him at the desk, and for the hell of it, offered his hand. Roberts, caught unawares, shook it.

"Always shake on a deal," said Mal. "The gentlemanly thing to do, and we're all gentlemen here, aren't we?"

"I know I am, sir," said Zoë.

They left the office. "Didn't like him," said Jayne, after a while.

"I'm sure he'll be heartbroken," said Mal. "He only had good things to say about you."

"Did he?" Jayne looked baffled. "When?"

"You didn't like him either, do you, Shepherd?" said Zoë.

"Oh, I had no particular strong feelings either way," said Book. "One thing caught my eye though."

"What was that?" asked Mal, since the Shepherd's opinion was always worth knowing.

"Did you notice," said Book, "that most of the leather in there was fake?"

Mal, having looked closely at the map of the city, now knew there were in fact two train stations in Neapolis. The passenger trains came into the station on the west side, a rather gaudy edifice that gave the tourists the kind of shiny entry to the city that they were expecting. Meanwhile, the huge cross-continental goods trains rattled into the north side station, and, here, mid-morning, Mal and his people found themselves watching the vast machine slow down and slot into place at the station. There was something about machinery working well that was deeply satisfying, Mal thought. These big trains, spaceships, they all promised something. A way out. A better future.

"Eight days this has taken to come down from Nashton," Book said, a note of admiration in his voice too.

"Good news for us," said Zoë. "Anyone with a mite of sense intending to steal from it would surely try their luck out in the wild."

"So you'd think," said Mal. "Which is why I'm hoping all we need to do today is stand around lookin' pretty and gettin' paid for the privilege."

Jayne spat on the floor.

"Pretty isn't necessarily our strong point," said Book. "But all signs otherwise are positive that this should all go smoothly."

Mal himself wasn't ready to say the job was done until the job was done, and he could see a few weak links along the way. Here at the train depot was one, with the cargo coming out into the open from the secured carriage in which it had been travelling. The unloading procedure was well routinized, which was a blessing and a curse. A blessing, since there should be few surprises; a curse, since anyone intending to rob the cargo would know the procedure. Each carriage on the train had its own distinct section for unloading separated from the others with force barriers. All Mal and his people needed to do was keep watch over their immediate section. They'd see and hear anyone coming long before they could do any mischief.

When the train came to a full stop, Mal keyed in the security codes to unseal the big automatic doors on the side of the carriage. There were ten crates under their supervision, each one on its own hover-pallet which inched out to be loaded onto the two trucks they were using. When the crates were on board, Mal and Jayne took one truck, Zoë and Book the other. The trucks too were automated, driverless, the route to Roby Docks already programmed in. There were upsides to this: no drivers meant fewer people around to watch for potential threats; all hands were on weapons rather than driving; and the remote monitoring meant that if the trucks were taken, they could be easily followed. But there were also downsides.

"Don't trust these things," muttered Jayne. "You can hijack 'em at range. Muck about with the computer controllin' 'em."

"Don't look for trouble where there is none," said Mal. "We can take manual control if we need to."

"This thing moves an inch off course and I start shootin'," said Jayne.

"No shootin'," said Mal. "Not today. Today everythin' is going to be smooth and sweatless."

And so far that seemed to be the case. Everything was moving forward on schedule. Mal gave the security codes to allow both trucks to leave the depot and move out onto the road. Their route out to the space port was empty: Roberts had naturally ensured them access to the fast-track lanes. Most people were slogging into Neapolis on the main route. Mal checked in with Zoë and Book. Everything was fine there, and everything remained fine as they curved south and west around the perimeter of the city and headed down toward the docks. Mal even got a chance to look left and admire the shining towers of the Platinum Mile.

"That's where I'm headin' later," said Jayne. "Once we're paid. Gonna have me the night of my life. Gonna find me a pretty girl and—"

"*Bi zui*, Jayne!" cried Mal. "I don't need to know the details!"

Jayne sat and sulked. Mal, with nothing else happening right now, thought about what he might do later. Go to a bar. Have a drink. Thing was, places like this, all bright lights and partying, they didn't much tickle his fancy. Open countryside, that was more his kind of thing. Maybe he'd hire himself a horse, take a ride out on the prairie… No, he thought, the black was best. He'd be glad when they left Bethel and all its glitz and pretense, and were safely back home, where they should be, on *Serenity*. The road swept by. How long now till payday? How long till they were back in flight?

The trucks moved smoothly toward the docks. On the north side, they came to an automatic checkpoint, where their Roberts-granted credentials allowed them access to a section of the docks kept separate for ships requiring extra security. The barriers came up, and the two trucks went through into a bleak, empty area with none of the crush and color of the main part of the docks, where *Serenity* was parked. That could be seen about half-a-mile distant, low grubby buildings behind a high wire fence. Here, there was only a handful of ships, each one a good safe distance apart. Nobody to be seen, just the occasional loading van moving about.

Asphalt roads cut across a field of flattened brown earth. The trucks rolled along one of these, drawing up alongside the *Millicent*. A solid little freighter, thought Mal, with none of *Serenity*'s charm. Still, if she got the job done, that was enough.

Mal and Jayne got out of their truck; Zoë and Book emerged from theirs, a little way behind. Mal gave authorization for the trucks to open up, and the cargo began to emerge on the hover-pallets. As the crates came out, Jayne nudged Mal's arm.

"You expectin' company?"

Mal, looking up, saw a loading van heading their way, scuffing up clouds of dust as it came. His hand went instinctively to his pistol; Jayne's did the same, and Mal would bet the platinum they were making from this job that Zoë and Book were on similar alert. The van pulled up about ten yards away. Dust billowed toward them. Mal shielded his eyes with his free hand, and saw two figures come out, wearing blue overalls. Dockers, presumably.

"There a problem?" Mal called out.

"Loading mechanism on the *Millicent* is on the fritz," one called back. "We brought the van here to help get those crates on board."

"Kindly meant, I'm sure," said Mal, "but I'll need to see some authorization for that."

"We got authorization," said the docker, reaching toward a pocket. Mal's grip tightened on his pistol.

"Mal," muttered Jayne. "Why're those dockers wearing masks?"

"Huh?" The dust was settling, and Mal peered ahead. Jayne weren't wrong…

"Hey," yelled Jayne. "Take off those gorram masks!"

For a moment, nobody moved. Then one of the dockers made a move to reach for something—a weapon? Jayne's pistol was out. From behind, Book's voice rose up, giving a fierce command. "Don't shoot!" Jayne, distracted, looked back over his shoulder, and, in that moment's hesitation, Mal saw what the docker was doing.

"Gas!" yelled Mal. "They've got a gorram gas grenade!"

The air began to fill with a thick, foul brown haze. Mal, memories flashing back to unhappier times under Alliance fire, covered his mouth and nose with his free hand. He couldn't see a damn thing, only hear and try to guess what was going on. He dived forward to where the docker had been standing and grabbed out, getting them by the jacket. Pulled them round. Caught a glimpse of dark angry eyes, and then felt a knee where a knee had no business going, and went down. The air was thick and Mal tried not to gasp from the pain. He heard the whine of hover-pallets, running feet, vehicles starting up, and Book, from a little way behind, shouted, "Zoë! Back to the truck!" Shots—from Jayne's gun—were being fired at random. "Jayne!" he yelled. "Stop that! You might hit one of us!"

The shooting stopped. The vehicles, from what he could hear, were moving away at speed. Slowly, the air began to clear and Mal, coughing, struggled to his feet and looked round. "Jayne!" he yelled, and saw a huge figure lurch into view.

"I'm here, Mal… Gorram filthy stuff, can't *breathe*!"

"Where's Zoë? Where's Book? Did you see which way they went?"

"Didn't see nothin' after that grenade landed, Mal."

"Did they chase 'em?"

"I said that I didn't see nothin'!"

The air cleared. Desperately, Mal looked round. His truck was still there; Zoë and Book's was not. The van was gone—and so were the crates. From the dust still rising across the field, he could see which way the van—and their other truck, he hoped—had gone. Roberts was going to kill them—if he ever found out.

"All right," said Mal. "Zoë and Book'll be on top of this. They'll find those crates and bring 'em back—"

"You dumb or somethin'?" said Jayne. "All they gotta do is throw another one of those grenades and they'll be away. Then that stuff'll be on a ship getting' ready to leave this stinkin' ruttin' planet. No wonder they didn't do the job out in the country. They wanted the cargo here, at the docks. We've done all their ruttin' work for them!"

And the worst thing about all this, thought Mal, was that Jayne was probably right.

Kaylee Frye, standing in the doorway of the engine room, looked regretfully at the sight of both Tam siblings fast asleep in her hammock, and wished with all her heart that she could somehow magically swap places with River. Why oh why did Simon Tam have to be so *shuai*? So very edible? Worse'n all that, why did he have to be so *proper*? Kaylee, given the opening, would bed this boy within *seconds*—and here he was, right now, in her gorram *hammock*, looking almost like you could eat him right up, and sometimes you couldn't help thinkin' that the 'verse was out to torment you...

Kaylee heard soft footsteps behind her and turned to see Inara. She nodded into the engine room. "Will you look at that?" she said, in a wistful voice.

"Well, at least he's getting some sleep," said Inara. "I thought we were going to have to roll him under the table earlier."

Kaylee sighed. There was no rollin' with Simon Tam anywhere, that was the whole problem... Inara laid her hand upon her arm and drew her away. "We should leave them in peace."

They went through the ship to Inara's shuttle. Inara took her usual seat, and Kaylee let her brush her hair. "You didn't mind waiting here on *Serenity* until the job was done, did you?" said Inara.

"In fact, I *do* mind," said Kaylee. "Job's only going to take a couple hours, or so Mal said. I could be out there, takin' a look round, havin' some fun—"

"Much as it hurts me to agree with Mal, it's probably the wisest choice," Inara said. "Mal's jobs do have a tendency to become... well, over-complicated at times. Staying on *Serenity* might turn out to be a sensible option."

"I thought Bethel was about as safe as a Rim planet could be."

"It's a strange world," said Inara. "From the outside, it could easily be mistaken for one of the central planets. The big resorts are beautifully maintained. As for the Platinum Mile—the security there would put anywhere on Londinium or Sihnon to shame."

"Plat'num Mile?" asked Kaylee.

"That's the part of the city with the main hotels and casinos. The Guild House is there, the main government buildings."

"Big mile," said Kaylee.

"Yes, that is something of a misnomer," said Inara. "But you'd easily think you were back in the Core."

"Not seen much of the Core," said Kaylee. "Not likely to see much of Neapolis either, if Mal has his way."

"Don't worry, Kaylee," said Inara, with a smile. "*Serenity* will have to stay for the duration of Carnival: I'm engaged for the whole of the last day. And I'm sure once the job is done, Mal will be happy for everyone to take a look round."

"He'd better." Kaylee bit her lower lip. "Reckon Simon could be persuaded?"

"I suppose there's no harm in asking," said Inara. "But…"

"But what?" There was a pause. "Inara?"

"Don't set yourself up for disappointment, Kaylee."

"Already disappointed here," said Kaylee. "A whole 'verse of disappointment with that one."

"Simon will work out what he feels eventually."

"Well, I wish he'd hurry up, because I ain't gettin' younger here."

Inara laughed. "Kaylee, you're still a baby!"

"Oh, don't you start. Mal's bad enough."

Softly, firmly, Inara ran her fingers through her hair. Kaylee sighed and relaxed. "Who's your client this time? Someone nice?"

"They're always nice." Inara paused. "Usually nice. This one is a local businessman. Young—almost as young as you," she teased.

"Shush! What kinda business is he in?"

"He owns several of the casinos on the Platinum Mile."

"Rich then?"

"I imagine so. Nobody went poor owning casinos. Just from playing at them."

"And handsome?"

Inara smiled. "Kaylee, you know that I choose my clients—"

"Because of their oh-so-charmin' personalities—yes, I know. But he is handsome, isn't he?"

"In this case, yes. He's very handsome."

Kaylee sighed. "And what will you be doing together? I bet it's all fancy."

"I suppose it will be," said Inara. "There's a reception in the morning. A recital in the afternoon. The usual."

Kaylee snorted. "Like I have any idea what any of those might involve."

"And, of course, there's the firework display on the final evening. That's a big event on the social calendar here—they call it the Big Bang. Anyone who's anyone is seen there."

"With a beautiful companion on their arm," said Kaylee.

"Only the very best people," said Inara.

Everything sounded so glamorous, so nice. Kaylee imagined herself in her big dress, Simon on her arm, off to some recital, whatever that might be. Simon would know, wouldn't he? He'd know exactly what was involved and what to do. If he'd only *ask*…

"We'll go to the ball," said a quiet voice. "You'll see."

River was standing in the doorway, eyes wide open, taking in everything around her. A shiver went down Kaylee's spine. Slicin' a piece from Jayne was one thing (and who among them hadn't wanted to do that at one time or another) but Kaylee had seen something the others hadn't seen. While they'd been rescuin' Mal from Niska. *Serenity* got boarded and Kaylee overwhelmed. And then, there was River, gun in hand, fellin' three men in a matter of seconds. This girl was an unexploded bomb, here on *Serenity*, where they should all be safest. Kaylee had put a little distance between them ever since. She hoped Simon hadn't noticed. She didn't want to hurt his feelings.

"River, honey," said Inara, soft as fine silk. "Would you like me to do your hair next?"

"Hair," said River, staring at Inara's hands as they worked. "Comprised almost entirely of keratin, a fibrous helicoidal protein. Grows from follicles found in the dermis of most mammals." She took a step toward them. "People think hair grows after death, but it doesn't. The corpse shrinks."

And there it was. Just when you thought you were getting halfway close to normal, River popped out something like that and… It weren't right. *She* weren't right… Inara tied Kaylee's hair back. "Come here, River," she said. "Your turn."

Kaylee went to sit on the bed, River drew closer, and, with a swift dancer's movement, lowered herself to sit cross-legged at Inara's feet. Gently, firmly, Inara set to work on River's hair. "Let's see to these tangles."

At Inara's touch, River sighed and closed her eyes. Kaylee felt bad for what she'd been thinking only moments before. Poor kid just needed a little tender loving care. A little human kindness.

"Where's your brother, sweetie?" said Inara.

"Asleep. He should sleep more." River sighed. "He's such hard work. Won't listen. Won't hear the words when they're said to him."

Kaylee sure could sympathize with that. Top three percent, huh? What was the point of all that learning and all those smarts when you couldn't see what was staring you right in the face? Maybe he didn't think she was much of a catch… Maybe he just didn't *like* her…

"Catch the girl and make her cry," murmured River.

"What?" said Kaylee, startled. "What're you sayin', River?"

River, her eyes still closed, went on, "Boxes. Catch the girl and put her in a box. She screams and cries and begs to go, go, go—but they won't let her. They take her and squash her. Try to shape her the way they want her. Won't let her be free."

"Shush, sweetie," soothed Inara. "You don't have to worry. We're safe here."

"Safe is momentary. Safe is transitory. Safe doesn't last. Can't last."

Inara was frowning now. Did she feel the same way about River? That there was somethin'... *uncanny* about her?

"River?" said Inara. "Do you mean we're in danger?"

"No," said River. "Yes."

"Sure am glad we cleared that one up," muttered Kaylee.

"We're not in danger, River," said Inara. "Not here. Bethel is safe—"

River's eyes opened. They were shining—it took Kaylee a moment to see they shone with mischief. A smile was tugging at her lips too. "I'll make more from this. More'n anyone. You'll see. We're going to the ball." She closed her eyes again. "Here they come," she said. "Two down, two to go."

The question of what that was supposed to mean was explained about two minutes later, when Wash's voice came through the communicator. "Kaylee? Inara? Mal's on his way back."

"That's... sooner than expected," said Inara, in a worried voice.

"Ain't likely to be good news," agreed Kaylee. She jumped to her feet and began to hurry toward the cargo bay. Soon enough, they heard the familiar grate of the cargo bay doors opening, and then the roar of a truck, coming back inside. The captain—who looked furious—was driving; Jayne in the seat beside him.

Two down. Two to go.

From behind Kaylee's shoulder, River said, "Not safe." She sounded weary, like she was tired of being proven right yet again. "Not safe."

"Mal?" said Inara.

"Don't ask."

"Damn Shepherd," growled Jayne. "Shoulda brung the doctor after all."

"Where's Wash?" said Mal, striding through the ship to the dining room. "Wash! Here! Right now!"

Kaylee chased after him to the dining room, where Simon (hair mussed from sleep, arms folded, shirt open at the neck, oh so *shuai*...) was standing in the doorway. "Oh," he said. "Is this the part where I have to do emergency surgery again?"

The captain shot him a filthy look. "Not this time."

"That's something, I suppose."

"You'll recall, Doc, what I had to say earlier about your sarcasm. If you ain't helpin', you're hinderin'. And I ain't in the mood today for more hinderin'.."

"Mal," said Inara. "What went wrong?"

"Shepherd went wrong," said Jayne.

Wash walked in. "Hey, Mal!" he said, cheerfully. "That was quick!" He looked round. His face fell. "Where's Zoë? Mal? Where's Zoë?"

Zoë, when she saw the loading van heading toward them, got an inkling that Mal's plan was going the way of many of Mal's plans, and began to move back toward her truck. When the grenade went down, then, she was in place to leap back inside, avoiding the worst of the gas. She heard the Shepherd call out, "Zoë!" he shouted. "Back to the truck!"

"Already there, preacher man," she called back. A

moment or two later, he too was scrambling inside, coughing a little, but not too bad. "They're taking the crates—"

"I figured that!" she said. He began switching the vehicle over to the manual controls. "Damn driverless," he muttered. Zoë took the opportunity to suck in a breath, lean out the window, and get the lay of the land.

"Which way?" said Book.

Dust was billowing through the brown fog; as good a clue as any. "Follow those clouds," said Zoë. Book obeyed. The truck kicked off at great speed. Quickly, through the dust, Zoë caught sight of the loading van, a little to their left.

"There it is!" No time to lose. Mal and Jayne could catch up later. "Get after them!"

Book swung the truck into pursuit. "Now where are they going…?"

"Another ship, I guess," said Zoë. "Get the cargo out of sight and off world as quick as they can—"

"Makes sense," said Book. "We've done all the carrying for them…"

But the van didn't stop. It picked up pace and sped across the field.

"Heading for the main road," said Zoë.

"One of the checkpoints'll stop them," said Book, confidently, only to say, moments later, as the van sped through, "—or not."

"So they're not takin' the goods off world?" said Zoë.

"Seems not," said Book. "Curious, that, isn't it?"

That was one word for it, thought Zoë, as their own clearances got them back out and onto an access road. Book swerved to avoid a solid little Mule trundling toward them. Once they were past this obstacle, Zoë saw what they were looking for: the van, with the hover-pallets behind, zipping away up toward the main road.

"There they are," Zoë said. "Hit the gas, preacher. They ain't gettin' away again."

He didn't need asking twice. The truck lurched forward, jerking them both, picking up pace. They rapidly gained ground on the van, which was held back by the weight of the cargo. When they came off the access route onto the flat straight main road, they began to gain on the van steadily. Inch by inch they drew closer. Zoë saw a masked figure at the back of the nearest pallet, pistol raised.

"Least we ain't heading into the city right now," said Book, far too cheerfully for a man in the middle of a chase where weapons were being drawn. "Traffic on that side of the road is murder."

Maybe so, thought Zoë, although to her mind there were more than enough vehicles over on this side of the road to keep both parties in this chase busy, dodging and weaving. She moved across her seat to lean out of the window and raised her pistol.

"I'd rather there was no shooting, Zoë," said the Shepherd.

"Shepherd," said Zoë, "there's always shootin'."

"You knock 'em off this road at speed," said Book, voice low, "there'll be more than us and them harmed. And this ain't anyone else's trouble but ours and theirs."

He had a point. Zoë ducked her head back inside. Just in time. A shot, fired by the person on the pallet, ricocheted off the side of the truck, right where Zoë's head had been.

"*Gǒu shǐ!*" muttered Zoë. She glanced at the Shepherd. His face was hard. "You changed your mind about the shootin' yet, preacher man?"

"Nope." He swerved to dodge another car, and brought the truck flying out safely on the other side. They were now maybe ten yards from the pallet and narrowing the distance rapidly. Zoë saw a sign overhead marking an exit and, at the very last minute, the driver ahead swung sharply to the right, leaving the main road.

"*Lǎo tiān yé!*" yelled Book, in most ungodly fashion, scrambling to react. "Shoulda seen that one coming!"

"Yes indeed," said Zoë. "Every single preacher I ever met knew exactly the best way to conduct himself in a car chase."

Book ignored this (but then he always ignored this kind of bait, like responding was well beneath his dignity), and sent the truck lurching right.

"Ow," said Zoë.

"Are you all right, Zoë?"

"I'll live," she said.

They sped down the exit road after the van, off the freeway, and out onto an access road that curved round and back under itself. The truck, to Zoë's way of thinking, was not entirely under control, and there were a couple of concerning moments before Book got the upper hand. "Nice work, preacher."

"God is good," he said, then: "Wonder where they're leadin' us," he muttered. The road they had come out on was empty, poorer quality, and stretching straight out across flat open country.

"I've no idea," said Zoë. "But I do know one thing. I'm done with chasin'."

Quickly, fluidly, she moved to hang out of the side window, and fired off a few shots. Not easy, bringing down a hover-pallet. There were stabilizers on either side, if you knew what you were looking for (Zoë did), but they were hellish hard to hit, even when both parties concerned weren't moving at speed, and the other party might start shooting back at any moment. Zoë ducked back in as a volley of shots bounced off the side of the truck. So now the game was tit-for-tat: Zoë trying to hit the stabilizers; the other party trying to hit her first. Nothing personal. Everyone just doin' their job. But the good times couldn't last forever, and one side had to get lucky. Suddenly, the driver of the van ahead braked. Dead stop. The Shepherd, in turn, hit the brakes and swerved to avoid the pallet.

"Hold on, Zoë, hold on!" he yelled, struggling to keep the truck under control. Zoë braced herself as the truck lurched off the road and came crashing to a halt in a cloud of red dust. She heard the van ahead start up again and speed away.

They both sat back.

"Are you all right?" said Book.

"Fine, Shepherd. How about you?"

"Thankful to the Almighty once again." He drew in a deep breath, and then slowly began to turn the truck back round. "They took one hell of a risk there. I could have ploughed right into them."

"They knew you were too good a driver."

"Huh."

Zoë looked up the road. The van and the pallet were out of sight now. "I guess we ought to head after them."

"I guess," Book replied. "But look—here comes more trouble."

Coming up the road toward them was another vehicle. Flashing lights. Official sign. Book gave a low laugh. "What do you think, Zoë. Up for another chase?"

The vehicle pulled up alongside them. Zoë considered their options, and said, "Not today, preacher. Our luck ain't up to it."

Simon, trooping along behind Inara and Wash, who themselves were following Mal and Jayne onto the bridge, once again found himself trying to piece together a coherent narrative from a chorus of voices that were far from being in harmony. Some were asking questions, some were answering them, some were cursing, and it seemed to Simon that all of them were shouting. *No, Wash, I ain't got any gorram idea where Zoë is, I thought she'd back here by now... Ruttin' Shepherd knocked my arm, woulda had 'em... Came out of nowhere, that's what... But where's Zoë, Mal? Where's Zoë?* Simon, hearing some residual coughing and a throwaway mention of 'gas', said quietly, "I suppose I should make sure neither of you are in immediate danger of asphyxiation."

As intended, this landed like a missile on a gap in the conversation. Everyone turned to look at him. He wasn't really worried—they'd be in a lot more trouble if that was the case—but he wanted people to shut up, and sometimes he couldn't just help himself. "If there was gas," he went on, straight-faced. "there might be damage to your lungs."

"What about my gorram lungs?" said Jayne, hand pressing against his side where his lungs weren't. "There a problem?"

"Never mind," said Simon. "I'm sure you'll both be fine. Am I right in saying that there's been some kind of a heist?"

"I wouldn't exactly call it a heist," said Mal.

"People in masks appeared out of nowhere and stole the valuable cargo which you were guarding under threat of violence," said Simon. "I don't have a dictionary to hand, but isn't that the literal definition of 'heist'?"

Mal, he realized, was starting to look about ready to punch him. "*Wā*, Simon," said Wash. "Do you always have to be such a jerk?"

"Mal…" murmured Inara, and the captain subsided.

"In our defense," Mal said, gathering together the shreds of his dignity, "there wasn't much in the way of actual violence. At least not on our part. Shepherd Book wasn't having it, for one thing."

"Stupid move on the preacher's part," grumbled Jayne. "I'd'a brung 'em down if he hadna got in my way."

"Oh well," said Simon, "I suppose there's still time for plenty of shooting."

"I'm countin' on it," said Jayne.

"You've still not said where Zoë is," said Wash.

"Nor the Shepherd," said Inara.

Mal didn't reply. Neither did Jayne.

"Mal?" said Wash. "What about Zoë?"

"Didn't see neither her nor Book after all that smoke went up," said Jayne.

"Like I said, I thought they'd have come back here by now," said Mal.

"But they haven't come back," said Wash. "They've not come back—"

"Not yet," said Mal. "But they will."

"Are you sure about that, Mal?" said Wash. There was a rising note of hysteria in his voice. "Only it's just that last time this kind of thing went wrong I got strung up and hurt and you got strung up and hurt and also bits of you came back before other bits and, oh, actually didn't you in fact *die*—"

"A temporary state of affairs," said Mal.

"That's not making me feel better, Mal—"

"Zoë and Book can take care of themselves, Wash," said Inara, softly.

"It's the other people who might be taking care of them that I'm worried about," said Wash. "Taking care of their ears, or taking care of their faces, or taking care of whole parts of Zoë which I don't want to talk about in polite company—"

The comm crackled.

"Saved by the bell," muttered Simon.

"It was just gettin' interesting," said Jayne.

"It's Roberts," said Wash, voice low and anxious. "Mal, what're you going to—"

Mal opened the comm. "Mr. Roberts," he said, with great bonhomie. "And how are you on this mighty fine afternoon leadin' up to the first night of Carnival?"

"I'm always well, Captain Reynolds. I am an exceptionally rich man who can do more or less exactly as he chooses. How did the job go?"

"The job? Well, the cargo arrived exactly as you described, sir."

"And?"

"And…"

"Don't lie to him, Mal," Inara murmured, shaking her head.

"There was what you might call a little interference in transmission," said Mal, "but two of my team are still out there and on top of matters."

"Two of your team?"

"Two of my finest," said Mal, not entirely inaccurately.

"I wonder who they might be."

"You want to know who my finest are," said Mal. "I hesitate to respond to that, sir, since there are other members of my team present, and I don't want to deal any unnecessary blows to morale—"

"I ask because two of your team are currently sitting in my library."

Mal cut the comm and swore profusely in a torrent that Simon couldn't entirely decipher, but considerable shade was cast upon the reputation of the mothers of more or less everyone present and, indeed, more or less everyone that Mal had ever had the misfortune to meet.

"*Shit*, Mal!" said Wash. "I knew this was gonna happen! I *knew* it!"

"How do you know he's telling the truth?" said Simon.

"Maybe he's just trying to go back on the deal. Ask him for proof—"

"No," said Inara, quickly. "Don't do that."

"I'm not much minded to ask for suchlike, Doc," said Mal, "given what happened last time—"

"No," said Wash, emphatically. "No *ears* this time. Not this time, not any time, not ever again with the ears."

"—but the doc makes a fair point..." Mal opened the comm again. "Far be it from me to disagree with you, Mr. Roberts, but all my team are currently accounted for—"

"Including the browncoat and the preacher?"

That'll be the proof we wanted, thought Simon, and watched Mal mutter something under his breath.

"You say they're in your library?" said Mal. "That over at your office?"

"Don't take me for a fool, Reynolds," said Roberts. "Do you think I'd tell you where they are so you can break them out? But if your hope was that they were out and about looking for my cargo and that they would bring it back before I discovered the mess you people have made—"

"You sure you got the right people, Mr. Roberts? I mean, plenty of folks out and about toting guns these days—"

"Oh, for God's sake, Mal," Inara muttered.

"A browncoat and a preacher isn't a combination that you see every day."

"Hard to deny that, Mr. Roberts. But maybe they'd'a been better left to get on with the job we agreed—"

"The job which we agreed was that you and your people would see that cargo taken safely from the train depot onto

81

the freighter. And that hasn't happened. So here's the new job on offer, Captain Reynolds. That cargo was worth five hundred platinum to me, and it's gone. Someone has to make good my loss, and that someone should be you. You've got till the Big Bang to bring me that five hundred you just cost me, or else I'll see a bullet through the brains of both of your finest."

"Now wait a minute—" said Mal. "No need to be talkin' about bullets and brains—"

"I'd say not," said Wash.

"I'm done now, Captain Reynolds. You get on with the new job and get back in touch when you have my money, or else you receive a couple of corpses in payment for all you've cost me." He didn't wait for the reply. The comm went dead.

"Mal…" said Wash.

"What in ruttin' hell did he mean by the Big Bang?" said Jayne. "Only one kinda big bang I'm interested in and—"

"It's the big fireworks display on the main night of Carnival," said Inara. "Which, Jayne, is tomorrow night, so perhaps you could start thinking more about the fact that Zoë and the Shepherd are in danger than about your—"

"Tomorrow *night*?" Wash goggled at her. "Mal!"

"All right, all right, *Bì zuǐ*!" Mal said. "Everyone shut up and let's think this through."

"Five hundred platinum ain't gonna be easy to lay our hands on," said Jayne.

"You think?" said Wash.

"Not in just over a day, no," said Jayne. "A little longer, maybe. You think maybe he'd let us have a little longer, Mal?"

"No, Jayne, I do not think he'll let us have a little longer—"

"Could we get some *help*?" said Wash. "Could the authorities help? I mean, he's threatened their *lives*, Mal—"

"Sheriff said if the job went wrong he'd have the ship," Jayne said.

"No help there then," said Wash. "So what then?"

"So now we have to find five hundred platinum in just over a day," said Simon.

"That's about the size of it, doctor," said Mal, "and I'd welcome some suggestions as to how we might go about achieving that."

"There's robbin'," said Jayne, ticking off on his fingers. "Whorin'," he said, with a leer at Inara. "And gamblin'."

"And for his next trick, he'll count past three," said Wash. "I think what Mal meant was does anyone have any *good* suggestions?"

"What was wrong with those?"

"Do you want to me *list* the reasons?"

"Jayne's not wrong," said Mal, to general consternation. "We have to find the money fast, and you don't come by that kind of money fast being honest. We ain't going to try to make that money."

"We're not?" said Wash. "Mal, he'll *shoot* them—"

"We ain't waitin' for that either," said Mal. "Listen. All of you. We're going to try to locate the merchandise. We find the goods, we get them back, we take them where they're meant to be—everybody's happy."

"Mal," said Jayne, "them crates'll be long gone. They let us bring 'em over to the docks for a reason. Whatever ship they loaded 'em on'll be halfway across the system by now. I say we go over to Roberts' place right now, point a few guns at him, get Zoë and the Shepherd back, and get the hell out of here—"

"Sounds like a good way to get us all killed," said Wash.

Simon glanced at Inara. She said, quietly, for his ears only, "This is going to go on for a while."

"Yes, that does seem to be the usual decision-making process," Simon replied. "I hate to ask this, but is there anyone down there that you can lean on?"

"I could make a few enquiries. But Jacob Roberts is a very powerful man on Bethel. I doubt people will want to go up against him. I suppose there might be a score or two to settle, but why would anyone do that for our benefit?"

Simon nodded. He stood for a while, watching as the argument went round in circles. He thought he might have an idea. "Inara," he said, "could you listen out for River for me? There's something I want to check."

Ava stopped to slip off her shoe and rub the blister forming on her heel. She had been walking for a couple of hours now, and the tenements on the north side of the city had given way to rows of small hotels and holiday villas, where the less conspicuously rich visitors to Neapolis stayed. Ava, who knew only the rough shacks of her home town, gawped at these places: the cool shady decks, where people were sitting sipping drinks before heading down to the Mile; the room and the space and the luxury. Maybe she'd been stupid to think that job at the hotel could ever have been real. Maybe places like this weren't for people like her.

As Ava made her way through this district, she became aware that the swell of people was heading in the opposite direction. She'd taken a good look at the map, so she knew where and why they were going: down to the Platinum Mile, where the party was underway; down to the shows, and the sights, and the food and drink, and the possibility (however slight) of making their fortune, of becoming one of those lucky people who didn't have to rent a room or two on this side of the river, but could buy a fancy house over on the east bank, up where the rich and fancy people lived their almost unimaginable lives.

Ava slipped her shoe back on. She saw a family heading her way—they looked nice, a momma and poppa and two little girls. Slowly, she approached.

"Excuse me please," she said. "Can you tell me the time?"

The poppa smiled at her. "Sure! A little after one thirty."

"Thank you, sir."

She saw concern flicker over his face. Maybe he saw that all was not right; maybe he got a sense that here was a girl in need of help. Ava felt a lump rise up in her throat, and she thought for a moment about asking these nice people for help, telling them what had happened to her, but then one of the little girls, running back, grabbed her poppa's hand and pulled him off down the street. After a moment or two, Ava decided that perhaps it was for the best. Wouldn't've been nice of her, to spoil their holiday with her troubles. And maybe they wouldn't have wanted to help. Maybe they'd have told her to go away. She couldn't have borne that. No, better that she looked after herself.

Slowly, the hotels became shabbier, the holiday villas in their own little grounds began to disappear. She came to a big road with trucks and hover-pallets shooting past and she crossed this, dodging through the gaps in traffic as people leaned on their horns and yelled at her from open windows. Reaching the other side, she quickly realized she'd crossed a barrier: the tourist district was gone, and she was in a very different part of the city. Industrial, commercial; more like home. She caught the stink of chemicals, fuel, burning tar. She came to a barbed wire fence, which seemed like it might prove a more difficult barrier, but wherever someone put up a fence, someone else wanted a way past, and she quickly found the place where a hole had been cut.

She slipped through, onto an expanse of rough asphalt. Weeds were growing in the cracks. As she walked across, the ground began to judder. She heard a deep, distant roar that rose rapidly to become almost unbearably loud and then—a little way yonder and overhead, and with a stink of fumes and a grumbling of reconditioned engines—a spaceship took off. Ava shielded her eyes to watch it leave. Wished she could join it out there in the black, far away from Bethel and her troubles here.

This end of the docks, nearest to the city, was where the shipping and freight companies were based. Ava passed through small streets of squat makeshift buildings; offices, mostly, and other amenities for visiting crew who weren't stopping over long enough or weren't paid enough to sample the delights of the Platinum Mile. Ava walked up and down for a while until she saw the sign she was looking for: *Mag Coirc Motel and Bar*. She went slowly past, and then crossed the street and walked back down the other side, all the while getting the lay of the land. The little motel complex, she could see, was laid out on a square: three sides of buildings, and the side facing the street left open so that cars and other vehicles could park in front of the rooms. The office was on the street front on the left, and the bar was on street level on the other side. Whoever had picked this place had made sure Ava could go straight to the rooms without having to pass through the office. She tried to work out where 107 would be. The rooms were stacked two stories high, and she was pretty sure that 107 was on the ground level, over in the right-hand corner. Now all she had to do was wait. Not before three, her anonymous friend had said, and yet not after three thirty.

There was an alley between two buildings where she could stand and watch, as long as she didn't mind the smell of garbage. Ava could certainly put up with that for a little while. She took a closer look at the bar. There was a handful of patrons sitting outside. Their mood was rough and cheerful; dockers, she guessed, or crew from the ships passing through. No worse or better than Uncle Nate's friends back home. On the wall outside, a chalk board with prices had been nailed up and, more helpfully from Ava's perspective, there was a rolling display of scheduled flights that also showed the time, ticking past. She had a little over forty minutes before she should make a move. Standing where she was, she might even see her contact arrive.

She leaned her head against the wall and stood patiently, watching the seconds tick by. There were tricks to this that she'd devised during the long train journey down from Evansville—close your eyes and count along, see how well you kept time; count up as the time got closer to targets— twenty past, twenty-five past, half-past, quarter to... Tell yourself stories about the people sitting outside...

A little before ten to the hour, a flyer pulled off the road and parked up in the motel courtyard. Was this her contact arriving? Ava leaned forward for a closer look, and then pulled back in dismay when she saw the two men getting out. One had a bushy black beard; the other wore a black T-shirt with a White Dragon logo on the front. The two men from yesterday... For a moment, Ava thought she might scream. Was this a set-up? Had this all been a trap? The two men walked round to the front of the building and struck up a conversation with some of the men sitting outside the bar. Ava shuddered, remembering the stink of the sweat on them, how hard they'd held onto her, how the one in the T-shirt had laughed as he brought the needle closer and closer...

They stood and talked and laughed. Ava checked the time on the display. Six minutes to. She willed them to move on... And then one of them—the one with the beard, the one she'd bitten—went inside. The other pulled out a chair at the table and sat down. At two minutes to, the first man came out again, followed by the waitress, a pretty girl who looked maybe a couple of years older than Ava. She took their order while fending off their advances with the kind of weary ease that comes from too much practice.

Ava watched in horror. If there was a back way into the motel, she didn't have time now to go and find it. She shoulda thought of this; she shoulda thought of making sure there were a couple of ways to the room… She was stuck now. Only way was through the courtyard. She watched the men settle into their chairs and checked the time. Two minutes past. She screwed her hands up; pressed her fists against her eyes; tried to decide what was best to do. *Twenty past*, she thought. She'd give 'em till twenty past, and then… Then she'd try her luck.

Simon, returning to the dining room about half an hour later, could hear straight away that the quarrel had got no further. Mal still wanted to steal back the goods. Wash still wanted to know how quickly this would help Zoë. Jayne still wanted to shoot someone, anyone, didn't matter who, and soon. Simon sat down at the table and listened politely for a while, waiting for a break in the argument. After a while, it became abundantly clear to him that such a thing was never going to occur naturally, so he attempted to intervene.

"Can I…?"

No chance.

"Just sayin' that if we go back to Roberts' fancy office and I show him what Vera can do then he won't be hangin' onto them for much ruttin' longer—"

"And I'm just saying," said Wash, "that that must be the stupidest plan I've heard since your *last* plan—Mal, I don't want her killed. I don't want her *hurt*. Is that too much to ask? Really?"

"Nobody wants nobody killed, Wash—"

"I have a suggestion to make," said Simon, to a general lack of interest.

"—but right now we're runnin' short of time—"

"It's actually quite a good suggestion," said Simon.

"—and even shorter on ideas—"

"If any of you would like to listen," said Simon, to a space on the wall just above one of the cupboards. "To my really quite good suggestion. Given the lack of any other really quite good suggestions—"

"—and I have to say that the good doctor here is starting to try my patience even further than usual... What," said Mal, "in the name of all that is ungodly, do you want to say, Doctor?"

"I have an idea," said Simon. "About how to get money. It's called 'working'."

His three colleagues looked at him dumbly.

"My patience is gettin' more tried by the second," said Mal. "Wearin' mighty thin—"

"Workin'?" said Jayne. "You mean as like... a job?"

"I mean as like a job," agreed Simon.

"The last job you came up with nearly ended up with you in the hands of the Alliance," said Wash. "Remember? The drug heist?"

"Anyone can have a stroke of bad luck," said Simon. His eyes came to rest on Jayne, who was looking anywhere but back. "Otherwise, I think it was a pretty successful heist. Admittedly my experience of heists is limited to that one, and, well, this morning—"

"I am done with heists," sai— ——
heists." He considered this. "No more h——

"There are other ways to make mon——
explained Simon, patiently.

"Hey," said Wash. "He's right! I think I even rem——
some of them. Before my life became filled with guns an—
shootings and near-fatal injuries and my wife getting taken
hostage by casino-running gangsters—"

"Wash, be quiet," said Mal. "Doc, keep talkin'."

"While you've been busy… doing whatever it is you've
been doing," said Simon, "I had a look on the Cortex to see if
any of the hospitals in Neapolis were advertising."

"Advertisin'?" said Jayne. "What, sellin' stuff? What do
they sell? Like, *bandages*? That don't make no sense—"

"No," said Simon, patiently. "Advertising jobs."

"Thinkin' of leavin'?" said Jayne, more hopefully than
Simon might have liked.

"Not today," said Simon.

"You're wasting your time talking to Jayne," said Wash.
"What did you find?"

"Something like Carnival," Simon explained, "it's
always a busy time for hospitals. There's usually a fair
number of injuries: fights break out, people do stupid
things. ER is always crazy. The same used to happen during
holidays at the hospital back in Capital City. I remember one
new year—" He looked at the stony faces of his audience.
"Anyway. There's a hospital, St. Freda's, that urgently needs
a temporary surgeon as cover over Carnival. And, as it
happens, I'm a very good surgeon."

Well, yes, for which we have all been thankful," said Mal. "And I'm not sayin' yes, and I'm not sayin' no, but, as a matter of interest—how much you think you could earn?"

"For a couple of shifts they're offering a hundred platinum. I could probably push them higher if they're stuck. It's not the whole amount, but it's a start."

Jayne spat his drink onto the table. "*How* much?"

Wash, almost in the firing line, said, "*Qù nǐ de*, Jayne! What is the matter with you?"

"He can make that much just for cuttin' someone open?" Jayne said. "Why can't *I* make that much just for cuttin' someone open?"

"It's not the cutting open," said Simon. "It's what you do when you're inside. Back home," he added, almost mischievously, "over a weekend like this, I could probably triple that fee."

"Well, you ain't home," said Jayne.

I don't need you to tell me that, thought Simon. "No," he said. "I'm not." He turned to the captain, who was looking pensive. "Does this sound like a plan?"

"Sounds like it might be a plan," conceded Mal. "But they don't just take on anyone who wanders in off the street says they're a mighty fine surgeon, top three percent, do they?"

"You did," said Simon.

Jayne laughed out loud. "He's got you there, Mal!"

"Yes, well, I ain't fussy," said Mal. "Don't you need to prove credentials, your qualifications, whatever they are, and so on?"

"I've got that covered," said Simon.

"So you can get into this clinic, hospital, whatever it is without trouble?" said Mal.

"Yes," said Simon. "But a reference would be useful."

"I can just about manage that," said Mal. "Might even manage something complimentary—about your surgeonin' skills, that is."

"They like it when previous employers comment on personality," said Wash, helpfully. "That's opened a lot of doors for me. You know—cheerful, friendly, obliging. I'm sure we can make up something, Simon—"

"Well, luckily for me, you won't have to," said Simon. "St. Freda's is owned and operated by the Companion's Guild. What I need, ideally, is a reference from a registered companion."

"Inara'll do that," said Mal, with what Simon thought was not entirely well-placed confidence.

"The thing is," he said, "I'll be using fake credentials, obviously, and I don't want to store up trouble for Inara as a result…"

"I think she can be persuaded of the merits of this idea," said Mal, rising from his seat.

Wash put a restraining hand upon his arm. "I'd leave it to Simon if I were you."

"Huh." Mal sat down again. "Maybe you're right on that score… Anyways, we still have the rest to come up with."

"I'll leave that to you," said Simon, standing in turn. "You might want to avoid situations in which you're likely to get shot, hit, otherwise wounded. I'm going to have my hands full."

"Hundred platinum," muttered Jayne, watching him go and shaking his head. "And for what? That ain't right. He ain't right. He ain't even taken a look yet at my lungs."

Simon found Inara with Kaylee in her shuttle. River was there too, curled up on the bed, eyes closed. When Simon explained what he needed, Inara proved surprisingly receptive to the idea, considerably more than he'd anticipated.

"I'm just glad that *somebody* is doing something," she said, with a sigh. "Besides, it's not as if you're lying about being a doctor." She smiled at him. "Nor about being a good doctor."

"If anything," Simon agreed, "the resume understates my skills." He saw Inara and Kaylee shoot each other a look and felt himself blush beetroot. "I… I… don't mean… I mean… it's frustrating, that's all, not to able to be accurate… I could probably earn more that way, for one thing—"

"It's all right, Simon," Inara said, her lips twitching. "I think we've all had cause to be grateful about how good you are."

"But look at you, cookin' up fake credentials on the sly!" said Kaylee, punching him on the arm. "You're takin' to this life like you was born to it."

"It was Shepherd Book's idea," admitted Simon. "He said it would be in my interest to have a handful of cover identities."

"Did he?" said Inara.

"He said the best way to do it was to take over the identity of someone who had died, but close enough to me in age and qualifications to look plausible."

"Shepherd's idea, huh?" said Kaylee. "I don't remember my Bible coverin' that kind of thing. Ain't it wrong to steal?" She bit her lip. "I mean, I'm not sayin' you shouldn't, Simon—you got to get by somehow, don't you?"

"Elbows," said River.

"What's that, *mèi mèi*?" Simon touched her gently on the cheek.

River leaned in to him, ever so slightly. "You're in it up to your elbows."

"Well, yes, it does give me a slightly queasy feeling, using a dead man's identity," Simon admitted. "But… I guess that's where we are now. Anyway, for the purposes of the next few days, I am Dr. Martin Naismith, I trained at the Mercy Hospital on Sihnon…" He pulled a face. "It's not a *bad* medical school, I guess, but I didn't even have it on my list of *potentials*—"

"Oh, Simon," sighed Inara. Kaylee was covering her mouth with her hand.

"Simon got offers from the best five medical schools in the central worlds." River said. "And three more offered to boost their scholarships to choose them."

"Hey," said Kaylee. "Imagine that."

"—and I *am* more or less what they need," Simon concluded. "In fact, I'm exactly what they need."

"Up to the elbows in blood and bone," agreed River. "Chopped off at the knees."

"River…" said Simon, unhappily. Which brought him to another problem: who would look after River while he was gone? He'd gotten the strangest feeling, recently, that Kaylee had been avoiding River. They'd started to form a friendship: they'd played games together during the long flights and Simon had even seen them gossiping and giggling. It had been a huge relief to him to see River doing something, well, *normal* again… But in the last couple of weeks, since they'd had to rescue the captain, Kaylee hadn't seemed so happy to hang out with her. Simon wasn't sure what had happened, and River wasn't telling. Simon wasn't entirely sure that River knew either. It was so hard to tell what River knew about her immediate surroundings. Maybe Kaylee had decided the whole situation was too complicated. Simon could hardly blame her. But who else could he ask? Inara was coming with him, Mal would presumably be off carrying out some half-baked plan or other… There really was nobody else…

"Kaylee…" he said, glancing over at River.

"I know what you're about to ask, Simon," she said, "and the answer's 'no'."

Oh. Well. That made it clear that whatever friendship there might have been between her and River was certainly over—

"Because I'm comin' with you," said Kaylee, with a bright smile.

"What?" said Simon.

"Well, I ain't missin' out!" Kaylee said. "I thought I might try this workin' thing too. Not like I ain't got no skills. I'm just about the best ship's engineer you'll find—"

"But there might be more trouble," said Simon. "Roberts has taken Zoë and Book already. What if he decided that another crewmember would come in useful?"

"Oh, you just want me for the babysittin'," said Kaylee, although without rancor. "But there won't be trouble if I don't go lookin' for trouble."

"I just think..." said Simon. He glanced at Inara, but she was keeping out of this conversation. And Kaylee's jaw was starting to set. Simon had come to recognize that look in recent months. It meant he'd just said something stupid, and that he should start getting ready with the apologies.

"If the captain and Jayne are going to be busy making an even bigger mess," Kaylee said, "it'll be better if there's another one of us out there makin' an honest livin'. You'll see," she added, stubbornly. "You'll *all* see. I'll cope just fine." She got up. "I'm gettin' my toolkit. I'll see you both in the cargo bay."

She left, in a huff. Simon ran a hand across his eyes. Why did everything have to be so difficult? Why did everyone around him have to be so *relentlessly* themselves?

"Wash will be here," said Inara. "River likes Wash. And I'll come back as soon as you're at St. Freda's. River and I get along fine, don't we, sweetie?"

"Nails," said River, holding out her hand.

"You'd like me to paint your nails?" said Inara. "I will, sweetie, after I've set up the appointment for Simon at the hospital." She brushed her hand gently over the girl's hair, and then went over to the comm. River sat staring at her nails.

"Human nails," she said, "are made chiefly of keratin. The colors are shiny and glitter like lights. Nails don't grow after you're dead either. The corpse shrinks, remember? Don't worry about me, Simon."

But Simon did worry about River. He worried about River all the time. When he slept, he dreamed about her. Sometimes, in his dreams, she was the girl who loved to dance, but more often she was screaming. And then, when he woke up, he was confronted with the reality of her, the mess that had been made of her, and the chaos he had caused by saving her. Everything Simon did was motivated by worry for her, and everything else (*Kaylee*…) was going to have to wait its turn.

"The girl within parentheses," said River. "Sealed and pushed away." She smiled, faintly. "Nothing is forever, Simon."

"I hope not," he said.

"The universe is finite," River explained. "The second law of thermodynamics shows that the amount of entropy in a system must always increase. More and more disorder. Heat death." She looked at her thin hand. "Besides, the average life span for the human male is only eighty-six years. Seventy-two on some of the Rim worlds."

Simon kissed her gently on the cheek. "Thank you, *mèi mèi*. That makes me feel so much better."

River looked straight back at him. Sometimes, when she looked at him like that, he could see the girl that she had once been—his sharp, gifted, and utterly annoying brat of a little sister. When she looked at him like that, he was torn in two: glad to see her back, even if just for a moment, and heartbroken to know it wouldn't last.

I'll help somehow, River, he thought. *I promise you I'll get you back, somehow. I just… haven't worked out how, yet.*

River held back, waiting for him. She rested her head upon his arm. "Don't be sad, Simon," she whispered.

"I'm not sad, *mèi mèi*," he lied.

"Don't lie," she said. "And don't worry either." She held up her hands. The nails were bitten to the quick. "You'll see."

Mal, as expected, was not in the least supportive of the idea of Kaylee leaving the ship and going into Neapolis. "I ain't got time for this."

"Mal," said Inara. "You're not being fair—"

"Inara, we got the most powerful man on the planet already holding in his less-than-tender custody two of my crew—two who can handle themselves better'n most on board this ship, *dǒng ma*?—and you think it's a good idea to let Kaylee go out there all on her lonesome. *Kaylee* of all people—"

"She'll be with me," said Inara.

"That supposed to make me feel better?" Mal replied. "'Cause it don't."

"Well, it should," Inara said, coolly, and Kaylee, who had been watching this row unfold, decided to intervene before things could get even a mite chillier. Kaylee didn't like it when Mal and Inara quarreled. She didn't like it when anyone quarreled, truth be told, but there was something particularly not nice about Mal and Inara being at odds with one another. Shook her in ways she didn't understand.

"Hey, Captain," she said. "I'm a big girl. I'll manage. All I'm doing is finding myself a little work, makin' a little money—"

"It's people gettin' the wrong idea about what you mean by work that worries me," said Mal. "Particularly given the company you're keepin'." He looked meaningfully at Inara, who shook her head in disgust.

"Mal," Kaylee chided him. "That ain't a nice thing to say—"

"Mal isn't very nice, in case you hadn't noticed," said Inara.

"Never said I was," said Mal. "But, Kaylee, I won't hear more of this. You ain't leavin' this ship—"

"Yes she is, Mal," said Inara. Stupid of the captain, thought Kaylee. If he'd shrugged and let them get on with it, Inara might have had second thoughts. Now she was diggin' in deep, and all to spite him. The captain was clueless when it came to women, and particularly clueless when it came to Inara.

"Come on, Kaylee," Inara said, pushing her gently on her way. "Let's leave the boys to whatever ludicrous plan they come up with. You and I have got better things to do."

They left the ship via the cargo bay doors, and Kaylee took a deep breath of the air of a new world. Truth was, the place stank of fuel and fumes, but Kaylee liked that too, and (she'd never told anyone she could do this, although she might have found they weren't particularly surprised by the information) she could determine the distinctive odor of at least seven different types of vessel in their immediate vicinity, not least that of an early Series 3 Firefly-class transporter.

Simon, carrying his bag and wearing his dark suit, came out of the ship, looking almost exactly like he had when he'd come on board *Serenity* all those months ago. Kaylee remembered him standing there, cool as you like, watching carefully as that big cube was loaded into the cargo bay. The cryo-crate, containing River, tucked away like a jack-in-the-box. They'd had no idea the trouble they were bringing on board, and even for all that, at least it meant Simon was on board. Hopeless, but on board.

"Hey," Kaylee said. "Ready to be the amazin' emergency doctor again?"

"I thought I was already," Simon replied.

"You know what I mean."

"I guess so… I… I don't like all the subterfuge, that's all."

"You didn't mind comin' on board *Serenity* under false pretenses."

"That… That wasn't practicing medicine."

"I guess…" Kaylee frowned. "I 'spose, if it were me in need of a medic, I wouldn't care whether he was posin' as the Joozy Frooty Bunny as long as knew which bits to take out and which bits to leave behind."

Simon began to laugh. Kaylee's heart took flight, soared upward, and sang a few hosannas. "Kaylee!" he said. "You really are funny…"

"Good funny or bad funny?" Kaylee said, hopefully, but she never did get an answer to that. Inara, who had gone ahead a little way out in the dockyard, came back, and said, "The cab's coming."

Well, thought Kaylee, taking a deep breath, *time for the second part of this workin' plan…* "All right, you two," she said. "Off you go."

"What?" said Inara.

"Shoo! Go! Vamoose!"

"Aren't you coming into the city with us?" said Simon. "I thought the plan was that you were coming into the city with us—"

"You think I'm going to find work as a ship mechanic at a casino?" said Kaylee. "No, right here at the docks is where I need to be."

Simon looked uncertainly back toward *Serenity*. "But won't the captain... I mean..."

The times he chose to become all gentlemanly and knight-in-shining-armor-y, thought Kaylee. Why did they never happen when she could do something about it?

"Captain Manners back there," Kaylee said, "can go whistle. I'll be fine, Simon! All I'm doin' is findin' some work. I promise I won't get into trouble."

The cab hovered up alongside them, and the doors slid open. "Simon," said Inara. "If we want to make the meeting, we've got to go now."

"Go if you're goin'," said Kaylee. "And have fun!" She looked at Simon and sighed. "Or... whatever it is that you do, Simon."

He nodded, with some reluctance, and they got into the car. Kaylee waved them goodbye then turned to look round the docks. You couldn't, she thought, mistake this place for a party, but she felt happy nonetheless.

"All righty," she said. "Here's me, and I'm *workin'*."

* * *

The cab, mercifully, was driverless, which meant Simon didn't have to worry about making mindless and awkward small talk to a stranger about what a fine place their world was and how much he was looking forward to sampling the delights of Carnival and yes, actually, he was a doctor and, no, no, it was fine to say you hated doctors, and of course he didn't take that personally. He watched Inara put her identification card into the slot. The onboard computer registered the booking, calculated the quickest route, and began to move on smoothly out of Roby Docks. Simon, looking back over his shoulder, saw Kaylee waving them goodbye. A wave of anxiety rushed over him. *Don't worry*, River had said. But how could he not worry? Until a couple of years ago, Simon's life had run like clockwork: school, MedAcad, hospital; free time at the family estate or at the estates of friends of the family; a few close friends that he saw regularly (less so, once he'd started trying to find River). These days everything had an almost inevitable tendency to collapse into chaos (if he was lucky) and violence (if he was not). He watched Kaylee's figure recede into the distance and turned to Inara.

"Do you think we should we have let Mal know that she was going off by herself?"

"I think we can leave her to get on with it," said Inara. "Kaylee's quite capable."

"Didn't you tell Mal that she'd be with you the whole time?"

"In fact, I didn't. I was quite careful not to say how long she would be with me."

"But won't Mal *mind*—?"

"Mal shouldn't be so trusting, Simon."

Simon took his glasses out of his pocket and fiddled with them. He knew he had a reputation for cluelessness, but he was as aware as everyone else on the ship of the powerful attraction between the captain and their "ambassador," which, for reasons best known to themselves, seemed to manifest chiefly as mutually assured destruction. People had their own reasons not to get together (Simon of all people knew that) but there was something about the way they kept each other at arm's-length… The undercurrent of… what was it? He looked sideways at Inara. Her face was still, but her eyes seemed bleak. *Desperation*, yes, that was the word… They reached out to each other, desperately, and then pushed each other aside with a similar hopelessness. Nonetheless, Simon didn't want to badmouth Mal to her, so he chose his words carefully. "Trusting is… not a word I'd generally associate with the captain."

"No?" said Inara. "You'll find as you get to know Mal better that he's a man of many hidden shallows."

Simon glanced back again over his shoulder. "Still, I hope she'll be okay…"

"Kaylee has plenty of common sense. She's far more capable than Mal allows for." Inara looked at him, directly. "She's a good girl, Simon. A very sweet and very lovely girl. She deserves every happiness."

Well, not even Simon could miss the meaning there. "I know," he said, helplessly.

"I think you'd find she wouldn't ask for very much. Kaylee doesn't take. She just gives."

"But the situation I'm in…" *She might get hurt. I didn't want anyone to get hurt, but somehow people still keep on getting hurt…*

"Kaylee knows all about that."

"Then there's River…"

And the simple fact was that River had to come first. Wherever Kaylee went, she made people into her friends. It was one of things that made him… Well, made him think she was special. But if this thing between them—whatever it was— never came to anything, Kaylee would survive. Kaylee would thrive. She would keep on making people love her, because she was so very loveable. But River… River had nobody to cling to, only a clueless older brother who was out of his depth, and floundering, and only just keeping his head above water. Suddenly, Simon realized that Inara's hand was on his, and that she was looking at him with something close to compassion.

"The trouble with some people," she said, "is that they're so busy saving other people's lives, that they forget to live their own. Don't make that mistake, Simon."

He stared down at her hand, resting upon his. Was this a clue to Inara? Was she telling him something about herself? Or was she talking about Mal? The car shifted upward, and Inara moved away, put some distance between them. "Look," she said, pointing out of the window at the cityscape rising into view, turning away so he could no longer see her face. "Neapolis. Life is short, Simon. Please, don't waste it."

* * *

Twelve minutes past the hour. Ava, still in her hiding place, was writhing in an agony of indecision. Soon, she would have to make some kind of move—either toward her only hope of safety or else away from this place entirely. When she thought about that latter choice, fear coiled within her. What would she do if she missed this appointment? Would she end up wandering the city until the people who wanted to hurt her found her? Would she try to reach the contact again, beg for help again? Would they be angry with her, turn her away? Ava rubbed at her eyes. It was too cruel: to have sanctuary held out to her like this, to come so close and yet still to be so stuck…

Quarter past the hour. Ava fiddled with the broken pieces of the mask in her pocket and wished she'd been more careful. Wearing the mask, she could have walked straight past. At seventeen minutes past, she watched the other flyer pull out of the courtyard and onto the road, leaving the route to room 107 even more exposed. At twenty-one minutes past, the waitress came out again to see if the party wanted more drinks. This, Ava knew, was her best chance, when they were busy with a pretty face. She lifted the shawl over her head, moved out of the alley, and walked up the road. When she was past the office, on the other side, she crossed back and began to move carefully back toward the motel.

She reached the corner of the courtyard. Let her breath out, slowly. Didn't risk a look at the fellas at the table with their drinks. Could hear them laughing and talking. Drew in another breath, looked across the courtyard. How much time had passed? Seemed an age. Was she too late, already? Ava turned her head to check the time on the display.

Big mistake. Even with the shawl, her face was not covered. The man in the white dragon T-shirt looked up and caught her eye.

"*Tā mā de hún dàn!*" he yelled, jumping up from his seat. "It's that ruttin' kid!"

For a split second, Ava thought of dashing over to room 107 and hammering on the door, in the hope that whoever was inside would let her in and deal with these people. But she knew in her heart that this was the wrong thing to do. These people who were trying to help her—maybe they used this place all the time, maybe she wasn't the first girl to come this way. Maybe these fellas had got wind of the place; were stakin' it out. Ava runnin' over and hammerin' on that door would mean the end of that. And that would mean that the next girl—the next Ava, lost in a big city and hoping against hope for someone to hold out a helpin' hand—there'd be nothing for her. Ava thought of the candle she'd lit, at that little street shrine. Seemed to her the Almighty hadn't been listening much to prayers the past couple of days. She turned her back on help, ran down the street like the Devil himself was at her heels, and as she ran she begged the little fat god: *Please—help me now!*

To a casual observer, it might have looked like the pretty young woman walking through the docks humming and swinging a bag of tools was meandering aimlessly around. An observer familiar with the place might wonder why such a pretty young woman couldn't find a more pleasant part of the city in which to take her daily constitutional, but in fact Kaylee Frye was not wandering about. No, Kaylee Frye was on a mission. She was listening, and listening hard, to everything going on around her. Not the chatter of folks sitting outside their ships, talking about when they were going into the city and how much they were going to spend or how much they were hoping to win and what they'd do with all that gorram platinum. Neither was she listening to the few people enquiring of ship's captains as to whether they might have cheap berth to get them off world. Other days, Kaylee might have been interested in them (although given the last coupla passengers she'd brought on board, Mal had politely requested she refrain from finding any more). No, today Kaylee wasn't listening out for passengers. She was listening to the engines.

Kaylee didn't know what it was about engines that spoke to her. She'd always been this way, sneaking out of the house to sit with Daddy while he fixed other folks' broken threshers and tractors and whatever else they brought his way. Poor Mom. She'd wanted a little friend to help her bake and sew and cook and clean, and instead she got Kaylee, puttering around after her daddy, clutching her own little toolbox from the age of six. She just had a way with machines. She guessed this was what it was like for other people and music or painting or sculpting, and while Kaylee wouldn't have been confident judging a piece of art or music, wouldn't have known how to say the clever things that people said about that (like Simon did, sometimes, and how that made her heart sink, 'cause then she felt like she wasn't good enough for a nice boy like him), she did know the sound of a Lambert nineteen hundred engine in dire need of tuning when she heard one, and when she picked up the first sorry note of its sad symphony, she quickly followed it back to the source.

Not a bad engine, the Lambert nineteen hundred, though Kaylee wouldn't have liked to spend her days trying to please one. *Zāo gāo*, but they were *moody* (*I mean, listen to the thing!*) and needed far too much in the way of spoilin'. Nothing like her beautiful Firefly. All you had to do there was shower love on her (which wasn't hard), and she always came through.

The Lambert, when she found it, was in good condition, clearly the recipient of much tender loving care. That was a good sign. That meant the owner was someone you wouldn't mind working for. Mean people were mean to everyone and everythin' around them. People who took care of their ship knew about takin' care. There was the captain, now, standing outside his ship, arms akimbo, and glaring up at his vessel with a look that combined both fondness and sheer exasperation.

"Hey," she said to him. "She's not soundin' so good."

"She's been grumblin' at me since Persephone," he said. "Shouldna pushed her, but you have to keep to the schedule these days or you ain't ever workin' again. What's a fella supposed to do, eh? Too many folks chasin' too little work."

"Yup," said Kaylee. She knew about that, not least because it was all Mal ever talked about these days. "You gettin' her fixed?"

"Well, I got a fella comin' in from Nashton," he said. "Says he's got experience with this partickler engine, but I bet he don't. I bet he knows the twenty-two hundred and he's plannin' on wingin' his way round her and takin' my money."

"Twenty-two hundred ain't nothin' like the nineteen hundred," said Kaylee, firmly.

He laughed out loud. "You and me know that, miss, but tell it to the fella from Nashton!" He looked more closely at her. "Hey, you're a smart little thing."

Yes, I am, thought Kaylee. "When's your fella comin'?"

"Later tonight," he said. "If he can get through all this gorram holiday traffic."

"Huh," she said. "You not plannin' on stayin' for Carnival?"

He wiped his huge hand across his brow. "You seen one parade, you seen 'em all. Besides," he patted his ship (yep, he loved her, for all her temperament, which only endeared him to Kaylee even more), "we ain't much of ones for parties, are we, sweetpea?"

That was it as far as Kaylee was concerned. Over the next few minutes, Captain Olsen had introduced himself properly, touched his temple when she introduced herself, the pair of them opened negotiations, and more or less sealed the deal.

"I'll have you back in flight before your fella from Nashton's reached town, never mind the docks," promised Kaylee.

"I got no doubt of that," said Olsen. "And there's five platinum for you when you do."

They were sticking out their hands to shake, when Kaylee heard a familiar voice behind her. "Only *five*? That all? Kaylee Frye, you sellin' yourself short again?"

Kaylee turned round. "Mal!" she said. "What're you doin' here?"

"Came lookin' to find you in the engine room," he said, "and found you missin'. Don't like it when members of my crew go missin'—" He loomed—there was no other word for it—positively *loomed* at Olsen.

"Mal, you need to go away," Kaylee hissed, "and *now*—"

But Olsen was already in retreat. "Sweetheart," he said, shaking his head, "looks like there's more trouble comes with you than will make you worth my while. I want a mechanic—not a mechanic and her daddy—"

"He ain't my daddy," said Kaylee. "He's a right royal pain in the—"

"Well, whatever he is," said Olsen, "he looks like he means trouble, so I'll thank you kindly for your interest, miss, but I think it's best I hold out for that fella from Nashton." He touched his temple again and went back off his ship.

"Wait! Please!" cried Kaylee, to no avail, as he disappeared inside. She turned to Mal and pushed him, hard. "Oaf," she said. "Idiot."

"Hey!" he said. "That ain't nice when I came all this way to save you."

"*Save* me? He was all ready to sign on the dotted line and you pop up and wreck my chances!"

"I didn't like the look of him, Kaylee. He had a mean eye."

"It was *none* of your business, Mal!"

"His left eye, in case you were wonderin'. Though I didn't much like the look of his right eye neither. That right eye had a surliness about it unfittin' for any man, never mind one you'd be hirin' yourself out to—"

"Oh, Cap'n, sometimes I *hate* you!"

Kaylee strode off, back toward *Serenity*. No point tryin' anythin' else. She knew how the grapevine worked. Word would soon be spreadin' round the docks about the little girl mechanic and her overbearing pa. She heard Mal come chasing up behind her and lengthened her stride.

"Look, Kaylee," he said, "you're on my crew and you're my responsibility. I've lost two folks already today and I ain't losing another—"

"Captain, I wasn't in trouble! I was doin' just fine! That job there would've put five platinum in our pockets, and now it's walkin' away, and I'll bet you and Jayne and Wash ain't yet come up with a better plan—"

"Kaylee, I don't want you out here by yourself while Roberts' men are out there and we're out of favor, understand? They find you, work out who you are, you think they won't think another hostage might come in handy? Think they won't try to harm you, hurt you, just to get back at me?

"It ain't always about you, Cap'n."

"Well, today it is, and I ain't havin' you bein' hurt on my conscience."

"Simon and Inara thought it was safe enough for me."

"And I'll be havin' words with them both when I see them again. In the meantime, we both of us should be gettin' ourselves back to the ship. I've wasted enough time on this already, and, in case you've forgotten, we are on a mighty tight schedule—"

She turned her back and strode off back through the docks toward the ship, muttering under her breath. "*Gēn hóu zi bǐ diū shǐ...*"

"Now, Kaylee, I could take some serious offence at that—"

"That's the idea, you *kě wù de lǎo bào jūn*—"

"All I was doing was making sure that you— Oof! *Wǒ de tiān da*, what just hit me?"

"I hope it was a wall," Kaylee said. "I hope it was a real hard wall and I hope it hurts for the rest of the week."

It wasn't a wall, hard or otherwise. It was a girl. A girl of maybe thirteen or fourteen years of age, breathless from running and clutching a purple shawl around her. "Sorry!" she gasped and looked back over her shoulder. "I gotta go!"

"Now wait up just one moment," said Mal, grabbing her arm, "you ain't goin' anywhere—"

"They're comin' after me! I gotta get away!"

"Mal," warned Kaylee, "I think we got ourselves that trouble…"

The girl's pursuers had arrived. One had a big black bushy beard, and the other was wearing a White Dragon T-shirt. Kaylee took an instant dislike to both of them. Not only were they chasin' this poor chick, but Kaylee hated White Dragon. They were a bad band. A *lousy* band. "Hey," said the one in the T-shirt, who seemed to be in charge. "Hand her over."

You could say what you liked about Mal (and Kaylee surely had plenty to say on this particular day), but his reflexes were a sight to behold. Out came the pistol from its holster, and the two men pulled up short and drew back.

"Now," said Mal, "I ain't the kind of man takes any situation at face value, because there's often two sides to a story, I've found—but there are some notable exceptions to such a rule, and that makes me think that you two gentlemen are going to need to come up with a mighty good tale to explain just how and why you're chasin' a girl this small down a street this nasty. 'Cause I'm hard pressed to come up with a reason that don't make me angry."

"I'm her daddy," said the man in the T-shirt.

"That right?" Mal looked down at the girl. "This your daddy, *mèi mèi*?"

"No," whispered the girl. "He ain't my daddy. Don't let 'em take me, mister! Don't let 'em hurt me!"

"Well, seems like we have ourselves a difference of opinion here," said Mal. "And since I'm the one holdin' the gun and you're the ones facin' it, I'd say my opinion right now carries a mite more weight than yours. So if I were you, gentlemen, I'd back off and melt away into the night. Afternoon. Whatever time it is. 'Cause the next thing comes from this side of the argument ain't likely to be talkin'. It'll be shootin'. Got that?"

There was a moment when Kaylee thought they were going to be stupid enough to try their luck. Then the one in the T-shirt jerked back. "This ain't over," he said. He pointed at the girl. "We'll find you, kiddo. Don't you be mistaken about that. In the meantime—" He zipped his fingers across his lips. "Keep those shut."

"Spoken like a truly fond father," said Mal. He watched them leave, then turned to the girl. "Care to do a little explainin'?"

The girl looked up at him dumbly.

Mal sighed. "All right. No need for me to be makin' you say anything you don't want. Where's your ma? Your pa?"

She kept staring at him.

"Well, then, maybe there's somewhere we can take you?" Mal said. "Somewhere safe. Somewhere that ain't here, with us, because as I may have mentioned, Kaylee, we got a world of troubles happenin' and no way through them yet that I can see."

"I ain't got nowhere," the girl whispered.

"Captain," said Kaylee. "If you weren't happy with me out here all on my ownsome, you can't be happy with leavin' her out here. Not with them fellas still around."

"Kaylee, we got enough on our plate right now without— Woah, now, stop that!"

The girl had made a grab for his gun.

By the time people got as far as needing Simon's attention, they were likely injured, scared, and saying the first thing that came into their heads. After telling him they didn't like doctors, the next thing they went on to tell him was how much they also hated hospitals. The antiseptic smell, the loss of control, the needles. Particularly the needles. People loathed needles. That was all fine. Simon didn't much enjoy getting needles either; far better to be jabbing than jabbed. But hospitals—Simon liked hospitals.

Simply putting one foot inside St. Freda's made him feel better. He was back on familiar territory again, the kind of world he understood, the kind of environment in which he

FIREFLY

excelled. His shoulders went down. Muscles relaxed that he had stopped noticing were tensed. Yes, this was safe ground, even walking in with false ID.

Before entering the building, Simon had taken the precaution of putting on the treated glasses which deflected retinal scans. So far, however, Inara's identification and her considerable presence had taken them past the front desk and into a pleasant waiting room. Tea was brought, in decent crockery.

"You know," said Inara, taking it upon herself to pour, "I'm not sure I've seen you look so happy."

"You should see me operate," said Simon.

"I *have* seen you operate," said Inara.

"I meant under normal conditions, not on *Serenity*."

"Does any surgery count as normal conditions?"

"It does when it's your job, Inara. The job you're trained to do."

"I understand," she replied, and handed him the cup. Jasmine tea. Tasted pretty good. Maybe some of these border worlds were a little more civilized than he'd realized.

Inara poured herself some tea and arranged herself to best effect in her chair. In his time on *Serenity*, Simon hadn't really got to spend much time with Inara. She was always polite (except when he made yet another mistake with Kaylee), and she was kind to River (which was a deal-breaker as far as Simon was concerned), but in general she kept her distance. This wasn't personal, he knew; she seemed to keep her distance from most of them. He couldn't quite understand what she was doing on board *Serenity*. She always said there were mutual benefits to the arrangement

116

on both sides, but the truth was that she was clearly way out of Mal's league.

Back on Osiris, Simon hadn't spent much time mixing in circles where companions were generally found. He wasn't really the type to attend elegant soirees, or dinner parties. He'd go to the ones his parents hosted, for his mother's sake, and make polite conversation with whoever they'd lined up for him this time as a potential marriage prospect, but otherwise he was busy studying and then working. One of his friends, for his sixteenth birthday, had a companion engaged for him by his parents. Simon's father had offered the same gift, but Simon had said no. Perhaps that had been a mistake. Perhaps, with a companion's tutelage, he might know what to do now about Kaylee.

Watching how doors opened in front of Inara was impressive. After a short wait, a young assistant came to escort them up to the executive level. He was polite to Simon, but he danced attendance on Inara, who treated him in turn with gentle, distant courtesy. There had, so far as Simon could tell, been no retinal scans. Parts of Neapolis might put on the kind of show you saw in the Core, but this really was a border world, closer to the Rim, and that showed in the details. The security, a little looser. The gloss, concealing shabbier corners. The office they were brought to was well appointed, however, and the man who greeted them was smart and glossy. His name was Mack Thorne, and he was the hospital's chief executive.

Thorne came round from behind his desk and, again, all the attention was on Inara. The Guild clearly held a lot of sway at St. Freda's.

"Great pleasure to have you here, Ms. Serra. Always happy to welcome visitors from the Guild."

She took his hand in that immaculately judged way which seemed to imply a special kind of intimacy while keeping a very palpable barrier between them. Thorne looked like he'd been awarded a big shiny medal. A short brisk chat followed in which Thorne satisfied himself that Simon was not some quack about to be let loose on his beautiful facility. They agreed terms (Simon inched his fee a little upward; not much, he didn't want to push his luck too far), and at last, they sealed the deal.

"I have to say, Dr. Naismith, you couldn't have arrived at a better time," said Thorne. "We had someone leave last week—I think they couldn't face another round of Carnival."

"When Inara told me that we'd be on Bethel this weekend I thought there might be some need for a doctor," Simon said. "I'm glad I'll be able to help. And I'm keen to get started…"

"Our senior ER physician is just finishing up in surgery right now. Dr. Nolan. She asked me to take you to her office. You can take a look at the recovery ward on the way past. We've enough time."

"That would be very helpful, thank you."

Thorne led them through the building to one of the wards. Inara waited outside. Simon admired the facilities (they were actually pretty good), talked to a couple of the ward nurses (both impressively sharp), and had a long conversation with a patient (who only had good things to say about Dr. Nolan, another good sign). Then on to another office, this time much less neat and shiny. Simon knew this kind of office. He'd had one like this back on Osiris. Smaller, but containing the same kind of chaos. You never quite had time to get to the bottom of all the paperwork.

"She'll be here soon," said Thorne. "I have to go, I'm afraid—"

"We'll be very comfortable here, thank you," said Inara.

Thorne gave Inara a besotted look, then went on his way.

"Happy?" said Inara.

"Yes," said Simon. "It's nice to be back in a hospital again." He looked round anxiously. "I hope the ID holds up."

"I'm sure it will. You need to worry less, Simon."

"I know… I want to get down to work…"

The door to the office opened and they both stood to greet the arrival.

"Sorry to keep you waiting," the woman said, pushing the door shut behind her with her foot. She was staring down at a sheaf of notes in her hand. "I have to say, Dr. Naismith, if you're as good in practice as you are on paper, we'll be glad to have you here over the next day or two." She looked up. The smile on her face faded immediately, to be replaced with shock. "Simon? Simon Tam?"

"Katarina?" Simon stared at her. "How are you… *Why* are you—?"

There was horrible silence, into which Inara said, very smoothly, "I wonder whether there been a misunderstanding."

"I don't think there's been a misunderstanding," said Dr. Nolan—no, this was definitely Katarina *Neilsen*, thought Simon, there was no mistaking her. They'd studied alongside each other for over four years, and she'd dated one of Simon's friends for a while. Will Carlsen. He and Simon had shared

119

rooms in their sophomore year. The relationship with Will had ended amicably enough, and Simon had thought about asking Katarina out. Carefully weighed all the pros and cons, then decided against. Simon had this habit of deciding against.

Slowly, Katarina walked round her desk. She put down her notes and opened a drawer. From this she took out a very compact hand pistol which Jayne Cobb (had he been present) could have told them was a Whitaker 380, which he considered "a girly kinda gun even for a girl." Still, Jayne himself might agree that if there was only one gun in the room, you would not want to be facing its barrel, however girly that barrel might be. Simon felt suddenly and extremely sick. Did she know the circumstances of his departure from the central planets? Was she going to sell him out?

"It's... it's good to see you again," he offered.

"Sit down," Katarina said.

"That's good advice," said Inara. "I'm sure we can get to the bottom of this—"

"I'd like *you* to be quiet, please," said Katarina. "It's Simon I want to talk to."

She gestured with the pistol and waited until they were both back in their seats. Then she came to sit herself on the edge of her desk, facing them. "Simon Tam," she said. "Whatever brings you to my office under a fake name, and with a registered companion in tow?"

Zoë and Book, in the back of the lawmen's vehicle, were, it seemed to Zoë, on a lengthy voyage of discovery round the northern edge of Neapolis. To the right, Zoë could see only the red desert stretching out into nowhere country, dotted with nowhere towns. Over to the left, the view was a mite more interesting. At one point the vehicle swerved upward to take advantage of emptier air space, and this new height gave them a good look down the river along the whole of the Platinum Mile toward the coast. A string of hot air balloons was spreading out in the distance, bright spots of color against the blue of the sky.

Book, who had been tremendously cheerful throughout this whole trip, nudged Zoë. "Will you look at that?" he said. "Very fine! I must say, Zoë, this sightseeing tour has been an unexpectedly welcome addition to our itinerary."

One of the officers up front shook his head. Zoë wasn't entirely sure that riling these two fellas was necessarily the best idea given the circumstances, but she had to agree with Book's take on the view. You didn't get to see the best of a planet from the docks, that was for sure, and in general you didn't tend to see the best while under arrest. If that's what they were. Zoë had been under arrest more than a few times during her career and was familiar with the customs and procedures on numerous far-flung worlds. But there'd been no official words, no cautions, no reading of whatever limited rights were granted to folks on here on Bethel, no informing them they were bound by law. Just put into the back of this car and driven… where? Not back to Roberts' office, that was for sure.

They crossed the river north of the city, and, on the other side, turned southward, passing over a dozen or so large private residences, each one set within its own green and pleasant grounds. Strange, thought Zoë, how rich people liked to grow grass to show they were rich. Zoë had grown up vesselside, where every piece of equipment had to be functional, and everything (and everyone) had to be making a contribution to earn their place. Look at all that wasted energy. Big flat squares of green—didn't even look pretty. Looked dull. Looked exactly what people did when they leaned toward the Alliance. Smoothed themselves out. No room for difference, for variety. Not if they were going to make themselves fit. Zoë didn't much care for a world like that. Liked rough edges, liked bumps and patches. That's where life was. Those houses down below seemed deadly to her. You couldn't breathe in a place like that.

The shore drew ever closer and, at last, the vehicle dropped slightly, and Zoë got a proper look at their destination. Big white house on the hills, with a good view over the sea. Set in yet more acres of dull green grass, and there was a swimming pool and courts laid out for some game—tennis, maybe? Zoë didn't really know how the rich went about passing the time of day. A request came up from the ground for them to identify themselves: pretty standard. All these private residences would have their own air space and their own security checks. When they passed through this, the vehicle began its proper descent, coming down to a halt in a courtyard at the back of the property.

"Not entering through the front door?" said Book. "That's mighty disappointing. I was hoping for a proper tour."

"Not today," said the slightly more talkative of the officers, who then instructed them out of the vehicle and into the house. Once inside, they were led along a back corridor, past a busy kitchen, up a flight of stairs and along another corridor, white-painted and hung with various pieces of abstract art. They came to a big door and were ordered to enter inside a large dim room: a library, the walls lined with heavy dark wood bookcases.

"Wait in here," said one of the men. "Mr. Roberts will be with you directly."

Zoë, peering through the darkness, saw big, curtained windows on the far side of the room. She went over to these and pulled them back, letting the light cascade through. She ran her hands across the window frames (solid) and tapped the glass. Force barriers shimmered. No getting out that way.

"Nice place," said Book, appreciatively. "He's turning out to be quite the book collector, isn't he?"

"Maybe so." Another waste of space. Books were heavy, held dust, and everything you needed was on the Cortex. Zoë, arms folded, took stock of her immediate surroundings. The window was a big bay. Two comfortable armchairs had been placed here to receive the light. There was a small table between them, and on this stood a red Buddha figurine. Bookcases round the other walls. But the centerpiece of the room was a huge pool table. Book was already at this, weighing one of the cues in his hands. Zoë, joining him, reached to touch one of the balls. "Oh!"

"Something the matter, Zoë?"

"The ball's real." She laughed. "Guess I'm used to holos."

"A lot about this city is fake," Book agreed. "Perhaps he keeps the real wealth for home." He nodded at the table. "Do you play?"

"Ain't played on table big as this. And I don't recognize the set-up."

"That's because this is billiards, not pool." Book examined the cue in his hand. "It's… fairly complicated. If we do end up being here a while, I can teach you—if you trust me to do the scoring."

"If I can't trust my preacher not to cheat me at games, what's the 'verse comin' to?"

He gave her a sly smile. "Have you checked the windows yet?"

"Yep. Nothing there." She went back and rapped the barrier again to show him.

"Huh. Nor through the door. I guess we'll be waiting here a while yet."

"Might be worth hearin' what Roberts has to say," said Zoë.

"Maybe." Book pushed out a breath. "There are worse dungeons, I suppose."

"You been inside many dungeons, Shepherd?"

"I was thinking of Adelai Niska," he replied. "I'd rather not find out whether Jacob Roberts is in possession of any similar facilities."

The door opened.

"Speak of the devil," muttered Book, as Roberts came in, two men bearing arms right behind him. He was wearing a red patterned robe, as if he'd been interrupted halfway through getting changed.

"Well," he said, looking past them both toward the window, "this is a most unwelcome complication to my day. I'm about to receive guests. It's First Night. I always have guests on First Night."

"We're mighty sorry to interrupt your celebrations," said Book. "Perhaps the simplest thing all round would be to let us go on our way and let you get back to your party—"

Roberts shook his head. "That isn't possible. I know that the job went wrong—"

"Ah," said Book.

"And now we must work through the consequences. For one thing, that shipment needs to be found."

"Maybe if those lawmen had left us alone," said Zoë, ever so gently, "we might have caught up with them as stole it."

"I have my own people on that. People upon whom I can rely completely." He pursed his lips. "I should have known better than to use outside contractors. But there we are."

"Mr. Roberts," said Book, "we're none of us happy at the way this job has turned out. If you let us back to our ship, then we—and Captain Reynolds—will surely be able to make amends in some way. At the very least, perhaps we might speak to him—"

"Captain Reynolds knows you're in my custody. And he's busy—"

"Busy?" said Zoë. Didn't sound like Mal. If she knew Mal—and nobody knew Mal as well as Zoë Alleyne—he'd be trying to work out a way to get them back. If he knew where they were. A mite too easy to picture the captain trying to break them out of Roberts' empty office.

"I've explained to Reynolds that he owes me for the shipment you lost," said Roberts. "That's five hundred platinum, in case you weren't sure. And I've explained that I expect to be paid in full by tomorrow evening."

Zoë, who was working very hard not to show any response to this, saw Book making much the same effort.

"Your task now—Shepherd, miss—is to sit and wait. When Reynolds delivers my platinum, you'll be free to go."

There was a pause as Zoë (and Book, she guessed) contemplated the likelihood of Mal doing such a thing. "Far be it from me to imply that Mal won't come good," said Book, "but what happens to us if for some reason he can't or don't deliver?"

Roberts looked at them with his very pale, very blue eyes. "Then you'll both be shot. I'll have your bodies returned to your ship."

"Ain't no call for that," said Zoë.

"I thought this was a law-abiding world," said Book. "More like the Core than the Rim."

"This is Bethel," said Roberts. "I'm the law here."

"In the end," said Book, "we must all of us answer to God's law."

"I'll take that risk," said Roberts. He blinked. "I must continue getting ready for the evening." He gestured round. "I hope this room is comfortable enough."

"Oh, it's charming," said Book.

"Good," said Roberts. He left, and Zoë heard the barrier fields hum behind the door as they were raised again.

"Well," she said. "Can't complain about his briefings."

"Yes indeed," said Book. "Concise. Clear. Convey exactly the information needed." He walked across the room to examine one of the bookshelves.

"Is this the time to be catchin' up on your readin', Shepherd?"

"You heard the man. We've got until tomorrow evening." He plucked a volume from the shelf, took it over to one of the chairs, and took his ease. "In the meantime," he said, "a little research surely won't do any harm."

"Well," said Simon, staring down the barrel of Katarina's gun, "this is… awkward?"

"School reunions," said Inara, in a pleasant voice. "They can be so very fraught."

"You haven't answered my question," said Katarina. "Why are you here, Simon? Why the fake name? And why the companion?"

"Well," said Simon, taking a deep breath. "It's all very complicated…"

"Keep it simple," Katarina replied.

Not for the first time, Simon wished for some of River's speed, or Book's smarts, or even Jayne's ability to punch someone out. His mind raced, and he tried to think of a convincing answer. He was fairly certain that she didn't know that there was a warrant out for him—she would have called for security by now if that was the case—and in fact now that he thought about it, she was looking pretty jumpy too… He knew a little of her background—comfortable, Core world, not fabulously rich—and he doubted she was all that used to guns either…

"I'll answer your question," said Simon, "if you tell me why *you're* using a fake name."

The barrel of the gun twitched up, ever so slightly.

"Simon?" said Inara, in some alarm. "What do you mean?"

"It's… It's just that the director of the clinic said that we'd be meeting Dr. Nolan," said Simon. "That wasn't the name you had at medical school, and while I know some people do still change their names when they get married, I don't see a wedding ring, and while you might take that off while you're in surgery, there's usually a mark on the finger where the ring would be—" *Cut the gorram crap, Doc*, he heard Mal snap into his ear. "—and besides…" Simon jerked his thumb behind him. "The name on the door said 'Dr. Karolina Nolan. But this is your office, isn't it? Katarina Neilsen. So that suggests to me… fake name."

"Oh, very good, Simon," said Inara. She might sound a little less surprised, thought Simon, with some irritation.

Katarina, pursing her lips, said, "You always were annoyingly smart."

"Yes, I know," said Simon. "I'm sorry about that. I know this doesn't look good, me here not using my name, but there's a perfectly straightforward explanation, and I'd like to have the chance to tell you what it is. But… well…" He nodded at the gun. "Do you think you could possibly see your way to putting that down?" He held out his hands, an open gesture. "It's just me, Kay. Simon Tam."

There was a moment when nobody moved and then, slowly, Katarina lowered the gun. "All right," she said. "But you've got some explaining to do. Not least what you're doing on Bethel. Last I heard, you were pulling down a fortune at that hospital on Osiris. What's brought you out to the border?"

Simon released a quiet breath. So she didn't know that he was on the run. Perhaps out here on the border worlds the news didn't get around so easily. It would surely be very different back home. He wondered what story had been passed around. There'd need to be something, given that the authorities could hardly let the truth get out. They would have tried to discredit him. *I heard Simon Tam got himself in trouble with a patient and now he's under investigation for assault... well, you know, he always was weird around girls...* Or maybe his father had pulled some strings, covered some of it up for the sake of the family reputation. *Did you hear about Simon Tam? Went postal and tried to jump off the Two-Mile Bridge. They've locked him up for his own good.* What would their friends have said, hearing whatever lies being spread about him. Probably tried to get his job. They were pretty cut-throat, some of them.

"I..." Simon went for the sympathy vote. "I burned out," he said. "It all became too much, and I had to get away. From the hospital, from Osiris, from everything, really. The new name... It lets me get some distance from who I was back there."

Was that even remotely plausible? Apparently so, since Katarina was looking at him with such real compassion that he began to feel bad for lying.

"Simon," she said. "I'm really sorry to hear that. You were a great doctor—"

"He's still a great doctor," said Inara.

"It... it wasn't medicine that was a problem," said Simon, "it was everything else."

"I understand," said Katarina. "Tough world. And not a nice set of people. D'you remember Will? Will Carlsen?"

"Yes!" said Simon. *Wā*, it was good to talk about home again. Talk about people he'd known, who'd known him before all this…

Katarina was shaking her head. "Did you know that the whole time we were dating, he was sleeping with Annette Stern? Annette *Stern* of all people! That *laugh*…"

"Oh," said Simon. "I… I didn't know that…"

"No, you wouldn't. Ugh, he was *such* a jerk."

"I guess he was…" Simon considered these revelations. Now that he thought about it, Will had been something of a jerk. Laughed, once, to hear that Simon wrote twice a week to his little sister. So much for the happy memories. "So, Kay… what's been going on in your life?"

"What's *my* good reason for using a fake name, do you mean?" Katarina sighed. "It's complicated."

"Yes," said Simon, "it usually is."

"I'm here undercover."

"Sounds… important?"

Katarina put the gun down on the table. Simon saw Inara's shoulders relax. Katarina said, "After I graduated, I took a job with the police in Capital City. Forensic medicine."

"You always did have a thing for corpses," said Simon.

"Well, they don't talk back!" laughed Katarina.

"No need for bedside manner," agreed Simon.

"If this is doctor humor," said Inara, "I'm happy not to hear any more."

"I did that for a while," Katarina went on, "and then a friend who's on the board of trustees at St. Freda's got in touch to ask me to come out here. That was about a year ago."

So well before his warrant was issued. Simon relaxed a little more himself. "Go on."

Katarina glanced at Inara. "I trust your friend here will be discreet?"

"Whatever is said in here remains between us," said Inara.

"It's just that St. Freda's is owned by the local Guild House—"

"I won't breathe a word," said Inara. "Although I didn't know that the Guild had such a presence on Bethel."

"Oh yes," said Katarina. "They got here immediately after the war ended. Snapped up some of the main real estate. I think they saw that the border worlds were opening up and that Neapolis was heading for a boom. They weren't wrong. They're one of the biggest employers around here, as a result. And not just companions."

"All the dependent businesses," said Inara.

"St. Freda's alone must employ several hundred people," said Katarina. "The Guild's very powerful here."

"But what's your investigation?" asked Simon. "What's going on?"

"Someone has been organizing the theft of various drugs and other supplies. Selling them off world to Rim planets for profit."

"Stealing medical supplies from a hospital," said Inara, shaking her head. "Isn't it terrible, Simon, what some people will do for money?"

"Yes," he murmured. "Appalling."

"Do you think someone at the Guild House might be involved?" said Inara.

Katarina seemed to consider her answer. "Yes, we do," she said, at last. "My friend asked me to look into it, so I came here about a year ago, under a different name. But the Guild's a hard nut to crack."

"If there's anything I can do to help," said Inara. "It's alarming to think that anyone at the Guild might be responsible and, really, even the suggestion of corruption is unacceptable. I'm very familiar with Guild governance, Doctor. I might be able to spot irregularities that an outside eye would miss."

Katarina looked at her thoughtfully. "You know, I wouldn't mind an expert opinion on the set-up here," she said. "Someone who knows the Guild, but isn't connected to the local house…"

"I'd be more than happy to oblige," said Inara.

Katarina sat for a while in thought. Simon and Inara gave each other relieved looks. Eventually, Katarina seemed to come to a decision. "All right," she said. "There's a party tonight at the Guild House. Hosted by the head of the house. Her name's Hilde Becker. It's a big event—one of the biggest private parties during Carnival. Tickets are like gold dust. I've been more or less instructed to attend. One reason I'm short-staffed," she said, bitterly. "But I don't have a guest."

"As luck would have it, I'm not engaged this evening," said Inara. "If you would like some company, and, perhaps, some insider information, I'd be glad to join you and see if there's anything you might have missed." Pointedly, she added, "Anything to help a friend of Simon's."

"In which case," said Katarina, "I see no reason why I should draw attention to the more creative aspects of your resume, Simon. Not least because I'm desperate for staff."

"And I see no reason why I should draw attention to yours, Kay. Not least because… well. Sounds like you're doing important work."

"Yes, it is important. Good. That's settled." She relaxed, ever so slightly. "You know, it's nice to see you again, Simon. I'm really sorry to hear about the burnout. You must miss Osiris. Very different out here."

"Yes," said Simon, unhappily. That, at least, wasn't feigned. He'd loved his job and would go back there in a shot, if the 'verse could somehow be rearranged to make that possible.

"You always seemed so on top of things!" said Katarina. "And you weren't competitive like the others. You weren't like the others at all." She turned to Inara. "Do you know, he was the only man in our year group that we didn't have to warn each other about?"

Simon hadn't known that and in fact wasn't sure he knew what she meant. "*Warn* each other?"

"You know," she said. "You weren't handsy like the others."

"Simon's practically a saint," agreed Inara. Simon looked for the glint of sarcasm in her eye but couldn't spot it. At least, he didn't think so. "We were very grateful he agreed to fly with us on board our ship."

"I can't quite picture him flying round the Rim," said Katarina.

"I think he's adjusted to the life very well—"

"This is actually painful," said Simon. "Can you let me get to work now, please?"

The two women exchanged amused looks. Katarina, coming round the desk, squeezed his arm. "It's good to see you again. And it's relief to think that there's someone of your caliber here this weekend."

Simon sighed. Like old times again. Maybe, for a while, he could pretend that the 'verse hadn't taken this awful sideways shift. That everything was back to normal, and his life had stayed on course, and he was home, doing what he loved to do best.

Katarina nodded at his glasses. "You won't need those, by the way. They've fixed the boxes on the walls here so that people think there's retinal scanning throughout the building, but they never installed the technology. That's this planet in a nutshell. Nothing's what it seems, and everything's done on the cheap."

"Not in theater, I hope?" said Simon.

Katarina smiled. "Anyone else would have asked whether or not that meant they'd get paid—but not you, Simon. The hospital's well enough equipped. Not by the standards of Capital City, but better than most border worlds."

And certainly better than stitching people together again in the medical bay on *Serenity*. "And I *will* get paid?"

"You'll get paid," said Katarina. "I'll make sure of that."

At the door to the office, she turned to Inara. "Ms. Serra," she said. "Thanks for agreeing to come along. If you let me know where you're staying, I'll bring a car over to collect this evening you. Around six thirty?"

Inara bowed her head with exquisite and precise courtesy. "That will be perfect. Have fun, Simon, if that's the right thing to say. And... do take care."

* * *

Back in her shuttle, Inara confirmed the engagement that evening with Kay, and then sent a wave back to Sihnon. Having made the decisions that had brought about her departure from House Madrassa, she didn't, in general, like to call on her old friends, but sometimes there were questions she could not answer alone. She needed her sisters.

"Guanyin," she said, smiling. "I hope this finds you safe and well. I'm… I'm well. I'm on Bethel right now, on the border, and there seem to be some question marks over the local Guild House. Some irregularities in how they are running a local hospital. Is there anything I should know? Is there anything you can find out for me? It would help the friend of a friend… Oh," she laughed, "you know how these things work! The head of the House is named Hilde Becker, if that helps at all. Thank you, *mei mei*. And it's been too long. We should try to speak properly, next time I'm near the Core."

She blew her friend a kiss, finished the call, and pushed aside the melancholy that always threatened whenever she interfaced with her old life. Instead, she began to prepare for the evening. Something to impress upon the members of the local House that she was from the central worlds. Something that made them understand the kinds of connections she had and, perhaps, send the signal that the House here on Bethel was coming to the attention of some powerful people back in the Core.

It was troubling, to say the least, to think that a Guild House might be involved in some ongoing corruption. Even small lapses threatened the integrity of the institution. The whole idea of Guild was built on trust. Clients needed to know that they were safe in these intimate spaces; that they could speak openly to their companions and not find themselves betrayed. Passing on information revealed in such a space; that was truly unforgivable. What Katarina had described— financial irregularity—was a different category of betrayal, and perhaps whoever was involved believed they had good reason to be diverting medicine off world. Since coming on board *Serenity*, Inara had seen much more of life beyond the Core, and she had come to understand that things were not so clear-cut out here. Still, there was no harm in some closer observation of how the Guild was operating here, and if it protected Simon, that was a good enough reason in itself. If the attendees were as high profile as Katarina said, she would surely learn something to help… not Mal, but Zoë and the Shepherd. Inara drew the line at helping Mal.

She looked in the mirror and considered the effect. Satisfactory. She heard movement behind her and turned to see River standing in the door, watching.

"River, honey," she said. "You don't have to stand there, *mèi mèi*. Come in."

River slipped barefoot across the room, like a ghost or a shadow. Poor girl… Simon said that she'd loved to dance. How old was she? Sixteen? Seventeen? She should be at some school or college, studying, stretching her brilliant mind as far it could possibly go, having fun, falling in love and out of love, and dancing, dancing, dancing…

River stood beside her. Inara took her hand. "I want to look like you," said River. "I want to go to the ball."

Inara's breath caught. River was so odd, so obviously gifted in ways that were not always entirely clear, that it was too easy to forget that she might feel the same as any young woman. Why should she not want to look beautiful? Why should she not get to experience the joy, the pleasure, the confidence that came from feeling comfortable within one's own body? So much had been done to hurt her. Her body must be a source of great pain, physical and mental, and that was truly tragic.

"There's no reason why you shouldn't," said Inara, and led her over to the chair.

Gently, patiently, and with infinite tenderness—Inara transformed the girl sitting before her. Combed out the tangles until her hair began to shine. Let her look through the closet until she found a dress that made her laugh out loud. Picked out a necklace, and earrings. A shawl for her shoulders. Made up her face so cleverly that River's youth and beauty were enhanced and not concealed. Made her giggle with a puff of scent. When she was done, Inara led her back to the mirror.

"What do you think, River?"

The girl was suffused with happiness. "Yes," she whispered, "you *shall* go to the ball…"

Inara placed a kiss upon her cheek. It was time for her to go. She left River admiring herself, and went into *Serenity*'s bridge, where she found Wash, poring over information coming in from the Cortex, looking for something that might help.

"Hey Inara," Wash said, throwing a casual glance back over his shoulder, "you look nice. You always look nice." He looked at her more carefully. "You look *particularly* nice."

"Thank you, Wash." She looked round, cautiously. "Where's Mal?"

"He went looking for Kaylee." Wash pushed back in his seat. "I wish you hadn't let her go off on her own. We're wasting time we should be using to get our hands on some money…" He looked at her more carefully. "Are you going *out*?"

"Yes," she said. "I have a party this evening."

"A *party*?" Wash, open-mouthed, goggled at her. "*Gǒu shǐ*, am I the only one with a sense of urgency round here about what's going on? Am I the only one worrying? There are *ears* in danger. There are *wives* in danger—"

"And Shepherd Book."

"There are ears and wives and preachers in danger, and nobody seems to care about any of this—"

"I care," said Inara. "This is a favor for a friend of Simon's."

"Woah!" Wash held up his hands. "Wait, back up, big news—Simon has *friends*?"

"Apparently so. And, no, Wash, I have not forgotten either Zoë or the Shepherd. The people at this party, they're important."

"Oh, well," said Wash, "if they're *important*—"

"If they're important, then they might be able to help. Or at least I might hear something that will help us." She sighed. "Where's Jayne? Did he go off with Mal?"

"He went off in a huff. I think he's gone to his cabin to cry on Vera's shoulder."

"At least you've all been using your time productively," said Inara. She turned to go. "I hope you're not planning to do anything stupid."

"Mal might be," said Wash. "But I'm definitely not. Well, I definitely am, but I'm not doing anything with the stupid right now. There's enough stupid goes on around here without me adding to the general levels of stupid, and I'm not that stupid. Is that clear?"

Wash had cause to regret those words about half an hour later. Abandoning his attempts to glean anything from local communications chatter, he got up, kicked his chair in frustration, hurt his foot, and after some magnificently robust cursing and some pitiful rubbing, made his ill-tempered way down to the dining room. There he was confronted with a vision that would haunt him for some weeks to come.

First (Wash would be at pains, when recounting this tale, to stress this was not the upsetting part), he saw River, dressed like something out of a fairy tale. That was nice, that part of the vision. Wash would certainly think of this at least once or twice a day over the next few weeks, and every single time he would get a goofy expression on his face that would make Zoë laugh at him. Yes, River looking nice was definitely the good part of the vision. The bad part—the completely unacceptably disturbing part—was Jayne, chomping on a cigar, and wearing a tuxedo. A dark blue velvet tuxedo with shiny lapels.

"*Wǒ de mā*," said Wash. "Has someone spiked the drinking water?"

"What?" said Jayne. "Something on my face? I washed it."

River pirouetted. The thing was, Wash thought, dragging his eyes away from the truly alarming sight that was Jayne to look properly at the girl spinning round before him, she looked beautiful. Really beautiful. There was a necklace and earrings and a bracelet, and the jewels looked like they were the real thing. There was make-up, and not too much of the stuff (Wash thought women looked better without, but what did he know about women?). There was a sweet scent of perfume. There was a long black dress, with shimmery stuff all over *(What was that stuff called? Did it have a name?)*, and the skirt of the dress had a long slit up one side, which revealed the existence of legs *(No, no, no!* Off *limits—seriously, there was so many good reasons not to be looking at the legs)*, and she was smiling…

"Are you coming to the ball?" said River. "You should come with us to the ball."

There was River and also—and Wash felt that this needed to be emphasized—Jayne standing next to her, wearing a blue velvet tuxedo. With shiny lapels. Tugging at the bow tie round his massive neck. And perhaps the most bewildering part of all this was that Jayne somehow looked *good*… "Jayne," he said. "Where did you…? *How* did you…?"

"Pretty cunning, huh?" Jayne preened. "Got it from that scary tailor on Prophet."

Wash sat down, heavily. He put his head in his hands. "I am so done with today."

"I'm done too," said Jayne. "Done waitin' round here any longer. Me and the girl—we're off, *dǒng ma*?"

"No, I do not understand," said Wash. How could anyone understand all this. "What? Where? Make me understand—"

"Casino," said Jayne, as if this was the only reasonable answer to that question. "Gonna win us some money."

"No," said Wash. "No, you're not. I forbid it. This, here, right now, is me forbidding that idea and anything associated with that idea. You, young man and young lady, have hit my limits—"

"Don't work that way," said Jayne. "Listen. Here's how it seems to me. The kid—she might be creepy, but she reckons she can work out how the wheels work. At the casinos. You know what I mean?"

The thing was, that Jayne was kinda making sense… Wash had seen River play knucklebones. She was invincible… *No*, he told himself. *Don't get pulled into this…* That way lay madness—terrible, terrible madness. "I know exactly what you mean. And I'm saying to you now that this is a bad idea. A really bad idea."

"And I'm sayin' it's worth a try," said Jayne, "because I ain't heard anythin' better comin' from neither you nor Mal. Someone's gotta get that money before Roberts does anythin' to Zoë and the Shepherd that can't be undone, and me and the girl think this is worth a try. You comin' or are you stayin'?"

"Red sun," said River, inexplicably. "Black dragon. The wheel turns and turns and turns. To everything there is a season." She frowned. "I cut that from the Shepherd's symbol and couldn't fix it back again."

"Well, as long as it's our season tonight, that's all I'm sayin'," said Jayne.

Wash opened his mouth and closed it again.

"What?" said Jayne. "What's the matter? You ain't seen me scrubbed up before?"

"No, I have never seen you scrubbed up before. I did not believe that scrubbed-up Jayne was a thing that was possible. I am alarmed," said Wash. "I am more than alarmed. I am frightened. I am more than frightened. I am *distressed*."

"Keep it civil," said Jayne. "It's your gorram wife I'm doin' this for, *dŏng ma*?"

"No, it's not," said River. "The money is too good."

"She's right," said Wash. "You'll want your cut. Do you two even have a stake to put down?"

This last, he realized later, was his mistake. That was when he acknowledged, even in this tiny and insignificant way, that what was happening in front of him was not the figment of a tired and worried mind, but was really happening, and, even more, had the slightest resemblance to a reasonable course of action. This was the moment—he would try to explain later—when they got him off-guard and reeled him right in to this shared insanity.

River started rattling off numbers. "Two, four, eight, sixteen, thirty-two, sixty-four, one-two-eight, two-five-six—"

"Stop!" said Wash. "Stop that! All right! All right! *Gou le*, I'll come! If only to stop you two from doing anything… from doing *anything*, anything at all."

The three of them stared at each other.

"What?" said Wash. "Why are you both looking at me?"

"Can't come dressed like that," said Jayne.

"You have to shed your skin," said River (and oh, no, it wasn't as if *that* wasn't troubling). "Put on a new one if you want to come to the ball."

* * *

The afternoon was wearing on and the preparations for the Roberts' First Night party were by now well underway. Zoë, standing by the window, had watched as a stage was built, and a firework display arranged. She'd seen huge floral displays arrive, a few dozen chairs laid out, and big round tables set. Watched people bring out silver cutlery and fine crystal glasses. Then the food was brought out on platters. Bottles and bottles of wine. Lanterns were placed along the terrace, and, as the sun went down, they were lit. Then musicians came out and started tuning up. At the sound of this, the Shepherd, who had, so far as Zoë could tell, done nothing more with the afternoon than slowly explore the shelves, picking out book after book, rifling through them, and then putting them back, at last came over to take a look.

"Ah," he said. "String quartet. That'll be pleasant. And fireworks too, by the look of things. Not the big show, but a nice display nonetheless."

"If it's all the same to you, preacher, I'd rather not be here for the party."

"Hm," said Book, folding his arms. "The day is wearing on, isn't it?"

"You've noticed."

"I'm assuming," Book said, "that Mal has been spending the time since our capture busily planning some kind of escape for us."

"Fair assumption," said Zoë.

"I'm also assuming that by now the situation has gotten

wildly out of hand, and that he's further away from mounting a rescue attempt than ever."

"Knowing Mal, that's an even fairer assumption."

The Shepherd leaned back against the wall. He looked to Zoë's eyes to be very relaxed, but she didn't take the Shepherd on face value.

"I imagine," he said, "that when the ransom was demanded for our release that the captain made some kind of ill-advised attempt to negotiate. Now he finds himself having to raise a large amount of money in a very short amount of time."

"So Roberts said."

The string quartet struck up, just as the first of the guests arrived. Well-dressed, very rich. Roberts materialized, the impeccable host, making them welcome. Drinks were handed rounded. More guests began to arrive. The music lilted on, sweetly.

"Nice," said Book. "Very nice. Mal will want to get the shipment back, I should think. He doesn't like people getting one over him. But whoever those folks were, they knew what they were doing. That cargo's long gone by now." The Shepherd shook his head. "No, that's a poor option. There's the casinos, of course, but I doubt Mal will be willing to gamble everything on, well, gambling. Seems to me those aren't the kinds of risks he generally takes. No, Mal's not a gambling man."

He was right there. Back in the war, Mal rarely threw in his lot in the card games the rest of them played. Kept his luck for the more life-and-death situations the 'verse threw at them. Hadn't changed, much. "You seem to have this all worked out, Shepherd, but I don't see where all this talk is leading us."

"Where it's leading me, Zoë," Book said, "is that I'm starting to think that you and I are going to have to take matters into our own hands."

At last. "Was hopin' you were comin' round to that way of thinkin'."

"Well, given there have been no updates on our situation, I see no reason why we should continue to make life easy for our captors." He looked out of the window. "Most of the guests are here now, by the looks of things."

"Have to say it's a mighty fine company."

"To my mind, they're a mighty fine distraction." He pointed over to one side. "I like the look of that red car, Zoë, what do you think?"

"Expect it would do what's necessary. Got to get to it first, though."

Book eyed her. "You know," he said softly, "I'd rather that nobody got killed."

"I know. But I don't want a repeat of earlier, preacher."

He shook his head. "No need for Jayne to be firin' that gun."

"Maybe. Maybe not. You can take that up with him when we're back on the ship. But if we're takin' matters into our own hands now, Shepherd, there's something I need to be sure of."

"Go on," he said.

"That the man standin' beside me is the man who can carry a gun, not the man who carries a Bible."

"I understand that, Zoë."

"I promise you, Shepherd—I won't breathe a word about anything you do today."

He began to laugh. "What happens in kidnap club stays in kidnap club, is that it?"

"That's about the size of it."

"Oh Zoë," Book said, with a sad smile. "It don't matter whether the others know or not. It's God that counts—and He always knows."

"If I get to the pearly gates before you, I'll put in a good word," said Zoë. "But what I need to know right now is—you willing to do what it takes to get out of here, Shepherd?"

"Let's take things as they come." He eyed her thoughtfully. "For one thing, we don't have any guns."

"Not yet."

Book smiled, dangerously. Zoë smiled back. Mal might not be one for men of the cloth, but she knew there was a reason she'd always liked Shepherd Book. He went back to the billiards table, picking up one of the cues and holding it much the same way that Jayne held Vera.

"I reckon someone could do some damage with one of these," he said.

"Reckon so," said Zoë. She looked round for something else to use, and her eye fell on the red Buddha. Little fella looked like he might do someone's head a mischief. She picked him up, only to discover, to some disappointment, that he was surprisingly light. Must be hollow. She put him back in place and, as she did so, the baize on the billiards table shimmered, and disappeared. In the space beneath, which had hitherto been covered by the holographic baize, was a very expensive flatscreen console.

The Shepherd burst out laughing. "Would you credit

that?" he said. "All afternoon I've been pulling books off the shelves hoping for that, and you're the one who finally hits the jackpot."

"You were looking for a *console*?"

"I was looking for something might give us some answers. What did you think I was doing? Trying to find something to read?" He gave her a wicked grin, most unsuitable for a man of the cloth. "I wonder what we might learn," he said, "if we took a closer look?"

Give the girl her due, Mal thought, she moved quickly for one so small and she made good use of the element of surprise. She nearly sent Mal flying. All more than a mite embarrassin', and he was going to have to make gorram sure Kaylee didn't mention that, once they were back on *Serenity*. But even catching him on the hop, the kid had no real chance against a man like Mal. He got his balance back quickly, grabbed her arm, and—ever so gently, yet ever so firmly—stopped her from biting him, a task to which she was applyin' herself with considerable diligence.

"*Tiān xiǎo de*, will you stop with that?" he said. "Who brought you up? Bitin' ain't right! Is that how you treat everyone who comes to save you?"

"I think it's just how she treats men who are grabbin' at her arm," said Kaylee.

"I ain't grabbin' her arm, I'm keepin' her teeth away from me, *dǒng ma*?"

But Kaylee was paying him no mind; all her attention was now on the girl. "Sweetie, it's okay. I know he looks like a mean old man, but he ain't so bad once you get to know him. I mean, he's an interferin' idiot who ought to know better, but his heart's more or less in the right place."

"Thankin' you kindly for that testimonial, Kaylee." Mal looked down at the girl. "If I let go, will you keep on tryin' to bite me?"

She shook her head.

"Will you run?" said Mal.

The girl glanced at Kaylee, who said, "I'll help, even if he won't. Please, honey, don't run."

"All right," the girl said. "I won't run."

Mal let go of her and she pulled away from him. Kaylee opened her arms to her and the girl fell into them and began to cry. "That's right, sweetie," she said. "You let it all come out…"

The girl cried on. And on, and on. Mal, conscious of time passing and everything that was at stake, said, "Any chance you could turn off those waterworks before tomorrow?"

The sobbing got even louder.

"Mal!" scolded Kaylee. "You're being a real *hún dàn* today!"

"That ain't nice, Kaylee."

"You're scarin' her even worse—"

"Scarin'? I ain't scary—"

"You just scared off the two men who were comin' after her and she was terrified of them!"

Despite herself, the girl gave a laugh. Kaylee squeezed her arm round her more tightly. "That's more like it," she said. "Sweetie, we're not from around here. Maybe we can help. We've helped already, haven't we?"

"I guess…"

"You hungry?"

"Uh huh," said the girl.

"How about we start by getting you somethin' to eat?"

The girl nodded. "Please," she said. "I'm *starvin'*."

"Okay, we'll find you somethin' to eat, and you can tell us your story. How's that for a trade?"

The girl laughed, weakly, and said, "Okay. I'll trade."

"Kaylee," said Mal, "it's mighty fine you settin' us up with a dinner date, but we're on a schedule here—" Kaylee turned on him, eyes flashing. Mal took a step back. "Woah!"

"She's a *kid*, Mal," Kaylee shot back. "She's all on her own and there are some bad men after her. You know, I didn't ask you to come after me, Malcolm Reynolds, so if you want to be on your way, that's fine. You be on your way and leave me and this girl alone and we'll see how we get on when those two apes turn up again and decide to do whatever it was they were tryin' to do before you came and stuck your oar in."

When did Kaylee Frye get this much fire in her belly? Mal, who knew when he was beat, frowned down at the girl, who stared back with huge wet eyes. Now he thought about it, she did look a mite peaky. He didn't like the look of that. Didn't like the look of the bruises on her arm, neither. And he knew he ought to know better, and that he had enough ruttin' problems of his own to be gettin' on with, but the truth was, he couldn't leave this kid out here by herself.

"All right," he groused. "Somethin' to eat."

"Back to *Serenity*?" asked Kaylee.

"No, not if them fellas are still around. Don't want 'em scoutin' out my ship. We'll find somewhere round here, fill this one, put her somewhere safe, and then she can be on her way. If that sounds satisfactory to you, Kaylee?"

"That'll do."

They found an all-day diner a couple of blocks away. "Get what you like," said Kaylee. "Mal's payin'." Mal opened his mouth to make it categorically clear that this was not under any circumstances going to be the case, and Kaylee moved in for the kill. "'Cause I ain't been able to make any money today."

Mal gave up. The sooner they fed this child and found her people, the sooner this wholly unnecessary delay would be over and done with. The girl didn't stint. Kaylee too decided she could manage another breakfast, but: "Coffee," growled Mal, when the waitress turned to him. "Black. Strong. Hot."

Pancakes arrived, piping hot and slathered in sweet syrup and strips of bacon and little berries, and the girl burrowed her way in. Kaylee stole a couple of the strawberries. Mal, catching the wholesome scent of the food, began to regret his abstemiousness. The girl ate her fill. When she was done, she looked up at them both, and seemed to remember her manners. "Thanks. Thank you. This was... This was kind of you."

Suddenly her eyes were full of tears again, and Mal had to say as how he didn't like the way she was surprised folks around her were being kind. "All right," he said, voice gruff. "You've had some supper. So now here comes the price tag."

She went stiff. "I ain't got no money, mister. And I won't pay any other way—"

"What?" said Mal? "No, no, no! No need to be talking about payin', not in a cash way and certainly not in a…" He swallowed. "Not in any other way you might be thinkin' of. All I was hopin' was that we might get your tale out of you now."

"Oh," said the girl. She stared down at her empty plate.

"Maybe," said Kaylee gently, "we might be able to help you."

The girl shook her head. "Don't think you can do that."

"You never know. You can trust us," said Kaylee. "But we can't help you until we know a little more about you…"

"We know those two fellas didn't mean you well," said Mal.

"No," she whispered.

"You know who they are?"

She shrugged. "Met 'em yesterday. Don't know their names."

"Can we get you back to your ma and pa?" said Kaylee.

The girl looked at her blankly. "They're dead."

"Sweetie, I'm sorry—"

"S'okay. Died years back."

"Then where's home?" said Mal.

"Grew up in Evansville. Up the river in the Croker Valley."

One of the mining settlements, Mal thought, recalling the name from the maps he'd seen. "Go on," he said.

"When they died, Aunty Eve, mamma's sister, took me in. Then she died and Uncle Nate… Well, he said as how we weren't kin, not really, but he'd look out for me till I was fourteen, and then I was my own business."

"Uncle Nate don't sound like a very nice man," said Mal.

"No," she whispered. "He ain't."

"How did you find yourself here in the city, sweetie?" said Kaylee.

"My fourteenth birthday came, he said he'd got me a present. A special present. Found me a job here…" She began to cry.

They got the rest of the story out of her in bits and pieces. They got her name, Ava Jones, and found out as how she felt scared and ashamed. Seemed to think the whole business was her own fault somehow. Turned out Uncle Nate had got her a job all right—sent her off by train down to the big city, and when she arrived, those fellas were waitin' to grab her and make use of her.

"They were goin' to give me a needle," she said. "Somethin' to make me sleep." She shuddered. "I knew it weren't right," she said. "I knew what they were plannin' for me…"

Kaylee put her arm around her. Mal knew what they'd had planned for her too. Get her hooked on some drug or other; keep her locked up in some whorehouse workin' for her next fix. *Uncle Nate*, thought Mal. *Evansville in the Croker Valley. I think I might be payin' you a call, when this is all done. Give you a special present in your turn…*

"How did you get away?" said Kaylee.

"Bit one and ran like… Well, ran like the Devil himself was after me, which I guess he was. I hid away and then…" She bit her lip, as if not sure as if she should carry on. She took a look at Kaylee's encouraging and kindly face and continued.

"A friend of my aunt's," she said, "when she heard I was

comin' this way, she gave me a card to use on the vidphones. Said if I was in need, to use it to make a call. So when I got away… When I got away, I did just that. That was yesterday. They folks on the other end told me to come out here, to the motel up the road, and there'd be someone to help me… But I had to get there at the right time. And when I got there, them two fellas were outside, and they saw me…"

So she'd run.

"Mal," said Kaylee. "We have to help."

Mal stared down into his cup. The coffee had gone cold. One little girl, and a couple of big fellas going to a great deal of trouble. It all sounded very familiar—and Mal had to admit he did on occasion have cause to regret taking in the Tams. And today he had enough to worry about. Zoë and Book were still in Roberts' hands, and the clock was ticking, and they were nowhere near layin' their hands on the platinum they needed…

"Captain," urged Kaylee. "We gotta do something. Get her where she's meant to be goin'."

"And where's that, Kaylee? Sounds like she missed her chance at that."

"There'll be somewhere she can go," she came back.

"I thought you didn't think I should be interferin' in other people's business—"

"You know what I meant by that. And it ain't this."

Mal sighed. Because Kaylee was right, of course—and no way was he leaving this girl out here, with people like that after her. But still he wondered—all this for one little girl. What was that old expression? "No good deed goes unpunished." River Tam—one little girl—had brought a whole heap of trouble along with her. Mal sure as hell hoped he wasn't going to regret this particular good deed either.

"All right," he said. "Let's start with what we've got. Show me that card you were given."

"Mal," said Kaylee. "Try to be nice."

"Please," he added.

Carefully, unwillingly, Ava took the card out. When Mal reached for it, she grabbed it away. "No," she said. "Ain't nobody getting their hands on this but me. It's my lifeline and besides…" She glanced at Kaylee.

"She was trusted with this, Mal," Kaylee said. "Someone trusted her not to give this to anyone else."

"All right, all right!" Mal threw up his hands. "But we ain't going to get far without usin' it again. Look, there's a vidphone over there. Ain't no harm givin' it a try—"

"But they told me what time to call," said Ava.

"Well, and now *I'm* tellin' you the time to try again is now, *dǒng ma*?"

"Don't let him bully you, Ava," said Kaylee. "He's a mean old man. But I think he might be right. How about I come with you?"

The girl agreed and Mal watched them head over to the vidphone near the back of the diner. The waitress came over, took a look at the state of his coffee, and brought him back a fresh cup and a bacon sandwich. He'd wolfed that and drunk half the coffee by the time Kaylee and the girl came back.

"We reached someone," said Kaylee. "She's given us a new location. We're to take Ava there as soon as possible. But…"

154

"Go on," said Mal, heart sinking.

"It's a little way outside the city." She carried on quickly before he could speak. "I'm takin' her, Mal. You can come or not, whatever you prefer, but I ain't lettin' this girl go off on her own—"

"Kaylee, chances are they won't want strangers like us seein' their safe house or whatever it is out there. Chances are they'll not want to let us go and that'll be two more of my crew held hostage, one of them me, and I ain't overly fond of being held hostage—"

"Mal! Will you just shut up for a minute?"

Mal shut up.

"You can do what you like," Kaylee said, and he could tell by her expression that there was going to be no persuading her. But I'm takin' her there." She turned to the girl.

"Come on, Ava, honey. I'll get you there. Captain Meanie can go f—"

"Kaywinnet Lee *Frye*!"

"Go fend for himself."

Late afternoon was tipping over into early evening. Carnival was here. Sitting in the car, Inara watched Katarina fiddle with the bracelet on her wrist. To Inara's eyes, the other woman seemed very uncomfortable. Perhaps she didn't enjoy dressing up and going to parties. Not everyone did. Inara had gotten the impression that Katarina, like Simon, would rather be at work this evening. Still, she could try to make the other woman feel more at ease.

"I've not visited Bethel before," said Inara, her voice light and pleasant.

"I suppose it's a little off the beaten track," replied Katarina.

"Most of my work until now has been on the central worlds," agreed Inara. "But I've noticed that people seem to be drawn out to the border worlds, one way or another. Perhaps the central worlds are too safe, too routine. Perhaps people like a little adventure in their life. Is that what drew you here?"

Katarina shrugged, and kept on playing with the bracelet. "Strange to see Simon Tam out here. If there was anyone fitted into life on Osiris, it was him. Hard-working, compliant... Not really the kind of person you'd imagine taking risks." Katarina shook her head. "Not Simon."

If only she knew, thought Inara. "Life on the central planets may be safe, but it can become very stressful in its own way," said Inara. "I don't know Simon very well—we've only really been acquainted a few months—but from what I've seen I get the sense he's over-achieved for most of his life. Eventually the strain shows." And while this was not what had happened with Simon, whom, Inara guessed, would still be happily at home back on Osiris were it not for River, she'd seen this kind of thing happen to friends in the Guild. Life became too structured, too imprisoning, and they had to break free.

"Simon always struck me as someone who loved his work," Katarina went on. "Someone who would choose to practice medicine even if the money was bad. I mean—the money certainly helps. But medicine was a vocation for Simon. Everyone used to say that about him. That he'd become a doctor because he cared. Strange that he should leave that world behind, to go travelling…"

Perhaps all this interest in Simon was merely someone trying to understand the decisions of an old friend, but Inara was starting to get the uncomfortable feeling that she was being questioned. Simon—and River—had to be protected. "Juggling that vocation with the politics of a big hospital must have become too much for him." said Inara. "This is just conjecture. I haven't pressed him for answers." She tried to shut this line of conversation down completely. "Like I say, we haven't known each other long, and it's his own affair."

But Katarina still pushed. "This ship you're on—they didn't mind taking on board someone using a fake ID?"

"The captain's a forgiving type." And while that was not, in fact, the first word that Inara would use to describe Mal (those were not repeatable in polite company), he was certainly minded to be merciful when it came to people causing trouble for the Alliance. Whatever else Simon might have done, there was certainly no doubt that he had caused, and was continuing to cause, a great deal of trouble for the Alliance. That alone would keep Mal on side, for a while at least. But would it last? What would Simon do, if Mal ever decided enough was enough? How long would he and River last, out here? Perhaps, Inara thought, Simon should be making plans that way.

"Yet Simon trusted you enough to tell you his name? His reasons for leaving?"

"People trust companions not to give away their secrets," said Inara. Would Katarina take the hint now and stop pressing her on this?

It seemed she did, since no further questions came. Inara looked out of the window. The sky was darkening, and the city lights begin to blaze. She studied them for a while. Was it her imagination, or were they becoming more distant? She said, "I thought that the Guild House was on the Platinum Mile."

"It is."

"But we seem to be heading away from the city?"

"Traffic's terrible, first night of Carnival," said Katarina. "That whole area around the Mile is more or less sealed off for transport. Not even these city cabs can get through."

"Yes, but we do seem to be going a very long way round—"

There was a pause. Inara felt the first cold trickle of alarm.

"The place we're going to is out of town," said Katarina.

"The head of the Guild House goes out of town on the first night of Carnival?"

"Her house—her private residence, I mean, not the Guild House—is out of town. And that's where the party is."

"I see…"

For some reason, Inara had gotten the impression that the party was happening at the Guild House, but perhaps she had misconstrued. Still, something else was nagging at the back of her mind. Her client for the following day was a wealthy businessman, and he had asked her to come to his private residence to collect him. This was located on the east side of the river. She'd taken the time to look at a map of Neapolis to get a sense of how the city was laid out. The Platinum Mile, the big hotels, the streets behind with the smaller venues and less well-appointed hotels, they were all on the flat plain that lay on the west side of the river. On the east side, the ground rose up, and this was where the private residences tended to be located, perched on the hillsides away from the noise and bustle of the rest of the city, looking down across the Mile or out to sea.

But they were not going that way. Rather, they seemed to be heading out into the country. Looking behind, Inara could see that bright lights of the Mile were slipping ever further away. Inara felt suddenly extremely vulnerable. Quietly, surreptitiously, she reached out to try the door of the car.

"That won't open," said Katarina, "if that's what you're trying to find out."

"No," said Inara. "I thought it might not." She took a deep breath. "Are we really going to meet the head of the Guild House?"

"No, I'm afraid we're not."

"Can I ask then where you're taking me?"

"You can ask." Katarina looked at her sideways. "I was wondering when you were going to work this out. Took you longer than I expected, to be honest."

"I had no reason not to trust you," Inara said.

"No?"

"Absolutely none. If I'm going to be kidnapped, I'd like to know why."

"Kidnapped?" Katarina gave a short, rather bitter laugh. "This isn't a kidnapping."

"No?" Inara swallowed down her fear. "I'm being taken somewhere under false pretenses, and—in case this wasn't clear—entirely against my will. Correct me if I'm wrong, but isn't that more or less the definition of kidnapping?"

"This isn't a kidnapping. If this was a kidnapping, there'd be violence. Needles. You'd know for sure that you weren't safe."

Inara fell silent, considering her options. She was not, she thought, in immediate danger. Katarina seemed on edge, but Inara suspected this arose more from being beyond her comfort zone than anything else. This woman did not lead the kind of life that Mal and the others did. She was far more like Simon—like Inara herself had been, until recently— navigating her way around a new world and not entirely sure of the part she had to play. But why had Katarina decided that she, Inara, was a threat? Why did she want her out of the way?

"Is this to do with Simon?" Inara said, at last. She would have to word this carefully, she thought, if she was not to give the Tams away.

"With Simon?" Katarina gave her a puzzled look.

"The reason you're… I hesitate to say 'kidnapping' again, since you're so averse to the term, but it's hard to think of another. Could we not simply talk—?"

"Do you really think I fell for his story about burnout?" said Katarina. "Simon excels at many things, but he's a terrible liar. And he *loves* being a doctor." She frowned. "He did look tired though."

Inara, still and quiet, watched carefully. Any answer might give away information which Katarina did not have, and Inara was not going to make so simple a mistake. If Katarina knew that Simon was a wanted man, why had she not immediately called the authorities to arrest him? No, Inara was sure that this wasn't about Simon. This was about something else. But what? Carefully, she observed the other woman: the tightness around the lips; the twisting of the bracelet. Body language fairly straightforward to read. She didn't seem agitated, not yet, which meant that she was unlikely to do anything foolish or irreversible, but she was certainly angry, and certainly anxious.

"I know why they sent you, Inara," Katarina said.

And what was that supposed to mean? "Nobody sent us. Nobody. I brought Simon to St. Freda's because he needed to earn some money, and quickly. The story that he told you was… not entirely accurate, but that part at least was true."

"I'm not talking about Simon!" Katarina shot back. "I don't know what Simon's up to, and I don't particularly care. What I care about is what you're up to." Now she was getting agitated. "How do you *sleep*? Knowing what's going on? Is it all about protecting the Guild's reputation? Is *that* it? Is that really what it's about? I just don't understand!"

Inara adopted her most soothing tone. "You're distressed. I seem to be contributing in some way and I'm sorry. But you're mistaken about me. I came to St. Freda's for no reason other than the one I gave you—to introduce Simon, to help him secure work. If there's something else happening, I don't know what that is. But if you could trust me, just a little, perhaps I can help—"

"You know, you're not helping yourself," said Katarina. "You might be better just keeping quiet."

Inara tried another tactic. "You do know, don't you, that harming or threatening to harm a registered companion is taken seriously? You'll certainly lose your post at the hospital and quite possibly your license to practice medicine—"

"Yes, I know how the Guild works. I know how you stick together—"

"But this will only happen if you keep on this current course. We can turn the car back round now, go back to Neapolis, and forget this happened."

"Do you think I'm an idiot? I told you that I know why you're here! You'll cover this up like you cover everything else up. It makes me sick."

"Dr. Neilsen," Inara said, a little more urgently now, "I arrived on Bethel yesterday. I have never visited this world before, and I have very little knowledge of the politics of the place. I have clearly walked into some local trouble, but I promise you that I have no idea what that is. I have no idea what's going on—"

"Local trouble!" Katarina shook her head. "That's one way of brushing it under the carpet, I suppose." She pushed out a breath. "How do you people *sleep* at night?"

They were well beyond the city limits now, well into the countryside, a sunburned yellow land of rocky scrub. Inara had by now lost all sense of direction. A small tendril of fear curled within her. She did not think she was in any immediate danger, but she nevertheless, for reasons as yet completely unclear, she had somehow allowed herself to be taken hostage. She thought about what Mal would say. She would never live this down. She reached for her purse—but Katarina was there first, opening the bag, and taking out the small device by which Inara could access the Cortex.

"Locater, hey?" said Katarina, as she altered the settings. "Were you anticipating trouble this evening?"

"It's a precaution I always take," said Inara, truthfully. Most clients didn't dare run the risk of falling foul of Guild law, but one could never be too sure.

Katarina slipped the device into her pocket. "You'll get this back later." After about half-an-hour, the car began to reduce speed. The light was diminishing rapidly. Ahead, a line of pine trees stood out in the open fields, seeming to form the boundary of a property. They turned at these, coming onto a narrow road that ran alongside them and ended in a high wall with gates.

Katarina ran her fingers quickly across the control panel. "It's me," she said. "Let me through." She glanced at Inara. "I have our guest with me."

Slowly, the gates swung open. The car slipped quietly into the confines of the property. Ahead, in the purpling light, Inara saw the dark bulk of a square-fronted adobe house. Big windows with lights behind drawn curtains. A wooden verandah stood along the whole front with a lamp at one end set between a couple of rocking seats. On the left of the building, outside steps ran up to the upper story; on the right was a little porch which led to the entrance.

The car descended, and stopped, a little to one side of the front door.

"Get out," said Katarina. "And don't bother trying to call for help or run. We're isolated here, and you're not going to get far in those shoes."

This was true, although Inara was considerably more adept at self-defense than perhaps Katarina realized. "I'm not going anywhere," she said. "I want to understand what's happening here—"

Katarina looked at her thoughtfully. "I'm starting to think you really don't know—"

"I don't," said Inara. "I really don't—"

"You'll find out everything you need to know once you're inside."

The door to the house opened. Inara glanced around. Once she was inside, escape would become considerably more difficult. She looked back at the car. "You won't get away that way," said Katarina. "Just go inside. They're expecting us. Please don't try anything. There are children present."

"*Children*?"

"Well, that shouldn't be a surprise—"

"I'll say again," Inara replied. "I don't know what's happening. I mean you no harm, and perhaps, if you trusted me, I might be able to help."

"Get inside."

Inara stepped over the threshold and into the house. The hallway was plain, unadorned; white walls and wooden beams, but the place was clean and well lit. She could hardly describe it as welcoming, however, given the woman standing directly in front of her, holding a pistol. She looked coldly at Inara.

"This is going to complicate things, Kay," she said. "Did you have to bring her here?"

"We can keep her here until we've moved everyone," said Katarina. "When we're gone, we'll contact the Guild House. They can come and pick her up."

Inara tried one last time. "Please listen," she said. "I've had no contact with the local Guild House since I arrived on

Bethel. If you think there's a problem there, it's possible that I can help—"

"She's been denying she knows anything all the way over," said Katarina.

"Well, she would, wouldn't she?" said the other woman.

"Katarina told me she was investigating the Guild for corruption," said Inara. "That isn't acceptable. That isn't how the Guild should work—"

"We know how the Guild works," said Katarina.

"I have contacts back on Sihnon," said Inara. "I can ask for a full investigation—"

"Ask for a cover-up, more like," said the other woman. The conversation was interrupted by a door opening at the far end of the hall. A girl, no more than thirteen or fourteen, poked her head round. "Anna," she said, "Izzy's askin' for you—"

"Quiet, sweetheart!" said the other woman, very quickly. "Tell her I'll be there in just a minute!"

Inara sighed and lowered her head. She was fairly sure, now, that she understood what was happening. "Katarina," she said, opening her hands. "I am not involved in this. I can help, if you let me—"

"You really think we're going to let anyone from the Guild help?" said Katarina. "They're all in it. All of them. The Guild, half of the sheriff's office, just about anyone who's anyone on Bethel." She glanced at the other woman. "With some notable exceptions."

"And we're not having it," said the other woman. What had the girl called her? *Anna*. "Not any more. Nobody's going to lay a finger on any of these girls, any more. I'm making sure of that." She gestured to Inara to move in front of her. "Come on," she said. "Come through into the kitchen. I think someone from the Guild should come face-to-face with some of the consequences of their actions."

Simon quickly settled into place at St. Freda's. One of the other doctors, a very tired young man in his thirties named Mayhew, took one look at him and said, "Merciful Buddha, I'm glad you're here. I've hardly had a break this week and tonight's going to be appalling." And that was that. Straight to work, as if he'd never been away, and Simon was quietly loving every second of being back where he was supposed to be.

The evening was unfolding more or less as predicted. A trickle of arrivals soon became a steady stream: drunks who had fallen over; gamblers who had gotten into fist fights; all straightforward enough. But a couple of hours into the shift, they got warning that a gunshot wound was heading their way. Priority patient too, no expense spared. Someone very important was covering the bill.

"I... wasn't expecting many shootouts tonight," said Simon.

"There's always a few," said Mayhew. "They can get the damn things out of the casinos but there's no way of getting them off the streets."

The ambulance arrived and suddenly, everything was much more like being on board *Serenity*. Mayhew moved forward and Simon let him take this one. He saw enough gunshot wounds these days. After a couple of minutes, though, he couldn't resist taking a look. Peering over Mayhew's shoulder at the patient, he saw a big man, broad, with bushy black beard, sweating and trembling. Breathing quick and shallow. Anxious? Didn't like doctors? So many people didn't… No, Simon knew, it was something more.

"You need to get a mask on this man," said Simon to Mayhew.

"What?"

"Do it now."

Fortunately for the patient, Mayhew wasn't the kind of competitive prick from one of the hospitals back on Osiris, and he did what Simon said straight away. Which was a good job, since it turned that the leg wound, while messy and painful, wasn't the real problem. The small puncture to the lung was.

"How?" muttered Mayhew. "How did he manage that?"

"Probably fell the wrong way when he went down," said Simon. "Does it matter?"

"I guess not…" Mayhew shook his head. "How did I miss this…"

Because you're tired, thought Simon, who knew how that felt, but there was something else too. Quickly, the man was moved out of emergency and was prepped for surgery. As Simon got ready, the thought occurred to him that the way he'd practiced medicine had changed. The past few months— seeing gunfights, participating in gunfights, patching up gunfights—he was different as a result. The way he went about his trade was different, as a result. Fights played out differently from how he'd imagined them. There was always something unexpected requiring your immediate and undivided attention.

Simon looked over at his patient. The mask, hiding away his beard, brought the upper half of his face more clearly into focus and, suddenly, Simon realized how young this man was. Nineteen, maybe, and very scared.

Simon put his hand upon the boy's forehead. "You're going to be fine," he said. "Really. You're in great hands."

It was all very well to decide to dress up and go off to a casino, but there was, still, as Wash had pointed out, the small matter of the initial stake. The three of them rummaged round and brought out whatever cash they had to hand. When Jayne laid his portion down on the pile, River ran her hands over the notes and coins.

"Blood money," she said.

"No, it ain't," said Jayne. "What would make you say a ruttin' thing like that?"

River gave him one of those clear-eyed looks that made you think she saw more than you realized and probably saw more than anyone else around her could see. Wash shivered a little, turned away, and started counting.

"There is no money," said River, "without blood. Without pain. Without lies."

"I ain't listening to that kinda crap any longer," Jayne said. "How much we got?"

Wash said, "A little over one platinum."

"'Spose it's a start," said Jayne. He eyed Wash. "That the best you can do?"

"What? What's wrong? I wore this suit for this for my wedding—"

"And Zoë still married you?" Jayne sneered.

Wash looked down at his suit. All right, so it was creased, but it was a nice suit. All right, it wasn't a nice suit, but it was a decent suit. All right, it wasn't a decent suit, but it was a suit. Well, it was trousers and a jacket in more or less the same color. The shirt, admittedly, wasn't so successful as the suit, and not particularly clean, but then he hadn't expected to be going out tonight. "I'm not going to an interview," he said, although he had over the years worn both suit and shirt for many unsuccessful interviews. "I'm going to make some money to save my wife's life."

"Just sayin' you can do it in style," said Jayne, tugging his shiny lapels. "*Dǒng ma?*"

Wash picked up the cash. River opened her little clasp bag, and he shoved the money inside. On balance, he thought, it was probably best simply to ignore the fact that he was now living in a 'verse in which Jayne was giving him fashion advice. Yes, much better to ignore that and instead concentrate on the fact that he was heading off into town in what was sure to be a wholly misguided attempt to win a fortune gambling at a casino with a gun-crazy ape-man and a troubled kid.

But the thing was, he thought, sitting in the car next to River as they left the docks behind, the kid didn't look troubled right now. She looked about as happy as he had ever seen her. All smiles and quivering delight. That alone made this whole crazy excursion worthwhile. No doubt they'd lose the whole stake straight off the mark, but at least there had been a couple of hours in River's day where she felt like a thousand platinum.

After a short drive, the car turned a corner and came out onto a wide boulevard. "*Wā*," said Wash, looking down the length of the road. Lights, everywhere, shining, glittering, flashing; whole buildings, drenched in color, and big signs promising people big bucks. Promising them that the whole 'verse was right within their grasp. All they had to do was come inside and play a little. Just a little.

"Plat'num Mile," said Jayne. "Huh. Ain't this a sight for sore eyes?"

Suddenly, River gave a shriek and pointed out of the window. Looking out, Wash saw the front of a huge casino, lit up glitzily in yellow and white and gold. The name of the venue was spread out across the front: *The Golden Balloon*. There was a huge flashing display next to the name. A golden balloon, with a figure inside, throwing out coins for all and sundry. *Come inside*, the display seemed to be saying. *Come inside and play a little!*

"The ball!" cried River, clapping her hands together. "We're going to the ball!"

"Oh…" said Wash, as enlightenment dawned. That was the thing with River. You thought she was coming out with nonsense, but it always paid off in the end. Other folks on *Serenity*—they just came out with nonsense. Wash not only included himself in this, he put himself top of the list.

"Here," said River. "Right here. This is the place!"

The car pulled over. The three of them got out. River ran up the steps to the doorway, Wash and Jayne chasing to catch up with her. At the door, they were stopped, and checked for weapons, and, once they were allowed through, they swapped their platinum in cash for a single plastic slip. River seemed to know exactly where she was going. She moved with speed and agility past the smaller tables, the kind where amateur games of poker were played, and small wheels were spun, and the occasional good win was made, but nothing big. She came at last to a halt before the biggest wheel in the house, spinning round and round, the brass ball landing seemingly at random on red suns and black dragons. Wash came up beside her, Jayne right behind.

"What's she doin'?" said Jayne, trying to get a good look over Wash's shoulder.

"I think… she's watching the wheel go round," said Wash.

"Freaky moon-brained kid," muttered Jayne. "She's gonna get us thrown out. They ain't gonna like her standin' and starin' like that. They'll think somethin' fishy's goin' on."

Wash was glad he hadn't mentioned the fact that River was also humming. Very faintly, you'd miss it if you weren't right up close, and while he wasn't sure whether this counted as 'somethin' fishy' (he suspected not), he was definitely sure that he didn't want to attract the attention of the kind of security guards that tended to lurk around a place like this. But River just stood there, eyes darting around the wheel, and humming to herself. After a moment, the hum became a little song, *"Red sun… black dragon… red sun… black dragon…"* It was so mesmerizing that Wash completely missed the very big man who had somehow come through the crowd and was now standing on his other side.

"Sonny," said the very big man, in a very quiet voice.

Wash nearly hit the ceiling. "*Tiān xiǎo de*, where in the name of merciful Buddha did you pop up from?"

"You don't mind that. But I'm here to tell you that you and your friend and the little girl need to place a bet or leave."

Wash leaned forward. "River. Did you hear the nice man? The nice, big man?"

"I heard," said River. She turned to the croupier. "What's the single biggest win there's ever been at this casino?"

The croupier grinned at her. "You feelin' lucky tonight, sweetheart?"

"Luck," said River, "is a word used in hindsight to create a sense of narrative cohesion about a series of events which are not necessarily connected."

The croupier burst out laughing. "Didn't ask what you were thinkin'! Asked what you were feelin'."

"Yes," said River, eyes on the wheel. "I'm feeling very lucky tonight."

An elderly gentleman, dressed for the occasion with top hat and a formidable moustache, standing a little way round, wheezed with laughter. "Good for you, little girl!" he said. "You know, with you standin' there alongside me, I'm feelin' a mite lucky too. And it's Carnival! Lay your bet, sweetheart, and I'll match it."

River picked up her slip. Her eyes roved around the wheel one last time, and she hummed a little. She placed the slip down. "Thirty-five," she whispered. "Black dragon."

The elderly gentleman cried, "And here's my slip— twelve, red sun! Shine for me, sun! Make my day!" He looked round the table. "Hey, you fellas! Where's your manners?

You ain't gonna let this little girl here bet all on her lonesome, are you?"

There was some general laughter and applause. Another man came forward and put a platinum slip down, on twenty-one, black dragon. After that, another half-dozen bets came in from various quarters. The croupier spun the wheel. Wash held his breath. Round and round went the ball, spinning and spinning and River was humming and then she laughed, and the ball was *landing*…

Thirty-five. Black dragon. Everyone round the table cheered and laughed, even the losers. The croupier handed back her stake, and her winnings. Two platinum slips. Wash let out a breath and Jayne cackled. "I gorram knew it! This girl's a genius. Come on, River—give us your next pick!"

She stood quietly for a while, and put down both her slips. "Thirteen," she said. "Black dragon."

"Come on!" cried the old man. "Come on, fellas! You don't want to be beaten by a girl, hey?" He put down two slips too, this time on fourteen, red sun. "I'm sticking with the sunshine, sugar," he said, nudging River. "Sun's gotta come up 'ventually."

The croupier spun the wheel. River won. More cheers; some gasps. They were starting to get attention from the next table along. River put down her winnings—four platinum slips—on eighteen, red sun.

"That's it, sugar!" cried her new friend. "Sun always comes up!" He fished around for a few more platinum slips, placed his bet, and cajoled a few more punters to pony up and join the fun. "It's Carnival!" he cried. "Live a little before the sun comes up!"

"Honey," said the croupier, softly.

"Yes?" said River.

"You asked me a question. And the answer's sixty-five thousand platinum," said the croupier. "The biggest ever win here. Do what you've just done, sweetheart, but do it fourteen more times."

A gleam of light appeared in River's eyes. She began to hum.

"*Zhe ge ji hua zhen ke pa*," muttered Wash, and from this point on he was looking far less at the wheel, and more back over his shoulder. Whatever River was seeing right now, Wash was starting to get far less pleasant visions of what the future might hold. More very big men. Very big, very unhappy men. He counted four, coming their way. River won again. And again. Everyone around the table cheered and placed a few bets of their own to keep her company. And four men came to stand nearby, and watch.

At Anna's instruction, Inara walked down the hallway. The girl in the doorway watched her, eyes popping at the sight of Inara's appearance. She said, "Is she... from the Guild?"

"It's all right," said Anna. "She can't do anything to hurt you."

Inara, shaking her head to hear this, went through the door into the kitchen, a clean white painted room with a red-tiled floor. The blinds were drawn, and the lamps were lit, and there was an air of subdued peace. At the heart of the room was a big wooden table, and around this sat half-a-dozen girls, talking quietly and eating supper. They too stopped to stare at Inara and she took a good look back. The youngest was maybe twelve or thirteen, a thin-faced girl who cut off a soft cry at the sight of her; the oldest surely not more than sixteen or seventeen. This one jumped up from her seat.

"Anna? Who's this? What's going on—?" Her hand had gone protectively onto the shoulder of the girl who had cried out, and who was now trembling.

"Izzy," said Katarina, her voice clear and calm, "everything's okay. We're in charge here. She won't hurt you."

"I certainly won't," said Inara. "If I can help—"

"You can help," said Anna, "by sitting down and keeping quiet." She gestured to a chair at one end of the table. Inara sat down, and lay her hands upon her lap, palms up, signaling as best she could that she was no threat. Anna and Katarina stood in the doorway for a while, in whispered, urgent conversation. Inara looked at the girl sitting beside her.

"Hello," she said. "My name is Inara."

The girl flinched and pulled away.

"You'll find that most of our girls don't react too well to the sight of a companion," said Anna. "Not after what's happened to them." She took a seat at the table across from Inara. "Shall I introduce you? That's Merry, next to you. She's fourteen. She grew up in Catsville, a little north of here. The Guild came to town last month, recruiting. Merry was flattered that they wanted her. They gave her a train ticket. Told her she'd be met at the station."

Fourteen, Inara knew, was too old to be starting companion training. Anyone with knowledge of the Guild would be immediately suspicious—but why would this girl know the details of Guild law? "What happened, *mèi mèi*?" she said, very gently.

"You don't have to say anything, Merry," said Katarina, "if it will upset you. You don't owe her anything."

Merry shook her head. "It's okay." She stared straight at Inara. "Got a train here to the city. When I landed, couple of men were waiting for me. Took me away and…" She shuddered. "Tried to drug me. When I fought back, they hit me, hard. But not the face. Said they didn't want bruises on my nice little face."

"Oh *mèi mèi*," said Inara. "My poor child…"

"That's happened to a few of you, didn't it?" said Anna. "Companion came to town, told you to come to the city, they'd train you or find you work. Others, told to get to the city and there'd be a companion there to meet them, or a job waiting for them. Next thing they knew, Inara, they were in the city, alone, and these men were putting needles into them, and they were in cryo-storage, until we got them out."

"There are a couple more sleeping upstairs," said Katarina. "They're not recovering so well from it."

"Emma here," Anna put her arm around the girl next to her, "was kept under for over a month. Over a month, Inara," her anger was rising. "They packed her away to sell off-world to who knows where—"

"This is not the Guild," said Inara. "This is not what the Guild does—"

"No? You sure?" said Anna.

"Guild woman who came to me," said Izzy. "Fancy dress, nice talk. Those men—they *hurt* me—"

"They must have looked like the Guild," said Inara, "but I swear to you that the Guild would not—"

"Stop it," said Anna, her anger coming through clearly. "Look at them. This is what they're doing here. Don't try to deny it—"

"All right," said Katarina, cutting through, her voice firm. "I think it's time for the girls to go to bed. It's been a scary time and you're all still recovering. So come on, bed, all of you!"

She stood by the door and encouraged them through. There were no complaints, Inara noticed, and this struck her as particularly upsetting. So docile. As if some spark had been scared from them. When they were all on their way, Katarina closed the door, and came back to the table. "I hope they'll sleep." She looked up, anxiously, toward the floor above. "Some of them already have nightmares. Flashbacks. The sight of you... Who knows what that will set off?" She sighed. "I'll check on them later."

"All right," said Anna. "What we need to know now is how much you know about what we've been doing. How you found out, and who else you've told. Does Hilde Becker know?"

"Katarina," said Inara, turning to her, "I've explained to you already. I've never been to Bethel before. I have no idea what's going on—"

Suddenly, a little chime rang out, a repeated sound.

"What the hell is that?" said Anna. "Kay?"

Katarina, digging into her pocket, brought out Inara's personal device. "Shit..."

"Is there a locator on that thing?" said Anna.

"I turned it off," said Katarina.

"It's an incoming wave," said Inara. "This might be helpful. Can I—?"

"You're not laying your hands on this," said Katarina.

"Then at least play the wave," said Inara. "It might help you."

With a nod from Anna, Katarina played back the message. As Inara had hoped, it was from Guanyin, back on Sihnon.

"*Mèi mèi*," said Guanyin. "It's been too long. I miss you. But you've posed quite a puzzle. There seems to be no information about a Guild House on Bethel. It must be very new."

Anna shook her head. "Several years now," she murmured.

"Even so, that's very odd. I'm going to look into this, Inara. Thank you for letting me know." She blew a kiss. "And you know—you don't need to have an excuse to contact me. Just to talk to you is enough!"

The wave ended.

"Who was that?" said Anna.

"Guanyin is a friend of mine on Sihnon," said Inara. "A priestess at House Madrassa. I didn't like what you'd said to me about the hospital supplies, Katarina, so I asked her to investigate. And she's investigating. Does that help?"

"Not," said Anna, "if it's the prelude to a cover-up."

"There won't be," said Inara. "The Guild stands and falls on its reputation. If people from the House here are responsible for what happened to those girls, then the Guild will punish, and severely. They do not take kindly to having that reputation tarnished. Believe me."

She watched Katarina and Anna waver. She herself was very certain. *Girls in boxes*, she thought, and the slow, deep rage lit inside her began to simmer over. "You have no reason to trust me," she said. "But I will do whatever it takes to bring the people who have done this to justice."

"Including the Guild?" said Anna.

"Including the Guild. If the Guild here on Bethel truly is behind this—then it can burn. And I swear," said Inara, "I'm here to help you light that fire."

At the Roberts' residence, Book was still laughing as he scooted over to the newly revealed console. "I said a lot about this city was fake!" He ran his hands over the wooden frame of the billiards table. "I was starting to take a strong dislike to our employer, but what kind of fella does this kind of thing to something like this? Never mind," his hands began to dance over the screen of the console. "Let's take a little look-see what's here…"

Well, this was turning into a wholly unnecessary distraction. "Preacher," said Zoë. "We were makin' plans to leave. Could we keep our attention on the task at hand?"

"In a moment," murmured Book. "This is too good an opportunity to miss. We've been here all afternoon—"

"I'm aware of that," said Zoë. "One reason I'm keen to get on our way."

"I've spent a lot of time hunting through those shelves," Book looked up, "and he has *terrible* taste in literature, by the way, so—please, Zoë, indulge me for a few minutes longer, and let me see what I can find out about Jacob Roberts."

"Time's marchin' on, Shepherd."

"Might find the override to the barriers on the door, for one thing…" He smiled at her. "Sounds to me like everyone's downstairs enjoying themselves. Roberts will be busy with their comfort and entertainment. You know, Zoë, this room has been a pleasant prison, all things considered, but I still don't take kindly to being taken away at gunpoint, and it strikes me that a man prepared to do that kind of thing will be prepared to do all manner of things of which the Good Lord might not approve. So let's get some leverage in our dealings with him."

Zoë conceded the point. "All right," she said. "But don't take all night."

"One thing I like about you, Zoë," said Book, after a few minutes, "is that you never trouble me overly with questions such as how it might be that a Shepherd would happen to know his way around security systems."

"We all got our pasts," said Zoë.

"We most certainly do," said Book, "and sometimes I find myself wondering about yours, Zoë. Before the war, I mean."

"Before the war I was a soldier."

"Nobody's born a soldier."

"Nobody's born a preacher. Ain't none of my business what your past might be, Shepherd," she said. "Expect you'll pay me the same courtesy."

He smiled and went back to his work. The smile didn't last. "Now here's something more than a mite concerning."

Zoë came to join him. "What am I looking at?"

"These are schematics for cryo-cases. Cold storage."

Zoë considered this. "Why would they be usin' cryo-cases to ship minerals?"

"Exactly the question I'm asking myself," Book replied. "I'm no geologist, but I'm hard pressed to think of what would need transporting under such precise conditions."

"Foodstuffs?" said Zoë.

"Well, they might ship them in, but they're surely not shipping them out. Not much farming to speak of on Bethel, not considering how much of the place is given over to desert." He looked up at Zoë. "You know what this reminds me of?"

"Go on."

"The case our friend the doctor used to carry his sister on board *Serenity*."

Zoë looked at the schematics. Size was about right. "I'm not sure I like what you're sayin', Shepherd."

"I'm not sure I like what I'm seeing, Zoë," he replied. "And I'm very sure that I don't like being made party to assisting such a shipment in its passage off world."

"You think that's what was in the cases we were guarding? People?"

The Shepherd carried on working his way through the files. "I don't know yet. I'd like to find out."

"Seems mighty strange Roberts would leave all this information lying about in his files for any passing stranger to find."

"Well, we had to hunt to find this console, didn't we? And let's say I can dig a little deeper than most."

"I ain't askin', Shepherd," she said. "What happens in kidnap club stays in kidnap club."

"The Good Lord is looking kindly upon you, Zoë Alleyne," he replied.

At least that was something. "You dug up any more?"

He didn't answer right away, and when he looked up, Zoë—veteran of some of the most brutal battles of a brutal war—shivered at the sight of his face. "They weren't minerals we were guarding. They were girls. Folded up in cryo-cases, concealed inside crates. Made to look like shipments of minerals for transporting off world. *Lǎo tiān yé*, Zoë, I hope these *tian sha de e mo* burn for this…"

Mask's slippin', preacher, thought Zoë, and gave him a moment to collect himself.

"Anyway," he said, "seems that was our job. To help that man downstairs ship those girls off Bethel and to the Good Lord only knows where. You know, I'm not happy about that."

"Ain't so happy myself, Shepherd."

He turned his attention back to the files, which seemed to cool him down a mite. After a minute or two, he said, "I've paid the ransom."

"How've you done that?"

"A little creative accounting. Moved some money from an account here, placed it in an account there, moved it on to Mal, moved it on again. Roberts' own money, coming back to himself." The Shepherd gave a low and not entirely nice chuckle. "God forgive me, but it's hardly the worst crime been committed on Bethel."

"You're not wrong there."

"Well," said Book. "Ransom paid, I believe we may consider ourselves free to go." He looked at her, dead straight. "But what do you say, Zoë? Shall we be on our way, or shall we stay a while, do some tidying up around here?"

"When you look closely, this place seems awful dirty to me," said Zoë.

"And to me," said Book. "I thought we might be of one mind on this. What do you say we clean house a little, before we go?"

Zoë looked at him. "You sure about that, Shepherd?"

He looked back at her, face hard. "God's work, Zoë. I believe we can consider such to be God's work."

There was a sound in the corridor outside. Quickly, with the merest of nods between them, and not a single word, they each grabbed a billiard cue, and took up their positions by the door. When the two men entered, they didn't stand much of chance against two such experienced—and deadly— professionals. Within a matter of minutes, both men were disarmed, back-to-back, and Book was tying them together. Zoë, meanwhile, was checking out their guns. When Book was done gagging them, she threw one of these to him.

"May I confirm," said Book, "that this remains our secret?"

"I won't breathe a word to a livin' soul," said Zoë.

At the diner, Mal got up from the table to pay for supper. The waitress said, "That kid with you, she yours?"

"Never met her before today," said Mal.

"She okay?"

"Better for some supper."

"Huh," said the waitress. "You're doin' a good thing, lookin' out for her. There's people round here, wouldn't lift a finger to help a girl like that. And those that would want to do her harm."

"People, huh?" said Mal. "What kind of people?"

"Powerful people. And the sheriff's office ain't no help these days. Not since…" She looked over at the table, where the kid had folded her arms like a pillow and put her head down on them. "Well, no matter. Supper's on me."

Mal thanked her kindly and went over to the vidphone. Then he went back to join Kaylee and the girl. "*Zāo gāo!*" he muttered, watching her gently stroke the girl's hair, "I wish somebody would make this gorram crew of mine understand how to take orders."

"I'll take it you're gonna help?" said Kaylee.

"'Course I'm gonna help," said Mal. "Think I'm gonna let the pair of you wander off into the night? There's a car comin' right now, take us where it is she wants to go."

"Next time," said Kaylee, "you think twice before interferin' in my business."

"Next gorram time, I will. And I'll still come after you anyways, little Kaylee."

Kaylee smiled at him. "I know you will, Captain. And that's why I'll always forgive you."

Mal looked out of the window. "Car's here."

Ava lifted her head wearily and looked at them through heavy eyes. "Is it time to go?"

"Sure is, honey," said Kaylee. "We'll make sure you're safe."

They went out into the evening and got into the car. More money going down the drain. All told, this was proving a mighty expensive weekend, and Mal hadn't even seen inside a casino, never mind started on making back the money owed to Roberts. Maybe when they turned up with this girl, someone would think of putting a little compensation his way for the pains he had taken. He looked again at the shabby urchin sitting in the middle, slumped against Kaylee's shoulder. Not gorram likely.

The car took them into open countryside; sparse land dotted with tough little shrubs and succulents. A line of trees up ahead, stood out, and this seemed to be their destination. The car dipped behind these and came up to a gate. Ava gave her name, and the gate opened. The car deposited them outside a well-kept square-fronted house. Lights on behind the curtains, and a lamp to light the way to the entrance porch. Mal went up and hammered on the door.

There was something of a pause, and then a young woman, who looked all dolled up for a party, peered out. She was holding a pistol, the barrel of this poking out round the half-closed door. To Mal's expert eyes, she didn't look particularly comfortable with this fact, but that was worse in its own way. Amateurs were unpredictable. They made stupid mistakes. She said, "Who the *hell* are you?"

"Whoa, lady!" said Mal, lifting up his hands. "I'm friendly—"

A voice called out from further inside. "Mal? Mal, is that you?"

Mal blinked. "Inara?"

The door opened a little further, and Mal saw Inara coming down the hallway.

"Mal," she said, "what are you doing here? And *Kaylee*?" She came up behind the woman at the door. "Katarina, these are friends of mine. Mal," she said, more sternly. "Explain yourself."

"Nothin' to explain. We gave someone a lift," Mal said, nodding back at Ava. "Certainly wasn't expectin' to see you here, Inara, and while your company's always pleasant this place doesn't seem the kind of set-up you're accustomed to—"

Inara rolled her eyes. The woman with her, Katarina, looked at Ava. "Are you the missing one?"

Ava inched forward. "I'm sorry, ma'am," she said. "I nearly got caught. These folks said they could help me. I didn't know what else to do."

Katarina sighed. "This safe house is looking leakier by the minute." She opened the door wider and said, "Get the girl inside, will you? I need to take a look at her... I'm a doctor, sweetheart, you're in safe hands now... As for you lot..." Her eyes flicked between Mal and Kaylee and settled on Inara. "These two. Can we trust them?"

"Yes," said Inara.

Mal opened his mouth to come back on that one, but one look from Inara made him change his mind about that. You didn't have to fight every battle came your way. "Ma'am," he said to Katarina, "I don't like to turn down an invitation, but me and my friends here are on a schedule, and now this young lady is in your tender care, we should be on our way—"

"Get inside," Katarina replied. "And shut up."

* * *

The main gaming hall of the *Golden Balloon* casino was overlooked by a gallery that ran round the whole upper floor. This was an exclusive space to which the very rich paid for the privilege of access to the more expensive champagne bars, and quieter booths to play for higher stakes. The owner of the casino, Joseph Liu, had spent most of the evening walking round here, greeting his guests, making sure his face was seen. Sometimes he would stop and look down at the hall, making sure the money was flowing his way.

There was a balance to be struck in a place like the *Golden Balloon*. People weren't fools. They knew that the scales were tipped in favor of the house. This was a business, after all—and Joseph's suit and watch and lifestyle were very expensive— but patrons were very good at ignoring this fact, as long as they knew there was a chance that some of the money flowing around might splash back in their direction. Every so often, you could hear a shout of triumph as someone made a minor killing at the wheels or the tables, or over at the holo-slots. Fifty platinum here, eighty platinum there—enough, perhaps, to pay for the winner's whole weekend here in Neapolis, with a little pocket money for drinks all round. The house barely felt these losses, the spectators felt they'd seen something special, and the winner was in seventh heaven. Everyone was happy.

But every so often a winning streak began to unfold that needed more careful monitoring. Such was the case at the Big Wheel right now. Joseph, looking down from the gallery, saw a man in a hideously gaudy shirt, another in a fine vintage dark blue velvet tux—and a girl in an exquisite dress, infinitely better dressed than either of her companions. How the hell did that set-up work, wondered Joseph. Were they her brothers? Her minders? Who the hell *were* these people?

"How much has she won?" he asked the very big man standing next to him.

"So far? Just over a thousand platinum."

"What was her initial stake?"

"She arrived with a single platinum slip. Stood and watched a while. Then… she just started betting. She's been doubling up every single time since."

Another huge cheer went up from around the Big Wheel. The girl pulled a huge pile of chips toward her and stared intently at the wheel.

"Two thousand, now," said the very big man. "But the thing is, Mr. Liu, we ain't losin'."

"No?" said Joseph.

"The folks around her—they've taken her to heart. Matching her bets."

Joseph laughed, quietly. As long as people round the table kept on doing that, and kept on losing, they were fine. And yet—and this was the magic of gambling—every single time the girl won the crowd round her seemed to consider it a personal victory against the house.

"Come on, sugar!" cried the elderly gentleman standing next to her. Emory Braxton. Joseph knew him well and knew he could stand to lose a fortune or two. "What's it gonna be next?" Braxton was already coaxing his fellows to match her bet, and a couple seemed to be up for the game.

"How many more times," said Joseph, "before she hits the record?"

"If she keeps on doubling up like this—five more bets."
Joseph calculated some odds. "It's not very likely, is it?"

"No," said his companion, unhappily. "It ain't."

"But?"

"But…" Another cheer went up. "Sir, she just keeps on gorram *winnin'*!"

Joseph signaled to one of the waiting staff and asked for champagne to be sent over. Then he made his way down from the gallery and across the hall. The wheel spun round and sung its tune. The folks round the table began to sing along with it, *"Wheeeeeee…!"* Joseph inched his way forward until he was behind the girl. She was humming. The ball settled. The girl won. Everyone cheered. The girl raked in more money. The house raked in more money. Joseph came to stand just behind the little man in the bad shirt, which, at closer quarters, proved to be not clean. The little man was already white with terror, and he jumped visibly when Joseph tapped his shoulder.

"*Rén cí de fó zǔ*, my poor heart," he muttered. He sized up Joseph immediately. "Please," he whispered. "Don't kill us. I didn't think she'd get this far…"

"Don't worry," Joseph murmured to him. "Everything's fine." The champagne arrived, and glasses were handed round. "And everything will *remain* fine," whispered Joseph, to the very frightened man in the truly awful shirt, "as long as you folks stay at this table and don't stray an inch until I tell you."

"What?" whispered the little man.

Joseph handed him a glass of champagne. "Right now," he whispered, "none of us are losing. Let's keep it that way." He tapped the glass. "Drink up. You're going to be rich."

* * *

Mal was taken down the hallway further into the house. Kaylee followed behind, talking to Inara. Womenfolk were always mutterin' and talkin' and schemin', with one notable exception. Zoë Alleyne was a rare find.

"You all right, Inara?" said Kaylee. "Thought you'd be at some party or other."

"It's been… an interesting evening," said Inara. "And, no, it hasn't turned out remotely how I expected. You'll find out, in a minute."

They were taken into a warm kitchen, where another woman was waiting for them. Another gorram woman with a gorram gun. In Mal's opinion, this had long since all got out of hand. The woman walked over to Ava.

"Are you our missing one?" she said.

"Yes, ma'am," said Ava. "I'm so sorry to have been the cause of so much trouble—"

"These things happen," said the other woman. "As long as nobody finds out about this place—" Her eye fell on the others. "Kay," she said, "who are all these people?"

"It's okay, Anna," said Katarina. "They're friends of Inara. They brought the girl here; they've been looking out for her."

Anna watched them cautiously as they came in and, when her eye fell on Mal, she lifted her gun. "*Lǎo tiān yé*, Kay, this guy was at the docks yesterday!"

"What?" said Mal.

"What?" said Inara.

"*What?*" said Katarina.

"One of the people guarding the girls at the docks," said Anna. "They shot at us!"

Mal looked round the room. "Whaddaya mean, girls?"

"Oh, Mal, for heaven's sake!" said Inara. "What is *wrong* with you?"

"Now, whoa whoa whoa," said Mal. "Everyone here needs to back up, just for one second." He was achingly conscious of being the only fella in this here room, and he didn't like the way that all these womenfolk were lookin' at him and what that might ultimately mean for his personal safety.

"Do you just take on *any* job?" said Inara. "Do you not do *any* checks?"

"I was paid to make sure a load of whatever-they-call-it, minerals, got from the station to the docks," said Mal. "Not *girls*—" He thought about the shipment. "Though now I come to think about it, they were some *big* crates—"

"They were cryo-cases," said Inara. "Each one contained a girl. They were shipping them off world! Oh, Mal!"

"Cryo-cases, huh? Is that right?" said Mal. Then, more coldly, "*Zao gao*, that son of a bitch Jacob Roberts—"

"Inara," said Anna. "Who is this exactly?"

"His name's Malcolm Reynolds," said Inara. "He's the captain of the ship I travel on and he's a *yú bèn de* idiot."

"That ain't nice," said Mal. "People have not been particularly nice to me today—"

"That's because you've been particularly annoyin' today," said Kaylee.

"But he wouldn't be involved in trafficking girls," Inara said. "Not knowingly, at any rate," she finished, pointedly. "Mal, you are *hopeless*."

"Neither knowingly nor willingly," said Mal, hotly. "Ma'am," he addressed Anna, "if you think I would be mixed up in that kind of business..." He shuddered. All them girls, in them tiny boxes. What kinda fella did that kinda thing? What kinda fella even *thought* of that kinda thing? "No way. No gorram way! We answered a call on the Cortex for some folks to take on a security job, guarding a shipment of minerals, but... No. Absolutely not. Are we clear on that? Because I want everyone to be very clear on that—"

"There's a lot I could say about Mal that wouldn't be complimentary," said Inara, "but he wouldn't be involved in trafficking in any way—"

"Well, thank you, Inara," said Mal, "for that nearly glowing recommendation."

"Please," piped up Ava. "He did help me. Him and Kaylee. He didn't have to, and I know he's worryin' about some of his people who're in trouble, and he didn't really have the time to help—but he did. And he paid for supper."

The waitress had paid for supper, but Mal thought he could correct the record later. "Well, that's all something, ain't it?" he said.

The two other women—Katarina and Anna—were looking at each other. By some unspoken means of communication (And how, exactly, did they do that, womenfolk? What could a simple fella like Mal do in the face of powers like that?) they came to a decision. To Mal's relief, that decision seemed to be that while he might well be a fool, he wasn't an evil fool.

"Sit down," said Anna, and Mal, who despite evidence to the contrary wasn't in fact so much of a fool, obeyed.

"I'm going to take this one upstairs," said Katarina, putting an arm around Ava's shoulder. "Get her comfortable."

Anna sat down opposite Mal. "And I'll try to find out exactly what's going on here."

As Mal (with helpful interjections from Kaylee and pointed commentary from Inara) explained the series of events that had found him and Anna on the opposite sides of a heist that morning, he saw the woman's expression harden.

"Jacob Roberts hired you?" she said.

"Like I say, we heard a call go out on the Cortex for the job. Came in knowing not much about the place," said Mal.

"You do that a lot," said Inara.

"Regretting I ever got involved," finished Mal.

"You do that a lot too," said Inara.

"You know, Jacob Roberts isn't a nice man," said Anna. "Anyone here could've told you that."

"I worked that out when he took two of my people hostage," said Mal.

"He was most likely behind the deaths of my parents, three years ago," said Anna. "Not that the sheriff's office were able to prove anything, of course…"

"The sheriff," said Mal. "We met him, over at Roberts' place. How deep is he in all of this?"

"Hard to tell," said Anna. "He was very friendly with my parents when they were alive… They owned some of the biggest sites on the Mile. But his investigation into their deaths went nowhere."

"Fairweather friend, huh?" said Mal.

"It's certainly looking that way," said Anna. "You know, we thought the Guild was behind the trafficking ring. But from what you're saying, Roberts is deep in the whole business as well."

"Much as it pains me to say it," said Inara, "the Guild house here must be recruiting young women up-country—"

"—and Roberts providing the means to get them off world," said Mal. "I'm starting to think I don't like this fella, nor his way of doing business. And I most certainly don't like being made party to his way of doing business." He shot Inara a quick look. "Tough, hearing the Guild's involved, huh?"

"I think there's more going on than that," said Inara.

"Guess we'll see soon enough," said Mal.

The door opened, and Katarina came back in, joining them at the table.

"How's Ava?" said Kaylee.

"She's fine," said Katarina. "I think she'll sleep now."

"Look," said Mal, "I don't want to make too big a deal of this, but thanks to your intervention this morning—which I ain't sayin' you didn't do the right thing, miss—but thanks to that nonetheless, I owe Jacob Roberts five hundred platinum, and he's got two of my people held as collateral. And *time*," he glared at Kaylee, "is starting to run out."

"When do you have to pay him by?" said Katarina.

"Tomorrow night," said Mal. "By the Big Bang."

"That's why Simon is at St. Freda's," said Inara. "We needed the money."

"Oh!" said Katarina. She laughed. "Simon should have held out for double what they're paying him. He's worth every penny."

"I bet," said Kaylee. Look at her, thought Mal, puffing up with pride on the doc's account. Not that she was gettin' anywhere. Fella couldn't see what was right in front of him. Girl like Kaylee—he should be honored by her attention.

"Five hundred platinum?" said Anna.

"Before the fireworks tomorrow," said Mal. "And since my main plan to get that was, not to put to fine a point on it, stealing back Roberts' merchandise from whoever had taken it away from, I am now without both plan and platinum—"

"Don't worry," said Anna. "I'll pay."

"You'll what?" said Mal.

Katarina laughed. "Anna's very rich. Disgustingly rich." She gestured round. "Who do you think bankrolls all this? The house, the whole operation. I think she likes being a gentleman adventurer."

"What I like," said Anna, "is seeing Jacob Roberts suffer. For that reason alone, I'll pay this ransom."

"Oh," said Mal. "Well, in that case, miss, if you're willin', I'll gladly take you up on that kind offer."

"See, Cap'n," said Kaylee. "Comin' all the way out here wasn't a waste of your time after all. Doin' the right thing never is."

"Not sure that's a claim that would hold up for long under too much scrutiny, Kaylee," said Mal, "but I ain't disagreein' that today seems to be pickin' up as a result."

"There's one condition," said Anna.

"Here it comes," said Mal, sinking back into his seat.

"I want your help to bring down Roberts. Captain Reynolds—you say you don't like what he does. But do you mean that? Enough to help put a stop to it?"

"What you sayin' exactly?" said Mal.

"You and your people—you're the ones that can prove the connection. Between the Guild House here and Roberts. Maybe we can pin something on Roberts and Becker that will stick at last."

"Oh… I ain't so sure…"

"Mal," said Inara. "You've done this kind of thing before."

"You heard what Ava had to say, Mal," said Kaylee.

"They've done this to other girls, Mal," said Inara. "And they'll keep on until someone stops them—"

"*Bì zuĭ*, the two of you! Please just shut up!"

"He'll help," said Inara.

"I suppose I will," said Mal. "Must confess I'm enjoy seein' old man Roberts' face when we bring him to heel. That man took on far too many airs and graces for someone up to neck in this amount of *niú shi*." He eyed Anna. "Easier if I have my two people back."

Anna smiled. "Consider yourself paid."

Around the table in the *Golden Balloon*, the champagne was now freely flowing, the punters gladly imbibing, and the girl in the black dress still winning. Over the course of the last twenty minutes, the word had spread that something big was happening. The crowd around the table had grown steadily larger, people pushing at each other for a view of the proceedings. They howled for joy as the wheel spun once again, and the brass ball, which seemed to them almost to be doing her bidding, obligingly dropped into place on eighteen, red sun. Joseph Liu, standing next to a worried man in a gaudy shirt, watched with interest—but not, as yet, with concern—as the girl collected the slips that represented thirty-two thousand platinum.

"Help," whispered the man in the bad shirt. "We're going to die."

"Not yet," said Joseph Liu, quietly. "Not quite yet."

"She gorram won!" yelled the big man in velvet. "She gorram went and won again!"

"Sweet Mary mother of Christ and the whole host of heavenly angels!" cried Emory Braxton. He took off his top hat, threw it in the air, and caught it neatly by the brim. "Sugar," he told the girl, "you're nearly there! One more go, sugar! One more and you've done it!"

"Lay your bets," said the croupier, when Joseph gave her the sign. "One more spin to go for the win of a lifetime. The wheel's been lucky tonight…"

"Not for me it ain't," cried one of the other punters. "I'm down a hundred platinum!"

The crowd laughed. They'd all lost a little, here and there. Joseph watched the faces around him carefully. Was this the moment when the magic wore off? When they all pulled back the curtain and saw how things really worked? That the house might not win, but it never, ever lost? The girl made her choice and pushed every last one of her slips forward. "Ten," she whispered. "Red sun."

"Come on, the lot of you!" cried Emory Braxton, may heaven smile upon heart and his bottomless wallet. "Can't leave this sweet little thing out there alone!" He took a mighty swig of champagne. "Who's in? I'm in! I got five thousand platinum here… Who else? We can match her bet! Come on, fellas! We're with you, sugar!"

"I'm in!" someone cried, from just behind him, while his wife hissed, "Jacky! No!"

Too late. The money was on the table. Fueled by the drink with which Joseph had plied them, egged on by Braxton, more and more people came forward, offering up amounts small and not-so-small that quickly matched the girl's stake. The croupier glanced over at Joseph, who gave the smallest of nods. Everything could proceed.

The crowd laid their stake. So did the girl. The croupier spun the wheel. Joseph watched the girl, trying yet again to work out how she was doing whatever it was she was doing. She watched the wheel, humming, for a couple of seconds and then, while it was still spinning, she relaxed and waited for what was clearly, to her, inevitable.

The wheel slowed. The ball rattled, and then landed, right on target.

Ten. Red sun. How did she *know*?

Whoops of delight and astonishment went up, and even the losers seemed not to mind they'd lost those stakes to make this girl a fortune. And particularly not when the slips were handed over, and her face lit up, and a river of laughter bubbled up from her. Emory Braxton laughed out loud. "See that?" he cried. "I told you, sugar! I told you! The sun always comes up!"

By now, the whole casino had ground to a halt. Huge cheers and applause rose up, a standing ovation for the little girl who had beat the Big Wheel. Joseph Liu, applauding with the rest of them, stepped forward and addressed the room.

"Ladies and gentlemen," he said. "What an amazing night we're having! This young lady has matched the biggest win we've ever seen here at the *Golden Balloon*. I hope I'm not being forward when I say I imagine you'll remember tonight for the rest of your lives. I know I will!"

Loud hoots of raucous laughter. Incredible, Joseph thought. They all believed somehow that the house had lost. The house never, ever lost.

"Our lucky winner here," he turned to the girl and whispered, "What's your name?"

"Joy," she whispered.

"Joy," he told the crowd, and a roar went up: *Bless you, sweetheart! Gorram princess! We love you, Joy!*

"Joy and I," said Joseph, "are going to go have a few drinks to mark this special occasion, and in the meantime, I hope you all enjoy the champagne I'm sending round—and a platinum slip for everyone in the building." Huge cheers. "Place your bets, ladies and gentlemen—it's a lucky night here tonight at the *Golden Balloon*!"

Joseph waved his hand again, and a couple of his larger staff appeared. Gently, the girl and her associates were moved away from the wheel and through the hall. "Please don't hurt us," said the little man in the hideous shirt. "I had no idea she was going to go that far. All we needed was five hundred—"

"Keep quiet," said Joseph, "and keep smiling. I'm not going to hurt you. I'm going to do exactly what I said. I'm going to pay you your winnings, and then I'm going to send you on your way."

The man in velvet looked disappointed. "Huh. Was hopin' for some shootin'."

"Not tonight," said Joseph. "We don't do things that way on Bethel. Not any more." At least, not in a place run by the Liu family.

He was as good as his word. In the back office, he paid up and passed round a little champagne, extracted the names of both men (as well as the name and location of their ship, just in case). They toasted their success; the little man, Wash, relaxed; and soon that was that.

"Well," Joseph said, once the ceremony was over, "it's been a pleasure meeting you all. And now it's time for you to leave. There's a car outside, ready to take you all back to *Serenity*, and I would warmly and respectfully ask that you do not return."

Wash was shaking his hand vigorously. "I promise that I am *never* doing anything like this again."

"Sixty-five thousand ruttin' platinum!" crowed Jayne. "I ain't never seen anything like it in my whole gorram life!"

The girl held out her hand, upon which Joseph bestowed a tender kiss. "Good night," he said. "It's been fun having you here."

"It was everything I hoped for," she said.

Joseph took her arm and escorted her back through the hall and toward the exit. On the way past, she stopped by one of the machines. She pulled the lever, the machine shuddered, and a single coin came toppling out.

"Biggest win now," she said. "No power in the 'verse can stop me."

Joseph picked up the silver coin, and, with the most beautifully executed bow, handed over the small treasure. "*Zhu fu ni, mèi mèi*," he said. "Enjoy the rest of Carnival."

Upstairs, the Roberts' residence was in near darkness, a single lamp at the far end of the landing just enough light to show where the staircase began. Zoë and Book inched their way noiselessly toward this and, once they were there, Zoë moved forward to look down on the hall. Fancy, as Kaylee would say, all white marble and gilt furnishings, and harshly and brightly lit. Not much in the way of cover there, and certainly plenty of folk about to cause them difficulties, should they decide to be troublesome. Music and laughter and chatter came up from the party in the garden below. As Zoë watched, a man in a fine gray suit, sporting a richly embroidered waistcoat, came into the hall and headed toward the staircase. She saw the bulk underneath his jacket where a weapon lay. Slipping back, she gestured to Book to hide. They both pressed into the shadows. When the man came to the top of the stairs, he went the other direction down the corridor. Zoë breathed a sigh of relief. She nodded the all-clear to the Shepherd, and he moved forward to get the lay of the land.

"No easy way out," Zoë murmured. "Soon as we enter that hall, we're seen."

"I don't mind," said Book. "I think I'd like to make our presence felt."

"You sure about that, Shepherd?"

"Quite sure."

He led the way downstairs. He seemed all fired up by new purpose, arising from his not inconsiderable anger. With any other man (Mal, say) Zoë would be a mite concerned right now, knowing that this kind of anger generally led to mistakes. Not with the Shepherd. To Zoë's expert eyes, he looked more alert, more focused, than she had ever seen before. When they reached the bottom of the stairs, Book turned to her.

"Ready to put on a show?"

"Reckon so, preacher."

They stepped out into the bright light. They strode side-by-side through the hallway and into a big reception room, where they found a handful of guests mingling, making small talk over canapes. There were gasps of surprise as they went purposefully past. Folks jumped out of their way and the conversation turned into fearful whispers.

"Guess we don't look the kind to have received an invitation," remarked Zoë.

"Roberts' mistake," said Book. "He should have played more nicely with us." He gestured with his pistol toward a pair of open doors that overlooked the garden. "Still, it would be impolite not to pay our respects to our host. This way, I think."

They went out onto a wide terrace that ran along the back of the house. Zoë looked out across the garden. There were, by her estimate, maybe fifty people out here, chattering and laughing, eating and drinking. The music from the string quartet wove around them. There was Roberts, at the heart of this great web of luxury, his arm around a beautiful woman—a companion, no less, by the looks of her. Best of everything for Jacob Roberts.

"Ah," said Book. "There he is."

People were starting to notice them. The music faltered. Book lifted up his pistol, fired a shot up into the air, and the music stopped, abruptly. So did the talk. Roberts turned around. The expression on his face when he saw Book standing there, pistol aimed at his heart, was one that Zoë would recall with considerable pleasure in later days.

"Jacob Roberts!" the man named Derrial Book cried out, and his voice, ringing out clear like the trumpet on Judgement Day, brought the whole gathering to silence. "Listen now to the word of God! *Vengeance is mine, sayeth the Lord, and recompense, for the time when their foot shall slip; for the day of their calamity is at hand, and their doom*," Book pressed his finger against the trigger, "*their* doom*, Jacob Roberts, comes swiftly!*"

Lǎo tiān yé, thought Zoë, *he surely ain't gonna kill him in cold blood?* Seeing Book's face, she wasn't rightly sure, and she made ready to knock the pistol out of his hand. Last thing they needed was a murder charge, with more'n fifty witnesses… The Shepherd's arm moved, shifting the target away from Roberts. Zoë saw Roberts follow the line of the pistol and realize exactly where the Shepherd was now pointing the gun.

"Jesus Christ, man!" Roberts cried out. "Are you *insane*?"

The Shepherd fired, right into the heart of the firework display. The first charge went off with a huge blast, sending off sparks sufficient to set the rest going. Bangs and sparks and all manner of explosives, going off all around. Folks began to scream and run for cover.

Book turned to Zoë and said, in a mild tone, "I'm ready to go now."

"Me too, Shepherd. Me too."

"As for our getaway… That fine red flyer we saw from the library window. I recall we were of similar mind?"

Zoë, more concerned now with the armed men hastening toward them, raised her own pistol and said, "We were indeed. And I hope, preacher man, I never have cause to find myself on the wrong end of your desire for retribution."

"Zoë," he said, "I doubt you capable of deeds requiring such." He took one last look at his handiwork and, with a satisfied nod, turned to run with her down the driveway toward the red car. Zoë leapt into the front and started the machine up. Book, in the passenger seat, leaned out of the window and fired his pistol.

The flyer rose and sped off. In the rear mirror, Zoë could see the flames of their purifying blaze rising up into the night. Book settled back into his seat.

"Did you hit anyone?" said Zoë. She looked back and saw a man with a beard clutching his leg in agony.

"He ain't dead," Book said crisply. "Tonight, and in this particular company, I'm not averse to causing a little wounding." He wiped his hand across his mouth. "And may God have mercy."

* * *

Inside, the big fancy car supplied by Joseph Liu was bigger and fancier than anything Wash could have imagined in his wildest dreams. Leather seats and polished finish. Drinks and—*Tā mā de*, were those snacks? A car filled with *snacks*? Grabbing packets of NutsSaltiNuts, he filled his pockets, opening a couple more of the tiny bags and stuffing down the contents as if the nuts were magical nuts that would disappear on the stroke of midnight.

"Nuts!" he said, indistinctly, his mouth full of them. "I love this world! I love this car!" Jayne, spread out in the seat opposite, reached for one of the open bottles of champagne and drank deeply. "Gorram *champagne*, Wash!"

River was humming and clutching the case of money—lots and lots of money. Wash clutched his head. "*Wǒ de mā*," he said. "How did you *do* that?"

"It was easy," said River. "The wheel sang to me. Sang to me in a major key. All I had to do was listen to her."

"I ain't got no idea what that ruttin' means," said Jayne, "and I ain't bothered. Sixty-five thousand gorram ruttin' *platinum*!" He took another swig of champagne and held out the bottle. "Neither of you want any of this?"

"Strangely not," said Wash. He found another bottle, and some glasses—proper, fancy, flutey, glasses—and poured out champagne for River and himself. They clinked them together. She giggled. "Bubbles," she said. "Nucleation sites. Caused by impurities in the glass. They tickle!"

"Whatever you say, River," said Wash, and drained his glass.

By the time the car drew up alongside *Serenity*, the three of them were more than slightly hysterical and considerably more than slightly drunk. Wash and Jayne grabbed half-a-dozen more bottles of champagne, and they tumbled out of the car and on-board *Serenity*. In the dining room, River put the money down on the table. She opened the case, slowly, and as she did, Wash and Jayne sighed with pure pleasure.

"Look at that," said Jayne, with a kind of reverence that would have warmed the Shepherd's heart. "Gorram *fortune*! I ain't seen a stack of cash like this in… Well, I ain't never seen a stack of gorram cash like this!"

Wash, trying to remember that there had been a *reason* for going out and doing this, said, "We should get onto Roberts. Get the ransom paid straight away. Get Zoë back—"

"Now hold on a ruttin' minute," said Jayne.

"Mal won't mind," said Wash. "He'll be back any minute, anyway…" (Where the hell *was* Mal, come to that…?) "Why wait?"

"I'm not sayin' wait for Mal, I'm sayin' I ain't wastin' my money on ransom—"

"Wasting?"

"I want to make sure I get my *share*—"

"You'll get your *share*, Jayne," said Wash, "just as soon as we've made sure that Zoë and Book are safe—"

"I ain't bein' cheated," said Jayne, doggedly. "Not again. Not over this one. Sick of bein' cheated. Not again. Not *ever*—"

"Honey," said a familiar voice, "is this *zhàn dǒu de yī kuài ròu* botherin' you?"

Wash spun round. "Zoë!" He was in her arms within seconds. "Why are you here? How are you here? Was there violence? Was there *wounding*? Are there *wounds*?"

"Not a single scratch between the two us," said the Shepherd, from behind. "Though you should see the other gentlemen. One of them won't be running marathons for a while yet."

Zoë unlocked her mouth from Wash's and tugged his shirt. "You plannin' on goin' to a wedding, sugar? You'll have to wash the stains outta this first."

"I've had enough excitement for one night," Wash said. "How did you two get away?"

"We got a mite weary waiting for things to happen," said the Shepherd, "so we took matters into our own hands." His eye fell on the table and the open case. "You know, I'm almost afraid to ask," he said, "but what exactly has been going on back here?"

"Much the same," said Wash. "No violence. Some minor wounding, maybe, more what I'd call scratching than actual gouging, and that was only near the end when I started to really panic. Mostly there was gambling."

"I'll say," said Jayne. "Went down to the Mile, Shepherd! Won me a gorram fortune!"

"You hit the *casinos*?" The Shepherd laughed out loud. "Damn, I wish I'd seen that!"

"You've seen enough fireworks for one night in my opinion," said Zoë.

"Maybe so," he conceded.

"All my idea," said Jayne, with considerable pride.

"All River's work," said Wash.

"How, River honey?" said Zoë, laughing. "How did you *do* this?"

"I'd like to know that too," said Wash. "I mean, I was *there* and I'd still like to know."

"I listened to the song," River said, as if this explained everything. "The wheel sang and I listened to her singing."

"See?" said Wash. "No idea. But it worked."

"We're rich," said Jayne. "I'm rich!"

"River's rich," said Wash. "Even richer, if we don't have to pay any ransom now." He looked at Zoë. "We *don't* have to pay any ransom now, do we? Roberts is all paid back?"

"Oh, we certainly paid back Roberts," said Book. "But I'd say he's as yet only received a small portion of what he's due." He looked at Jayne. "What the *devil* are you wearing?"

When Simon finished surgery, he was off shift, so he took his time cleaning up, and then went to look for somewhere to sit by himself. As ever, after the intensity of theater, he had a powerful desire to be away from other people—outside, ideally. Signs round the hospital indicated there was a small roof garden, so he took the elevator up there. It was nothing magnificent—just a small, paved area dotted with shrubs and potted plants and a few benches—but there was nobody else out there to bother him with conversation or demands. He fell back on one of the benches and sat watching the bright lights of the city. In the distance, he could hear music; laughter and raucous voices rose up from the street below. Carnival was happening, a long way from Simon. He didn't particularly mind. He breathed deeply, the cool night air clearing his head. As was his habit, he ran through the previous few hours' work, checking his decisions and confirming he'd done everything right. He checked the time. He had a few hours to kill before he was expected back again. He yawned and ran his hands over his eyes. He was tired, as ever; more pressingly, he was also absolutely ravenous.

He went in search of the staff canteen, where he secured and then devoured a huge bowl of noodles. He sat back and closed his eyes. Suddenly, he was struck with an overwhelming desire to be at home, but when he tried to visualize where this might be, he found he couldn't quite pin down the location exactly. He tried to imagine his apartment back in Capital City, but the place was getting hazy in his memory. For some reason, he kept on thinking about the little lights that Kaylee had hanging up in her cabin on *Serenity*.

Someone sat down opposite. Simon opened his eyes. It was Mayhew, nursing a plastic cup of plastic coffee. "Hey," he said, "sorry to wake you."

"I wasn't asleep," said Simon. "Just dozing. You know."

"Yep," said Mayhew. He had four little sachets of sugar in front of him. One by one, and very methodically, he opened them, tipping the contents of each into his coffee, and stirring vigorously. He took a deep swig. "Nice," he said, "Instant diabetes. You know, you were really good earlier."

Yes, thought Simon. *I know. I'm a* great *doctor.*

"I missed it completely," said Mayhew. "But you know that."

Simon wasn't generally sympathetic with the mistakes of other doctors. You weren't there to make mistakes, you were there to be excellent, at all times. But for some reason, his heart went out to Mayhew. "Well, you're tired."

"So are you."

That was certainly true. "When you're faced with something messy and obvious, it's easy to miss something less messy and obvious," he offered.

"Hmm, not just that," said Mayhew.

"I've… I've been traveling round the Rim a while now. Sometimes thing happen unexpectedly, and often you're the only doctor around…"

"I see," said Mayhew. Simon, hyper-conscious these days that any attention could bring all kinds of problems, watched the other man carefully. He liked this man. He hated lying to him. But he would have to, if it was the only way to keep him—keep River—safe.

"Is there any chance," said Mayhew, "that you could be persuaded to stay? I'd have a word with Kay—"

"Oh," said Simon, caught completely off-guard. "Oh… I… I'm… I have to leave Bethel the day after tomorrow… I'm… I'm expected somewhere else."

"Oh," said Mayhew. "Well, that's a shame. I think you'd fit in here." He finished his coffee. "*Gǒu shǐ,*" he muttered. "This stuff is like horse piss." He looked at Simon. "I'd say let's go out for a drink, this being Carnival and all, but to be honest you look like a man who could do with a few hours' sleep. I know I am."

"I think you're right," said Simon.

Mayhew stood. He picked up his cup and flattened it in his hands, ready for the recycler. "See you in the morning."

"Yes," said Simon. "See you in the morning." He waited until Mayhew had gone before standing up. More than anything, he wanted to see River and make sure that she was safe. Sleep could wait.

Mal, with Inara, Kaylee, and Anna Liu following close behind, strode into the cargo bay of his ship, ready now to start putting a plan (whatever that might be) into action to secure the release of the preacher and his corporal.

"Hey, sir."

He looked up to see said corporal leaning on the gantry and pulled up short. "Zoë? What're you doin' back here lookin' so cheerful? Someone pay the ransom while I was out?"

"Didn't much like our accommodations, sir," she said. "Shepherd and I thought we'd prefer to be back home. Hope that suits?"

"Fine by me," said Mal. "Fine and dandy." He took the metal steps two at a time and nodded at Book, who had come out to join her. "Much in the way of trouble?"

"Fair amount," said the Shepherd. "They'll be cleaning up a while yet."

"Only just started with the trouble we're sending Jacob Roberts' way," said Mal. He turned to introduce Anna Liu, who was standing behind him, looking at his two crewmembers with considerable interest. "This here's Ms. Liu."

"We've met already," said Anna, and, seeing Mal's puzzled expression, added, puckishly, "at the docks. Remember?"

"Oh yes," said Mal. "Long story," he said to Zoë and Book, "but Ms. Liu was the one stole the shipment from us this morning."

"And that's good because… why?" said Zoë. "My lungs are still aching from that gas grenade got thrown about at the station—"

"I'm sorry about that," said Anna.

"Ms. Liu here tells me that the Guild has been up to all kinds of mischief," said Mal. "Worse'n that, seems they and Roberts are deep together in some real unpleasantness—"

"You mean trafficking girls," said Book.

"Huh," said Mal. "You're well ahead, ain't you, Shepherd?"

"I keep myself informed." Book nodded at Anna. "Pleasure to meet you, ma'am, and I hope we'll be able to help. You know, Mal, I don't like finding myself party to criminal activities without my express permission. I'm assuming we're intending to do something about this?"

"Some of us have been already," said Anna, wryly.

"And seems our presence might have messed up the good work being done by Ms. Liu on this matter," said Mal.

"Ah," said Book. "Unfortunate. In which case, I hope we're planning to make amends?" He looked at Mal. "A little penance never did anyone any harm, Captain."

"Most times I'd disagree," said Mal, "but not on this score." He strode toward the dining room.

"Sir," said Zoë, "You might want to prepare yourself—"

Mal halted, mid-step. "What? What now?"

"You know, Zoë," said Book, "I think Mal should see this for himself."

Mal, entering the dining room, was confronted with one of the more challenging sights of his life: Jayne, in blue velvet tuxedo, quaffing champagne, sitting in front of a whole heap of cash. "Hey, Mal," said Jayne. "Made me a fortune."

"River," said Wash, "*River* has made herself a fortune."

Kaylee, looking at Jayne, said, "*Wǒ de mā…*"

"Jayne," said Inara. "I'm not sure I've ever seen you look so dashing."

Jayne smiled at her, mostly with his teeth.

"This day," said Mal, "is rapidly startin' to count among one of my least favorites. Wash—I was gone couple of hours at most. What did y'all…" He waved his hands at the money, "…*do?*"

"I did nothing," said Wash. "I want everybody to be quite clear on that score. All I did was try to make sure people kept out of trouble. I'm not saying that I was particularly successful in my task, but that's what I tried to do."

River hoved into view. She looked… She looked nice. Real nice. River stared at him. "I turned thoughts into money."

"Yes, of course you did," said Mal. "I'm no clearer to understandin' how, why, when, whether or not I need to be angry—"

"Ain't hard, Mal," said Jayne. "Went out poor. Came home rich."

"*River* came home rich," said Wash. "I don't know how many times I have to say this…"

"Weren't just River—"

"Speaking of which," said Mal, cutting through, "River, you're lookin' fine and I find myself wonderin' whether I see a companion's hand behind … whatever this all is?"

But Inara was laughing. "River, sweetie," she said. "Did you have this in mind when you came to my shuttle?"

River looked only slightly penitent. "Had to look the part." She really was dressed uncommonly nice, Mal thought, taking a proper look at her. Dressed how you might look if you were plannin' a night on the town… Dots connected. Pennies dropped. "Did y'all hit the *casinos*?" he said. "Wash? I turned my back for *ten minutes*—"

"More like a couple of hours," said Wash, as if this served somehow as a defense.

"Which one?" asked Anna. "Which casino?"

"We went to the ball," said River, happily.

"She means the *Golden Balloon*," said Wash and, when Anna began to laugh, he went on, "What? That mean something to you?"

"Tell me it's owned by Jacob Roberts," said Mal.

"No," said Anna. "Unfortunately, not. The *Golden Balloon* has been in my family for four generations. My older brother runs the place."

Book laughed out loud.

"*Tian xiao de*," said Mal, "is there anyone on Bethel ain't gonna be pissed with us by the end of today?"

"We should go, Mal," said Jayne. "Get while the goin's good. We got Zoë and the Shepherd back, ain't we?"

"Simon's not back," said Kaylee.

"Soon," murmured River.

"You say that like that's a bad thing," said Jayne.

"Your suit is worn at the elbows," said River. "You should be patched."

Jayne subsided. Mal, firmly, said, "We ain't going nowhere. We've caused trouble for some good people," he nodded at Anna, "and our services were bought under false pretenses. We'll be settin' all that straight before we think of headin' off anywhere, *dǒng ma*?"

"Also," said Kaylee. "*Simon*'s not back."

"Heard you the first time," said Jayne. "Still not seein' the problem there—"

"That's enough," said Mal. "We got comp'ny," he nodded at Anna, "and seems to me the least we can do is offer her some champagne. Her brother paid for it, after all."

This was met with general agreement. A bottle was shaken, by Book, with much brio, and big cheers rose up when the cork popped. They poured the champagne out into chipped mugs. They toasted River. They toasted Jayne's suit. They toasted Anna's brother. They were trying to think of something else to toast when Simon walked in. He glanced round the room, taking in everyone present, his gaze coming to rest on the open champagne bottles and the nuts strewn around the table. He threw his jacket across the back of the nearest chair. "I hate every single one of you," he said. "Not you, River..." He peered at her. "*Mèi mèi*, what... what are you *wearing*?" He looked at the open case. "What exactly has been going on?"

* * *

Someone (Simon was pretty sure that it was Book) pushed him into a chair. Everyone, he saw, literally *everyone* was back on-board ship, which meant that spending the whole day working under a false identity was, presumably, rendered entirely *moot*, and also while he'd been up to his elbows in guts, people here seemed to have been drinking *champagne*, and there was someone here that he didn't even *recognize*…

"Hi," she said, waving from down the table. "I'm Anna. I'm a friend of Kay Neilsen. Are you the doctor she hired for the weekend? The one she studied with?"

"Yes," said Simon, struggling to find his manners. "It's… very nice to meet you… Look," he said to his immediate colleagues, "I'm sorry, but I'm tired, and there are champagne bottles open and while it's nice to see you both safe and, you know, *alive*, I'm not sure why Zoë and Book are here, exactly—"

"Don't spoil the party, Doc," said Jayne. "We're tryna celebrate."

River handed him a mug which turned out to contain champagne. "Is it champagne," she said, "if it doesn't come from Earth-that-was?"

Plaintively, Simon said, "I am too tired for this. I've just come from theater—"

"You've been at the *theater*?" Jayne scoffed. "Thought you was supposed to be workin'—"

"There was a gunshot wound," Simon said. "To the left thigh."

"Ah," said Book, his interest piqued.

"He also had a punctured lung," said Simon. "Which I spotted. Which I operated on. Which probably saved his life."

"Ah," said Book, more thoughtfully.

Simon tried the champagne. It was slightly flat. He put the mug down and someone (definitely Book this time), put a hot cup of tea into his hands, and a packet of peanuts on the table next to him. "It's possible," said Book, with a suspicious note of apology in his voice, "that Zoë and I have a little insider information on those particular wounds."

"You're the one takin' the rap for that, preacher," said Zoë. "I only did the driving."

"I'm not actually sure that's a defense, Zoë," said Book. "Particularly as we stole the car. But then I do doubt any of it'll be coming to a court of law."

"There was *shootin'*?" said Jayne, with considerable disappointment. "And car-jackin'? You went shooting people and stealin' cars without me?"

"You seem to have made quite the evening of it anyway," said Book. "And if it's any consolation, the action was over very quickly. Although it was quite… flashy."

"It was a very professional operation," said Zoë.

"I know all about those," Simon mumbled into his tea. He'd saved someone's life tonight. Who cared? Nobody here, that was for sure.

"No room for amateurs, Jayne," said Wash. "Not when Zoë's there."

"I don't know how you're insultin' me, little man," growled Jayne, "but I know you are, and I ain't happy about that—"

"Leave it to my wife," said Wash. "The professional."

"And the preacher," said Zoë.

"And the preacher," said Wash, happily. "Who is also wholly professional. Not to mention a 'holy' professional…" He performed the scare quotes. His colleagues looked back at him, unforgivingly. He reached for the champagne bottle and filled up his mug again. "I am not appreciated here."

"I appreciate you, honey," said Zoë. "But you can quit talkin' now."

Simon (having by now drunk a mug of champagne, most of a cup of tea, and eaten some nuts) was starting to rally slightly. "Is there an explanation? For champagne? I'm guessing it has something to do with… the very large amount of money in the suitcase on the table in front of me? Also, I have questions about why are Book and Zoë back here? Did the ransom get paid?"

Book said, "In a manner of speaking."

"Yes," said Mal. "No. No." He looked around. "Where are we on that right now? Does anyone know?"

"I've made fifty platinum so far," said Simon. "Do we even need this money now?"

"No," said pretty much everyone.

"Good," said Simon. "I'm quitting medicine. I'm going to retire."

"No, you won't, Simon," River said, with great confidence. And obviously she was right, because he loved being in surgery and he would even turn up for his next shift at St. Freda's because they were short of staff and he wouldn't let them down. Simon stared helplessly at the case. "Where has all this money come from anyway?"

Jayne looked at Wash and Wash looked at Jayne.

"You tell him," said Jayne.

"Why me?"

"You like talkin'."

"True enough," said Wash. "So, what happened was this… Actually, could someone pour Simon another drink first? Because I think he's going to want it." Someone did, whereupon Wash picked up his story again. "So you see, Simon, the thing about Neapolis is that there are an awful lot of gambling establishments—"

The story unfolded and slowly, ever so slowly, with many interruptions and annotations, the explanation for why River was dressed up began to penetrate through the fog of fatigue weighing down Simon's mind. He looked at Wash in undisguised horror. "You took River to a *casino*?"

To their credit, his colleagues were suppressing their laughter pretty well.

"I want to make it very clear," said Wash, "that when I woke up this morning, taking your sister to a casino was not in my plan for the day. It was not even something I would have considered a possibility for today or indeed any other day—"

"I asked you to look *after* her!" cried Simon.

River, across the table, was humming quietly.

"It was Jayne," Wash pointed at him.

"Huh?" said Jayne.

"It was all because of Jayne," said Wash. "He was the one who came up with the whole plan—"

"Oh, so it *was* my idea," said Jayne. "Them'll be my winnings, then—"

"She's not *well*," said Simon. "How could you be so *irresponsible*, both of you—"

"She seemed to be having a good enough time," said Jayne, with a shrug. "Maybe you should loosen up. Let her live a little. She might get less crazy, *dǒng ma*?"

"They made a plan between them," said Wash. "There was nothing I could do in the face of the planning. The plan was all-out planned before I had any idea there was planning going on. I only went with them to make sure that the plan went to plan." He pointed at the case on the table. "Look!" he said. "Look at that. Don't look at me! River's rich, Simon! She's rich!"

"And me," said Jayne. "Me too. I'm rich."

"Zoë," Wash concluded, "protect me."

"You're on your own on this one, sugar," said Zoë.

"I only let them do it to save you," Wash said.

"And I love you for that," she replied, "but I had everything covered."

"Look at her, son," said Book, quietly, in Simon's ear. "She looks about the happiest I've seen her since you came on board."

River, still humming, smiled at him. Her lipstick (*Lipstick? River?*) was smudged, its imprint on the mug in front of her, which he assumed held champagne (*River? Champagne?*) And she did look… well, *happy*…

"She's safe and sound," murmured Book. "Don't begrudge her living a little."

And Simon found that he couldn't. "All right," he said. "I guess… Everyone's home again, and safe, more or less…"

He eyed the preacher. "I'd like to know how you two got away. I mean, if the answer to the question 'did we pay the ransom' is somewhere between 'yes' and 'no', then—why and how are you here?"

"I'd like to know that too," said Kaylee.

"Oh, it wasn't so hard," said Book. "Once we put our mind to it."

"Shots were fired," reported Zoë. "There was a small explosion." In the clipped tones of one used to briefing a commanding officer, she recounted all that had occurred.

"You blew up Jacob Roberts' First Night party?" Anna burst out laughing. "*Tā mā de*, that's the best piece of news I've heard in years!"

"The Good Lord himself kicked over a few tables at the Temple at the sight of the money-lenders," said Book, virtuously. "I'd like to think he might have reacted in a similar fashion, confronted with the nature and depth of Jacob Roberts' depravity. But I have to say, I'm interested in this man you treated, Doctor. Wounded…" The Shepherd patted the top of his left thigh, "round about here, would you say?"

"Yes," said Simon.

"Big black bushy beard?"

"Ye-es…?" said Simon, suspicions rising. *No way*, he thought. *No way did I spend this evening clearing up their rutting mess yet again…*

"Huh," said the Shepherd. "I suppose there's not likely to be two of them out there."

"Pity you didn't shoot Roberts," said Anna.

"The chance did arise," admitted Book, "but I think I'd like to see him suffer more in what we might call a spiritual manner."

"You mean hit him in the pocket," said Wash.

"Oh, at the very least," said Book.

"My concern," said Mal, "is less what we have planned for Jacob Roberts and what he has planned for us after your show this evening. I'm expectin' a lot more in the way of trouble from that quarter as a result."

"Surely not more trouble, Mal," said Inara, dryly. "How could that possibly happen?"

"Because we're just so gorram charmin'," said Mal. "And in the meantime," he looked at Anna. "Between us all we've discovered a great deal more about Jacob Roberts and the kind of business he conducts, and I'm both displeased to learn I've played some small part in this, against my knowledge—and I'd like to see some way toward making amends for our part in interruptin' work bein' done in that respect by you and your people, Ms. Liu."

Quickly, Mal filled the rest of the crew in what he and Kaylee had been doing all afternoon; their discovery of the network that Anna and Katarina were running to help the girls and young women trapped by Roberts and the local Guild.

"Good work that doctor friend of yours is doin'," said Mal to Simon. "I guess not everything comes out of the central worlds is a waste of time and space."

"Punctured lung," mumbled Simon through a life-giving mouthful of nuts. "Saved his life."

"I care," said River.

"Now listen up," said Mal. "We find ourselves at something of an impasse. We've managed, in that way we have about ourselves, to make ourselves an enemy of the nastiest man in town—but we now know a great deal about his less-than-savory business. We've caused some trouble for some good people," he nodded at Anna, "and seems to me we might consider doin' a little tidyin' up around the place before we leave."

"Why ain't we leavin'?" said Jayne. "In case you hadn't noticed we're sittin' pretty on top of a fortune right now."

"Because, as I just explained," said Mal, "though it seems my words failed somehow to penetrate your skull, we've caused some good people some big problems."

Jayne shrugged. "Ain't causin' me any problems I can see."

"I'd prefer not to leave," said Book, softly, "until this matter has been resolved."

"Might this be a good point to approach the authorities?" said Wash. "I mean, isn't there a sheriff in town who might take people trafficking seriously?"

"There is a sheriff, yes, but he's not one I'd trust overly," said Mal. "We met him, remember? Seems to be well in Roberts' pocket. But you might have a different perspective on this, Ms. Liu?"

"I don't know," said Anna. "Back when my parents were alive, Zhao was a good friend of theirs."

"Easy to be friends with powerful people," said Mal.

"Men from the sheriff's office took me and Zoë over to Roberts' residence," said Book. "I got the impression they were accustomed to running messages for him."

"I think he's in a difficult position," Anna said. "Roberts and the Guild are so powerful these days that he's limited in what he can do."

"Disappointin' to hear about the Guild," said Mal, with the air of a man who didn't sound particularly disappointed.

"It's not the Guild," insisted Inara.

"No? Looked like 'em to me," said Mal.

"My friend on Sihnon was surprised to hear there was a Guild House on Bethel. It's all extremely irregular," Inara said, unhappily. "And before you say anything, Mal, it's not in the least typical either. My friend is investigating. Let's wait till I hear back from her before jumping to conclusions, shall we?"

"Guess we'll find out where the Guild stands when you do," said Mal. "But we'll take as read that—typical or not—the head here is in it up to her neck with Roberts."

"We know that from the ground," said Anna. "Out in the towns. The Guild arrives, recruiting. We don't see those girls again…"

"*Rén cí de fó zǔ*…" Inara shook her head. "We have to put a stop to this."

"Indeed, be a shame if the Guild was to look bad," said Mal. "Myself, I think the sheriff is the one we need if we want this all to unravel. But I ain't in the way of seein' yet how that thread should be pulled." He looked at Simon. "You up to speed now on everything, Doc?"

Simon, who thought that by now he understood pretty much everything that had happened, said, "I think so. My day does seem to have been wasted slightly…"

He checked the time. Four hours until he was expected back at St. Freda's. The others were talking again about Roberts, and the Guild, and what could be done. Quietly, Simon stood up, finished what was left of his champagne, grabbed his jacket, and slipped out of the dining room. He'd only gone a few steps before Kaylee caught up with him.

"Hey you," she said. "Where you slopin' off to, middle of the party?"

"Back to the hospital."

"The hospital?" she said. "Why?"

"My next shift starts in four hours." From the dining room, they heard a roar of laughter. "I'd like some sleep first and I'm not going to get any here."

"Simon," said Kaylee. "Don't you get what's happened? River's just won a fortune. Zoë and Book are back. We don't need the money any longer—"

"No," he said, "but I signed a contract—"

"Under a false name! Simon, stay! Mal and the rest will have this whole business with Roberts finished up first thing, we're gonna have the whole day to go into Neapolis, do whatever we like, and how often do we get the chance to do that, and with so much *money*—"

"I know," he said. "But it's their busiest weekend and they're short of staff and Katarina's a friend and…" He held up his hands. "Kaylee, I'm a *doctor*."

"Oh, Simon, why do you always have to be so…" Nice? Thoughtful? Responsible? Not handsy? From the look on her face, Kaylee wasn't thinking of anything close to that.

"Simon…?"

And now here was River, slipping down the corridor toward him. Her hair was coming loose, strands tumbling down the sides of her face, but she was still glowing. "Don't go. Please."

"River, it's only for a few hours—"

"I don't want you to go."

"You and me both," muttered Kaylee.

"They put her in a box," said River. "She didn't dream and when she woke the nightmares began..."

Simon closed his eyes, very briefly. He'd tried so many combinations of her medication, and still the nightmares seeped through. The worst thing was knowing that he was the one who had put her in that box, that it had been the only way to keep her safe.

"River," he said, "you'll be fine. Everyone's here—"

"I want you to stay, Simon."

"I'm only going to be at the hospital. Just for a few hours."

Kaylee said, "Let him go, sweetie. We'll make our own fun." She reached to take River's arm. At least they were friends again. River murmured something. *"Beware the white dragon..."* He supposed it meant something—even River's most cryptic statements usually turned out to mean something, but not always immediately. Sometimes not for weeks, and you couldn't lead your life round what she said.

"Here," she said, pressing something into his hand. "Lucky charm."

Simon, opening his palm, saw a silver coin.

"Biggest win ever," she said, with pride.

Kaylee was smiling. "You gotta admit, Simon," she said, "it's pretty funny. I mean—did you *see* Jayne's suit? Would you even've thought that was *possible*?"

Maybe it was Kaylee's smile; maybe it was the thought of those shiny lapels; maybe it was simply River looking happy, but all in a flash, Simon did see the funny side. He began to laugh. "River, you're incredible! All that *platinum*…! Never let it be said that the Tams don't pay their way on this ship."

River stared at him. "I made more money than you."

Simon bent to kiss her on the top of her head. "Of course you did, *mèi mèi*," he said. "Of course you did."

The night wore on. River Tam, barefoot now, but still wearing the black dress, drifted like a ghost through the ship—listening, listening, always listening. River didn't miss much. River didn't miss anything.

In the dining area, Jayne and the Shepherd, the last ones at the table, were finishing the champagne. Jayne was complaining. "My ruttin' idea," he said. "I'd better see my gorram share…" And: "I'm sure you will," the Shepherd was saying back, affably. "Your fair share." River wasn't fooled by appearances. River too was a box of secrets, waiting to be opened.

She drifted on, listening… In their cabin, Zoë and Wash, entangled together, were loving and laughing as usual. "It was *velvet*, Zoë. *Velvet*," said Wash. "Dammit, who knows what the hell else he keeps hidden away in that cabin…" And Zoë, placing kisses on her man, said, "Don't bear thinking about…" River loved them; loved their love.

She glided through the darkness. In Inara's shuttle, three women—Inara, Kaylee, and Anna—sat and talked about the girls, not much younger than River, and how each one of them had left home looking for a better life, and all that happened to them, and what might happen to them next. *So many girls*, thought River. *Girls in boxes, trying to get free…*

River moved on. She went into Simon's cabin. Taking one of his shirts, she folded it into a pillow, then she lay down on his bed and pressed her head against the shirt. She let her mind wander further, and found him, sleeping, at last, peacefully. "I'm sorry, Simon," she mumbled. "Sorry I broke your world. Sorry that it can't ever be mended…"

But for tonight, River did not want to be sad. She blew a kiss to her sleeping brother, and let her mind float on into the city. She moved through the streets, feeling the lights and the laughter. Felt warm. Happy. For just one night, but she had climbed out of her box and heard the music and *danced…*

All of a sudden, the joy stopped. She heard them—the voices, crying out for help. She jumped up. On bare feet, she ran to Mal's cabin and hammered on the door. After a moment, Mal materialized, sleepy-eyed and grumpy. "*Lǎo tiān yé,*" said Mal, when he saw who was there. "River, it's late! We got us a busy day tomorrow…"

"They took the girl. Tried to put her in a box," said River. "She's crying, crying crying—"

"I know. We took her out to the house in the country and she's safe there—"

"Not her. More girls. Lots of girls—"

"That's right," said Mal. "All of 'em, safe in the country. Remember? With Anna's friend. Simon's friend—"

"Little children that come to him suffer." River—who could see and feel more these days than she could ever put into words—struggled to make him understand. "He won't let them go, Captain. In case they tell their stories. Bear witness."

Mal. Latin for bad. Not this Mal. He was not bad-bad. He was good-bad. This Mal she trusted nearly as much as Simon, and here he was, the good-bad Mal, trying to find the meaning behind the words. "What're you tellin' me, River? What're you tryin' to say?"

"The girls," she said, struggling to make him understand. "He won't ever let them out of the box..."

The ship's internal comm crackled to life. Book's voice came through. "Mal," he said. "I think you should come up here. We may have a problem."

Tā mā de, thought Mal, as he ran down to the bridge, *but that girl ain't right...* Not for the first time, he wondered whether letting her stay on board was one of his wiser decisions. "What? Shepherd, what's going on?"

Book's face was grim. "We got a message. From Katarina Neilsen. Asking for help."

"Help?" said Mal. "She still there?"

"He won't let them tell their story," whispered River. Look at her now, standin' in the doorway there like some ghost. "He'll put them back in boxes. Nail down the lids."

"Message got cut off," said Book. "Mal, you said you left them at some house in the country?"

"That's right—safe house of Anna's."

"I think there may be some trouble brewin' over there."

"Nail down the lids and light a pyre," whispered River.

Mal hit the comm and roused the crew. Anna tried to reach Katarina and the house using their secure codes but couldn't raise anyone. "Thought the place was safe," said Mal. "Any idea how they found it?"

"Best guess?" said Anna. "They tracked the car that you and Kaylee used to bring Ava to the house. Those driverless cars— their routes get logged, and the sheriff's office can get access to that. If Roberts was having your movements followed…"

They'd led his people straight there. "All right," said Mal, "time we were on our way."

Within minutes, he and his people were strapping on weapons. Book offered his services, and Jayne was pretty cheerful about the turn of events.

The five of them piled into the red hover-car that Zoë and Book had taken and were quickly in flight. Anna kept trying to reach Katarina, but with no success. They were soon beyond the city limits, out into open country, and darkness. On Anna's advice, they came to the house via a back route which she guessed would not be known to the attackers. As they drew nearer to the house, they saw a red flickering light. Mal's fury began to rise. "*Ai ya tian a*," he said. "Those gorram bastards have set fire to the place."

"*Ren ci de fo zu, qing bao you wo men*," whispered Anna. "The girls… There were a dozen girls there!"

"Oh, now, that ain't right," said Jayne. "Didn't you say some of 'em were kids, Mal? That ain't right."

"May the Good Lord protect them," murmured Book.

"Hoping we can do considerably better than that, preacher," said Mal. "Being here in the flesh and all, and not in the spirit."

"The spirit guides each one of us," said Book.

"A powerful desire for vengeance is guidin' me at this moment, Shepherd, but this ain't the time for that argument," said Mal. "Zoë, you ready?"

"Always, sir."

Mal dropped the car, very suddenly, almost to the ground. Zoë kicked her door open. Anna said, "What the *hell* are you doing?" but her voice was drowned out when Zoë started shooting. When shots were returned, Mal banked the flyer up again.

"Get a good look, Zoë?"

"I'd say about half-a-dozen of 'em, sir."

"I like them odds," said Jayne.

"I'd strap in if I were you," said Book, to Anna. "Things are going to get a mite bumpy for a while."

As befitted a man of the cloth, he was telling the truth. Mal took the flyer round overhead three more times. On each occasion, Zoë and Jayne strafed the ground below, and shots were sent back up. By the third time, however, these were more in the way of a token protest. "Think we got 'em on the run, sir," said Zoë.

"For a while at least," said Mal. "But they'll be back."

"We should take a closer look at the house," said Book. "See if there are any…" He sighed. "See if anyone got out."

Mal, in agreement with the Shepherd on this score at least, brought the flyer down as near to the house as he dared. The fire was now raging through the building. The air was thick and the stench was terrible. *Sons of bitches*, thought Mal, *if a single one of those girls is still in there, I'll hunt you down, Jacob Roberts, and I'll see you burn…*

"Sir."

"Yes, Zoë."

"I'd like take a look round. Maybe some of 'em got out in time."

"Take a look," he said, "but I ain't hopeful."

"I'll come with you, Zoë," said Book. "Got to keep hopin' against hope, Mal."

Anna, who knew the grounds, went with them. Mal turned back to the house, where the roof looked like it was on the verge of collapsing. Sad truth was that he couldn't see anyone making it through this conflagration. First few minutes were what counted, getting folks out as quick as you could. He doubted those fellas would've let anyone get out. Shot them if they tried. Left them to the flames and the smoke if they didn't… *Kids*, thought Mal. Kaylee weren't much older than some of them. River the same age…

"Mal," said Jayne. "We got incoming."

"Those boys want more?" said Mal. "'Cause I got a barrel-load to give 'em—"

"Summat else," said Jayne, pointing up. Mal saw lights in the sky—the bright beams of headlamps and the flashing beacons of about half-a-dozen official vehicles. They were moving at speed and, as they drew closer, sirens began to wail.

"Huh," said Mal. "Seems like Sheriff Zhao has decided to show. Question is—which side he is on?"

Anna Liu led Zoë and Book toward the left-hand side of the house. "Where you takin' us?" said Zoë, still a mite suspicious of the other woman.

"There's steps round the back of the house from the upper story into the garden," said Anna. "If Katarina knew the house was under attack, she'd have taken the girls that way."

"Seems to make sense," said Book. "Shall we go?"

Zoë nodded, although with some misgivings. Truth was, she knew little about Anna. Didn't know whether she could hold her own in a fight, couldn't tell whether she was amateur or professional. Sure, she'd got the better of Mal at the docks, but that weren't always a good guide, and she'd planned for that. None of this, tonight, was planned.

They got as far away from the house as they could and made their way round the side of the property. The fire crackled behind, casting a grim light over them. They went down a wide, tiled passage filled with green shrubs and other dry weather plants, coming at the far end to a long wall. Three steps led down to an iron gate, which stood open. "Hopeful sign," said Book.

"Either that, or someone's ahead of us," said Zoë, and clutched her pistol more firmly. Through the gate was a big garden of the kind found in these hot climes, mostly flagstones with beds set in them, homes to succulents and other hardy plants. In the center of the space was a big palm, hung with yellow lights. Everything was still and quiet.

"So what is there this way?" said Zoë. "Any place to hide?"

"There's another gate in the far corner," said Anna. "Beyond that, there's a little swimming pool—"

"Nice place you've got here," said Zoë.

"I'd like to think I've made good use of my fortune," said Anna. "Near the pool there's some changing rooms. Kay might have taken them there for cover."

"Seems as good a place to try as any," said Book. "Zoë?"

Zoë nodded her assent and gestured to Anna to lead the way. As they drew near the far side of the garden, a new sound began to fill the air.

"Sirens," murmured Book. "Reckon that might be back-up?"

"Ain't relyin' on that bein' so," Zoë said.

"Might be wise," he murmured, "given the sheriff."

They passed silently through the gate to the pool area. Lights fixed into the walls and on the ground gave some illumination, of an uneasy kind, with many shadows. At the far side, the dark blocks of the changing rooms huddled together. Behind them, back toward the house, the sirens were getting louder. Kind of noise might make a man jumpy. "Stay here, will you, Shepherd?" murmured Zoë. "Keep an eye out for anyone unwelcome."

Book nodded and took up position near the gate, one eye on the way they had just come. Zoë and Anna went round the pool, passing a couple of low lounge chairs and then round to the dark huts. Zoë tried the door to the first; it was locked. "Sauna," muttered Anna. "Haven't used it for a while."

"Shame," said Zoë. They moved on. The room behind the second door was empty. Between this hut and the next was a garden area, about six feet long, filled with clumps of potted cacti, some low on the ground, some loomin' up with their long arms from the shadows. Suddenly, from the far side of the pool, Book yelled out, "Zoë! Behind you!"

Zoë swung round. Saw the dark figure of a man, pistol raised, heading toward them. Now where'd he come from? Side of the huts, maybe? "Stay still," she ordered. "Lawmen're here. Ain't no use tryin' anythin'—"

The man laughed. "Lawmen're on our side," he said. "You ain't worked that out yet?"

"Maybe," said Zoë. "Maybe not." She started moving backward, very slowly, thinkin' that one of the doors to the huts might come in useful as cover. Let her fire a few shots off. The man kept headin' toward her. "You're the one needs to stand still, lady," he told her. From the corner of her eye, Zoë saw Book, soft-footed and hidden by shadows, start to make his move round the edge of the pool. This would be another good time, she thought, for him to forget all them scruples about usin' a gun. But perhaps he was hopin' this still could be brought to an end without any shots fired. Zoë kept moving back, ever so slow, toward the next hut along.

The man came past the sauna, and past the first changing hut. "Lady," he said, as he drew past the cactus garden, "stop movin'—"

He didn't get another word out. Suddenly, someone came out of the shadows, and, with one well-aimed blow, smashed a potted cactus hard against the man's head. He went down like a stone, the pistol tumbling from his hands. Zoë darted forward and kicked the pistol into the pool. She looked up into the frightened face of a young woman. She looked a lot like Simon Tam did when he found himself in the middle of a fight.

"Katarina Neilsen?" said Zoë.

"What?" said the woman. She stared wide-eyed at Zoë. "Who are you?"

"Name's Zoë Alleyne," said Zoë. "Came with Mal Reynolds. I'm here to kill anyone tries to hurt a single one of you." She looked down at the man lying on the floor amidst pot shards and smashed-up cactus. "Though I have to say, you're doing a mighty fine job of that already."

The police vehicles landed. Mal counted maybe a dozen officers and, when a couple of those headed his way, pointing their pistols at him and Jayne, both men decided the sensible thing to do right now was to put down their weapons and put up their hands. The officers fanned out around the property. A few minutes later, Mal heard a series of rapid shots being fired. All the officers returned, this time with three men in their custody. These were shoved unceremoniously into the back of one of the vehicles. With the area secured, people from the fire department arrived, and started work putting out the fire. Not that much of the house would be left standing after this, thought Mal. Roberts' men had done a thorough job there.

Mal heard voices behind him and turned to see Sheriff Zhao heading his way.

"Captain Reynolds," Zhao said. "I recall that when we met the other day that I asked you to do your job smoothly, without any trouble, and please to leave no trace of your presence here on Bethel. How d'you think you're doin' on that score?"

Mal watched as part of the roof of the house fell in. "In all honesty, Sheriff, I would have to say that we're doing badly."

"So would I," said Zhao. "You know, this ain't the only thing on my mind. I heard there was a little trouble over at the Roberts residence last night."

"Is that so?" said Mal.

"Yup," said Zhao. "Word is a browncoat and preacher were seen leaving the place in a red car. A stolen red car." He looked at the vehicle matching this description that was parked a little distance away. "You able to shed any light on that?"

"Not personally, Sheriff, no."

"And you able to shed any light on all of this?" Zhao gestured round at the chaos.

"Well," said Mal, "depends on what you want to know…"

At this moment, Book emerged from the shadows. "I think that I can tell you most of what you want to know, Sheriff," he said. "But, if you don't mind me sayin', I'm fairly sure you know already the manner of man that we're dealing with in Jacob Roberts. And I believe that when you hear some of what we have to say, and show you what we have to show you, you'll be a mite better disposed toward us."

"I ain't a religious man," said Zhao, "but out of respect for your position, Shepherd, I'll hear what you have to say."

"There's a dozen girls here," said Book. "Roberts had them taken from their families. Drugged them, and stored them in cryo-cases to sell off-world. And when someone tried to help them, Roberts came after the girls, and he ordered them burned alive rather than living and able to testify against him. Are you ready to hear more, Sheriff?"

"I am," said Zhao. He looked around. "But not here. Back in the city." He waved at a couple of his men to come over. "I sincerely hope, Captain Reynolds, that you and your people aren't going to do anything foolish and end up getting shot resisting arrest."

"Arrest?" said Mal. "What exactly have we done to deserve that kinda treatment?"

"For one thing, I'm lookin' at a red car over there that ain't yours," said Zhao. "And for another thing—I still want to get to the bottom of what's been happening over at the Roberts residence. A lot of important people at that party, gentlemen, and I've spent the time since listenin' to them shoutin'. A lot of them askin' what I'm doin' about the fright they had. Word gets around that the city ain't safe durin' Carnival and folks round here stand to lose a great deal of money—"

"Marcus!" someone called out, and Zhao turned.

"Miss Liu," he said, and his voice became oddly warm, like a fond father might address his daughter. "What're you doin' out here? These fellas here haven't laid a finger on you, have they?"

"What, Zoë and her people?" said Anna, in surprise. "No—"

"Hey—!" said Mal.

"Hush, sir," suggested Zoë.

238

"They've nothing to do with this," said Anna. "Jake Roberts is behind this, Marcus, and you know he is—the same man that killed Mother and Father."

Zhao was shaking his head. "Miss Liu, you know I weren't ever able to prove that—"

"This time I think we have him, Marcus." Anna's mouth was set in a hard, straight line. "This time we're going to put him behind bars."

Which was fine by Mal Reynolds, as long as there wasn't any chance that they were all going to be sharing a cell.

The roof of the house collapsed. "All right," said Zhao. "I think we'd best take this back to base."

Simon was still smiling at the thought of all the platinum when he arrived back at St. Freda's. *Mèi mèi*, he thought, *nobody has ever made me laugh the way you do…* He found a room in the temporary accommodation set aside for the medical staff, lay down, and had three of the best hours sleep he'd had in months. He woke refreshed, alert, and ready for whatever the day might throw at him.

It was still early in the morning. Checking admissions, he found out that some people had been brought in suffering from smoke inhalation; Mayhew was already with them, so Simon didn't need to worry. There was nothing else immediately pressing, so he took the opportunity to go and check on the patient from the night before. He was in a private room—paid for by his employer, Simon assumed. Was that employer Jacob Roberts? Book seemed to think that he might have had a hand in the young man's injury, but Simon didn't particularly care either way. What mattered was how well the operation had gone, and how quickly the patient was recovering.

The young man was awake, lying back against the pillows, still very pale behind his dark beard, but looking much better. Simon was struck again at how young he was when you looked closely. Young and miserable.

"Good morning," said Simon. He picked up the patient's chart. Read his name for the first time: *Michael Doherty*. He put down the chart and went over to the drip on the left-hand side of the bed. "How are you feeling today?"

"Are you the doc?" said Doherty. "You're the doc from last night, aren't you? The one who…" Water began to seep from his eyes. "Oh, mister," he said, "I'm gonna shake your hand…" He grabbed Simon's hand with his huge paw and made good on his promise.

This happened sometimes (not as often as you'd imagine), and Simon was embarrassed every single time. A grateful patient showered him with thanks and praise. Made a fuss of him. Named a hamster after him. But Simon was only doing his job, doing what he'd been trained to do and, until recently, had been paid ridiculous amounts of money to do. And yet here was this big man, who was not a particularly nice piece of work if even a part of what Zoë and Book said was true, with tears rolling down his cheeks, speaking breathlessly as he pumped Simon's hand and thanked him.

"Anything," he rasped. "I'll do anything for you, Doc."

"All you really need to do is rest up and get better," said

Simon, gently extracting himself. He checked Doherty's blood pressure and then checked his retinas.

"You know," said Doherty, "I been lying here thinkin' ever since I woke up."

"Thinking?"

"Thinkin' 'bout things, what I done, how I got here…"

Carefully, Simon sat down on the edge of the bed. This was something else that happened sometimes too. People want to confide in you. It did no harm to listen for a while. Someone would come and get him if he was needed.

"How you got here?"

"I mean… Not last night… More'n that…" Tears started leaking out of his eyes. "I done some real bad things, Doc."

"I know," said Simon.

"There's these girls," said Doherty. "Not much more'n kids, some of 'em…"

"I know," said Simon.

"And I guess I didn't think about 'em much…"

"How long have you been working for Jacob Roberts?"

"Three, mebbe four years?"

How old would that have made him when Roberts got his claws into him, wondered Simon. Fifteen? Sixteen? Just a kid himself…

"And now, I'm thinkin'… I made some bad choices…"

Simon sighed. He knew about that.

"You, Doc. You look like the kind of man makes good choices…"

You don't know the half of it, thought Simon. "I've been lucky," said Simon. "I had a lot of opportunities…"

Doherty reached out for his hand. "How do I put myself straight, Doc?"

"I think," said Simon, "that you know the answer to that. It's… it's never too late."

That seemed to do the trick. Doherty smiled up at him. "Guess you're right, Doc. Never too late."

Simon stood up. He was thinking, and these thoughts were very unwelcome, about Jayne Cobb, and what kinds of opportunities and choices made a man like that. Simon turned to go, but he didn't get far. There was a man standing in the doorway, blocking the exit.

"I'm afraid it's not visiting hours until later," said Simon. "Even in the private rooms. He needs to rest now—"

"Shut up," said the man. Simon took a closer look at him. Months on board *Serenity* meant he read situations differently these days. Looked for threats. Looked for the best way out. And he definitely couldn't get past this guy. He was massive, and he was armed.

"You're not touching this patient," said Simon.

"Ain't here for him," the man said.

"Me?" said Simon. "What have I done—"

"You're with Reynolds, ain't you? On *Serenity*?"

"What? But—" Simon didn't get further. The guy punched him in the face. Simon crumpled, falling heavily, the side of his head hitting the bed. The man advanced toward him. He was wearing a black T-shirt with a logo in the shape of a white dragon. River's whispered words, *Beware the white dragon*, just before he left, came back in a flash. *I hate my life*, thought Simon. White Dragon kicked him, hard. Simon closed his eyes. *River*, he thought. *I'm sorry. But why do you always have to be so... right?*

Because she was his brilliant little sister, of course; the girl with all the gifts, the one out of the two of them who was going to go further than anyone had ever gone before; the sister for whom Simon would do anything, absolutely anything, up to and including throwing himself into harm's way, if that would save her. And it wasn't enough. Nothing he did was ever enough.

There was a sudden, crashing noise. Simon wondered why there wasn't any more pain as a result and opened his eyes. Everything was quiet. Some pained, ragged breathing; someone moaning. Pushing himself up, Simon saw that White Dragon was lying half-conscious on the floor, blood all over his head. Simon turned to look at Doherty, who was sitting up in bed, gasping, and holding in both hands the metal frame for the intravenous drip.

Ai ya, tian a, thought Simon. *He swung that round and he hit him and wǒ de mā that must have hurt...*

Simon, scrabbling over to White Dragon, quickly checked the head wound. Not immediately life-threatening. He heard footsteps running down the corridor outside and wondered whether he might let someone else clear up this particular mess. His head was really hurting now, and he was starting to see flashing lights. Still, he had one more patient to check. Just to be sure. He looked at Doherty, who had fallen back against the pillows. His breathing was rough and ragged.

"Thank you," whispered Simon, reaching to take his hand. Other people were here now. Perhaps he could leave things to them. Let someone else take care for a while. "Everything's okay," he said, as much to himself as to the man on the bed. "Everything's going to be okay…"

"Said I'd do anything for you, Doc," Doherty muttered. "Meant it."

You've seen the interior of one police station, you've seen them all, thought Mal Reynolds, but the truth of the matter was that there was never much in the way of dignity in being hauled off unceremoniously in the middle of the night to one of these *gǒu shǐ* places. It was heaving, full of *fèi wù* and other crap, drunks maudlin and furious, combatants from every side of fights big and small, and the occasional subdued victim, waiting to give their statement and then get out of the gorram hellhole. Mal's eye fell on a young man sitting quietly in the corner. He was wearing a white coat and sporting the makings of a fine black eye. Mal's temper took an upward swing.

"Well, well, well, look what the cat dragged in," said Mal. "Doc, what is it about your face compels folk to land a punch?"

Simon Tam, to his credit, did not implode. "I gather that people just don't like doctors." He took a look at who had arrived: Mal and Zoë, Book and Jayne, and about half-a-dozen sheriff's men. Mal guessed they made quite the party. "Hi everyone," said Simon. "Are you under arrest again?"

"I… ain't entirely sure," said Mal, looking round for Zhao.

"Not just yet," said Sheriff Zhao, from behind him.

"How about you, Doc?" said Mal, shooting Simon a pointed look. "You in some kind of difficulty here?" What he meant was: *Is your cover blown? Is this real trouble?* The doc at least had the sense to get his meaning and shake his head. *Not that.* The boy wasn't stupid, that was for sure. He was just a jerk.

"Someone came by the hospital looking for people on your crew," said Simon. "I got hit, and he got hit."

Jayne guffawed. "Like to shake that man by the hand. If it were a man. Girl could take you out, Doc."

"Hope you at least got a punch in, son," said Book.

"I didn't hit anyone," said Simon, firmly. "I'm here to make a statement."

"Captain Reynolds," said Zhao, "I'm guessin' that from your familiarity with this young man he is yet another ever-lovin' member of your ever-lovin' crew."

"No," muttered Jayne.

"Yes," said Mal, "he's one of mine." Kinda touching, he thought, the way the doc looked cheered at this claim being laid. Though he might think differently when the arrest started formalizin'.

"Doctor, preacher, coupla browncoats, and…" Zhao looked at Jayne and sighed. "Well, I guess it takes all sorts to keep the world spinnin' on its axle. Anyone else signed up with you yet to put in an appearance, Reynolds?"

"I think you've met most everyone," said Mal. "Oh no, there's a registered companion too. Never know when one will come in handy."

"Registered companion. Regular circus troupe, aren't you?" Zhao called over a couple of his officers and sent them off with Jayne and Zoë to get their version of events. He nodded at Simon. "All right, sonny, you come along with us. Me, your captain, your preacher—we're going to get to the bottom of this *niú fèn* and ain't nobody leavin' this buildin' till I'm satisfied."

It was truly fascinating, thought Simon, watching Mal try to find out whether an officer of the law was amenable to taking a bribe. He himself might have been tempted to approach the whole business with somewhat more delicacy, or perhaps not at all, but Mal seemed to have decided to lay his cards down flat on the table.

"I'm going to be frank with you, Sheriff," he said.

Zhao settled back into his chair. "Best all round, Captain Reynolds."

"We happen to be in the way of being able to offer you a substantial bribe—"

"Shepherd," whispered Simon to Book, "aren't… I mean, aren't there *laws* about this kind of thing? Only, I don't want to find myself an accessory—"

"Give the captain a moment or two," murmured Book. "I think he has a plan. Leastways, I hope so."

"Now wait," Mal said, holding up a hand to stem Zhao's rising fury, "I haven't finished yet. Because I have the feeling that you are a man of principle, one who has been strugglin' with the kind of powerful people he's been forced to deal with in this city and strugglin' to cope with the way they go about their business. Am I right?"

"You're near the mark," said Zhao. He didn't look quite so angry now. "I don't need a bribe. But I do need money."

"That," said Mal, "was the direction in which my thinkin' was tendin'."

"Money, but not a bribe?" whispered Simon. "I... I'm not following the distinction?"

Book hushed him. "Listen. You'll work it out soon enough."

"A man in your position—fancy hat, fine office, all well and good—might find himself not so powerful as he seems," said Mal. "Man of principle such as yourself—stuck dealin' with folks more powerful than him, strugglin' to stop them doin' their worst, findin' out even men in his own office ain't the most loyal—"

From the look on the sheriff's face, this was certainly sounding familiar.

"And it seems to me," concluded Mal, "that a little platinum in the right places might swing a few loyalties in a more lawfully minded direction."

"It'll take more than a little money," said Zhao.

"Just so happens that right at this moment, we ain't so short of money," said Mal.

Lǎo tiān yé, thought Simon, a smile creeping over his face, *Jayne is going to rutting explode*... He sincerely hoped he would be there to see that. But this was River's money, he thought, that Mal was spending. He opened his mouth to say something about this, but Book's warning hand and Mal's expression stopped him short.

"Now," said Mal, with a nod in Simon's direction, "I have to confirm with the young lady in possession of these funds that she's happy with the plans I have for a portion of her fortune, but I'm hopin' she'll see my reasoning. Because it strikes me that you might make some good use of what we have. Help you clean things up a little round here."

"I might," said Zhao. "But, you know, the problem with such is that it's never a deep clean. Wipe up some of the muck, but it comes back again. Requires more in the way of attention. What I need," said Zhao, "is to get the *source* of all this pollutin' cleared away for good. And that has to be done fair and square, if I'm gonna keep this city nice and shiny."

Simon, putting the pieces of all this together, thought he understood. Roberts had half the sheriff's office on his payroll. Mal had offered Zhao the money to buy people back—but that wouldn't help, as long as Jacob Roberts was still operating.

"If you have a way to do that, Captain Reynolds," said Zhao, "we might be more in a position to do business."

"We could testify," suggested Book. "Roberts hired us to help smuggle girls off world. I learned a great deal while I was… Now how should I put this? *Visiting* his residence."

"You folks put your heads over the parapet," said Zhao, "and all manner of questions arise. And they ain't small questions neither. Who blew up Jacob Roberts' party? Who shot their way out, causing injury to a young man who I hear is still in the hospital as a result of the damage he took? Who, in order to get away from the scene of the crime, compounded their error by stealin' Carleson James's brand new Huxton 44 flyer, shipped in last week at great expense in time for Carnival? And from what you were sayin' just now, Shepherd—which, may I add, by some miracle of your maker I didn't hear—who was it hacked his holy way into Jacob Roberts' private files via the personal console in the library in his residence?"

"Ah," said the Shepherd. "Some interesting questions you pose there."

"*Shén shèng de gāo wán*, preacher," muttered Mal. "Sounds like a certain someone had his own gorram Carnival. He'll be requirin' considerable penance—"

"Now you fellas think for a moment what a mighty fine lawyer, brought in at great expense from some central planet by Mr. Roberts, would make of all this? Whoever and whatever happened, *you* fellas," said Zhao, "ain't gettin' anywhere near a court of law."

"Which I myself count a rare blessin'," said Mal. "But we need someone to stand up there in court and tell the truth of what's been happenin'. Otherwise Jacob Roberts is going to be runnin' this world in perpetuity."

"You need someone on the inside," said Book. "Someone willin' to speak up."

"And Roberts either got them all squared off," said Zhao, "or in fear of their lives."

The captain, the sheriff, and the preacher, fell silent.

"Can… can I say something?" said Simon.

"Doc," said Mal, "the grown-ups are thinking."

Simon sighed. "Really," he said, "I think I have something useful—"

"Doctor," said Book, his voice kindly but firm. "This is a tricky situation."

"I really think I can help," said Simon.

"Let the boy speak," said Zhao. "God knows you two ain't been comin' up with any bright ideas the past coupla days."

"It's… It's just that, the man in the hospital," said Simon. "The one who works for Roberts and got shot in the leg at the party…" His eyes flicked to Book, who nodded his appreciation for the passive voice there. "His name is Doherty—"

"That's mighty interestin', Doc," said Mal, "but I ain't seein' how it helps here—"

"Michael Doherty. He's nineteen years old. He had a punctured lung. I operated and, well, it saved his life. He was very grateful. He said he'd do anything for me." Simon looked again at Book, this time for guidance. "Would that help?"

The three older men looked at each other. Mal shrugged. "Worth a shot. Nice thinkin', Doc. And nice work, savin' his life and all."

Now they care, thought Simon. "It's my job," he said. "But thank you anyway."

"And you think he'd turn?" said Zhao. "Really?"

"I believe so…" Simon thought about Doherty confiding in him. Talking about his life going wrong. Wanting to turn himself round. "Another one of Roberts' men came to get me," explained Simon. "He'd worked out I was part of Mal's crew."

"Roberts' people here could find that out easy enough," said Zhao.

"He came at me." Carefully, Simon touched the side of his face. Those bruises would be coming along nicely. "Doherty intervened… He hit his friend pretty hard…" Simon was still worrying about the damage done there to his patient. He'd have to ask Kay… "Anyway, I got the impression that

Doherty was ready to make the break with Roberts. He said he wanted to turn his life around."

"Young man's seen the light," said Book, with quiet satisfaction. "Far better early than late."

"You know," said Zhao, "I think maybe I should get some of people—my *own* people, I mean, ones I most certainly trust—over to that hospital. Get them to keep a little eye on that boy." He turned to his console and organized the watch. "Good work, son," he said to Simon. "I'm impressed."

"Yes, Doc's truly a marvel among men," said Mal, pushing up from his seat. "We done here?"

"Nearly," said Zhao, and Mal fell back down again. "I still got one big problem."

"Speakin' frankly, Sheriff," Mal said, "I'm not sure how many more of those I can solve and I'm not rightly sure how many more of Bethel's problems are mine—"

"The Guild," said Zhao.

"The Guild?" said Mal.

"Putting away a local gangster is one thing," said Zhao, "and I ain't sayin' it's a small thing, but the Guild—now, that's somethin' else." He shook his head. "You know, we were all glad when the Guild arrived, opened that House of theirs here. Thought those ladies would be a benefit, civilize this place in some fashion."

"Ain't ever straightforward with those ladies from the Guild," said Mal. Book cleared his throat, and Simon saw him put his hand up to cover his mouth.

"Ain't that the truth," said Zhao. "And, from what Ms. Liu's been tellin' me, it's worse'n that. Up to their neck in this trafficking business." He frowned. "What kinda people do that kinda thing?" he muttered. "What kinda people seize girls like that, stick 'em in boxes with a view to selling 'em on…? You know, I ain't married, Captain Reynolds—"

"Lucky man," said Mal.

"And I ain't got daughters nor sisters nor even a coupla favorite aunties, but I know what's right and what's wrong. And what Roberts been doin'—that ain't right. Anyways, the Guild are a headache. They're powerful, see? And not local powerful. Off-world powerful. As good as messin' with the Alliance, as far as I can see—and however much platinum you fellas won yourselves this weekend, there ain't that much money to be won on the whole of Bethel. I still got the Guild to reckon with, and that ain't a small thing."

Mal was shaking his head. "'Fraid I ain't got much pull in that direction, sir."

"No?" said Zhao. "You said you were travelling with a registered companion. Might you have a little pull there?"

Book gave a low laugh. "Falser words were never spoken."

Mal shot the Shepherd a filthy look. "It may well be that I could ask for a favor or two. Not for myself, you understand. But on account of those girls."

"Reckon so?" said Zhao. "Be a big help to me."

"You let us go," said Mal, "and I'll get my best people working on this problem."

"His very best people," confirmed Book. "By which I mean—neither of us."

"Well," said Zhao, leaning back contentedly in his seat. "In that case, fellas, I think we can most certainly call this a bribe."

* * *

"You did *what* with the gorram money?" said Jayne, back on *Serenity* about an hour later. His expression was pretty much everything that Simon had been hoping for. More, actually. A kind of slack-jawed, stunned rage, how he imagined a large animal might look when hit by a hunter's dart. Best of all, this was making River happy. She was sitting with her legs up, arms wrapped round her knees, her eyes sparkling as she watching the conversation unfold.

"You heard," said Mal. "Got to help the girls, eh, River?"

She nodded. "Got to help the girls."

"Mal," said Jayne, "if this is a joke, it ain't gorram funny—"

"Kept back double what Roberts was paying us," said Mal. "Split between us, that's a good enough payday for anyone. Best payday we've had in a while."

"Highly appropriate," said Book. "*This stone that I have set up as a pillar will be God's house, and of all that you give me I will give you a tenth—*"

"But it ain't a tenth!" said Jayne. "It ain't nowhere near a tenth! And it was my ruttin' money, Mal! My gorram bright idea to go to that gorram casino! There'd be no ruttin' money without me and my bright idea!"

"Have to say you don't always have the brightest ideas when it comes to makin' yourself a little money," said Mal, "but this was one of the better ones, *dǒng ma*?" His voice went hard. "What do you say, Jayne? You wanna share with the others some of your worser ones?" He gave Jayne a look so vicious it nearly took Simon's breath away. And it worked. Jayne shut his mouth, immediately.

Wǒ de mā, thought Simon. *I thought trying to sell out me and River was the worst of it. What else has he done we know nothing about?*

"Besides, the way the tale was told to me, River was the one did the work," said Mal. "Spun the wheel, picked the numbers and the signs—"

"Ten," agreed River happily. "Red sun. The wheel sang and I picked up the tune."

"Whatever that means," said Mal, "exactly that. Which to my way of thinking makes this River's money—and River knew what she wanted done with it."

She certainly did, thought Simon. The bulk of the money had been split two ways. Half had gone to the sheriff to do what was needed to buy off the people in his office. And the other half had gone to Katarina and Anna, to help the girls in their care set themselves up, and to look after any other waifs and strays that came their way. *My sister the philanthropist.* Almost from the moment she was born, River had never ceased to amaze him.

"Catch the girls," River said, swaying back and forth in her seat. "Make them smile. They'll be safe now. They'll be happy. Never ever ever put back in their box."

Simon, hearing her, had to look away. He thought of her arrival on *Serenity*, when Mal opened her cryo-case, and she fell out screaming. Life had not been easy since then, but Simon knew one thing for sure. *I'll never regret the choices I made,* mèi mèi. *Never.*

"My thinkin'," concluded Mal, "is that everyone here can be content—more'n content—with what they're taking away from their time on Bethel."

"Gorram girl's brain's addled," muttered Jayne. "My bright idea." But no more complaint came from those quarters. Whatever hold Mal had over Jayne, it was enough for the minute.

Speaking for himself, Simon was certainly content. So he'd won himself another black eye. That was fairly standard, these days. On the other hand, there was the money he'd made at the hospital, which was unequivocally his, and earned entirely legally. Almost entirely legally. Sufficiently legally, given his current circumstances. Very soon, he would be in bed, asleep, which was really all he'd wanted all along. But most of all, River was the happiest he had seen her in ages. She, head tilted, was looking at the state of his face. "Lucky charm," she said. "Saved you."

Simon reached into his pocket for the silver coin. "You hold onto this, *mèi mèi*. It's yours—and, you know, you're my real lucky charm."

Zoë, having given what passed in her world for a statement, which largely consisted of words denyin' much and affirmin' little, was happy to find herself back on *Serenity*, and even happier to learn what Mal wanted her to do next. What she wasn't so sure about was the presence of Anna Liu on this particular mission.

Zoë still wasn't sure what to make of Anna Liu. Seemed

like the woman knew how to carry a gun, but nothing good ever came of working with amateurs. Still, this was Anna's world, and from what Zoë had heard about her parents she had a serious stake in this whole business, so perhaps she'd do for the job at hand. She'd have to. Zoë eyed her thoughtfully as she came into the cargo bay.

"Any news on those girls?" she said.

"Kay's with them," said Anna. "They're all fine. One or two breathed in a little more smoke than was good for them, but they're going to be fine. Those who aren't staying in the hospital tonight are back at our residence. Zhao's got some of his people keeping an eye on the place."

"Good," said Zoë. "And Kay?"

"Shaken, but she's okay."

"Huh," said Zoë.

"You don't like me, do you?" said Anna.

"Don't know you, Ms. Liu."

"You think I'm an amateur."

"Are you?"

"Maybe." Anna, she saw, was looking at her coat. "Were you in the war?"

"Some," said Zoë.

"Browncoat."

"One name for us. Not the worst."

"I was too young for the war," said Anna. "I thought at the time that I understood what was going on. You know what teenagers are like. Never short of opinions."

Zoë wasn't sure she cared to hear this rich young woman's opinions of the war. As far as she was concerned,

Bethel had picked sides when its wealthy citizens had decided to stay neutral.

"I thought of running away. Joining the Independents."

"Last thing we needed," said Zoë, "was more bright-eyed kids playin' at soldiers."

"I worked that out," said Anna. "And you know what? I realize now that wasn't my war. These girls—they're my war."

Zoë thought about. "Then I reckon that we're on the same side. For today." She looked up. Inara was coming out of her shuttle. She looked devastating. Well and good, thought Zoë, since there was a mite more warfare ahead of them yet today.

Zoë had never been inside a Guild House before, and while it was more or less what she might have guessed, she still felt like a fish out of water. The furnishings, well, they were perhaps more or less as expected; lots of curtains and cushions and fussy little bits and pieces of whatever they were. Zoë wasn't averse to comfort, but vesselside life was a mite more austere. The smell—well, she didn't mind that so much; these days she was used to the occasional waft of incense drifting from Inara's shuttle. And now she thought about it, she wasn't so surprised to find that this was a working building. The salons, where the companions met and socialized with the clients; the big reception rooms, for parties, Zoë guessed, and suchlike; and the doors that led to more private, intimate spaces.

Inara was moving with ease through the place, of course, and while there were many beautiful people here, Zoë could see the difference. The extra gloss and polish. Inara shone like the biggest jewel in the crown. They were led through the main hall toward the big stairs. Zoë, looking round, saw signs on all sides of the preparations for the big party that the Guild was hosting that night. They went upstairs, walked along a richly carpeted corridor, and came at last to a wooden door that opened onto a room that looked, to Zoë's eyes, something between a private office and a boudoir. Hilde Becker, the head of the House, was waiting to meet them.

They were strangers, but she and Inara greeted each other with warmth; a kind of sisterhood, thought Zoë, must exist between companions. Hilde led them over the window, where three low but comfortable chairs were set up around a pretty little carved wooden table. The inevitable pot of tea was there, and three cups. "Do sit," said Hilde. "I'll pour."

As she made good her promise, Inara arranged herself comfortably in her chair. Zoë sat with both hands upon her knees, watching Hilde carefully.

"Thank you for finding the time to see me this morning," said Inara. "I'm aware that this evening is the highlight of the Guild's social calendar, and that you must have a great deal to do."

"It's nice to welcome visitors from the central worlds," said Hilde. "Bethel has its own charms, but it is, ultimately, somewhat provincial."

"I travel a great deal around the Rim," said Inara, pleasantly. "But I do consider Sihnon to be my home. I'm in regular contact with my former house there. In fact, I received a wave from them just this morning."

"Yes?" said Hilde. She passed a cup to Inara, who accepted it gratefully.

"Yes," said Inara. "They've been very interested in all that I've had to say about Bethel. To the extent that they're sending their own people to come and see about the House's arrangements here."

Zoë was now watching Hilde very closely.

"One thing puzzled me," said Inara. "They were surprised to learn that there was in fact a Guild House here on Bethel."

"I'm surprised in turn to hear that," said Hilde. She picked up the pot again and poured out a cup of tea for Zoë. Zoë took the cup and put it straight back down on the table.

"And one that's been in operation for several years," said Inara. "If I understand correctly."

Hilde smiled. "Perhaps their records aren't as good as they would like."

Inara laughed. "Oh, Ms. Becker, we're both trained companions, and you know as well as I do that if there's something in which the Guild excels, it's attention to detail." She took a sip of her tea. "All of which helped, I imagine, when you arrived here."

"I don't know what you mean—"

"How would people here know the difference? This tea is very pleasant, by the way."

"Thank you. What do you mean by 'the difference'?" Hilde was holding the teapot again, making ready to pour a cup for herself, but had stopped to look at Inara.

"This is not an official Guild House, Ms. Becker. It may look the part—it's practically indistinguishable—but you and I both know better. Who here on Bethel would know what questions to ask? Just after the war, a confusing time… People happy to welcome the Guild here. Quite a coup for Bethel. Few questions asked."

Hilde resumed pouring. She filled her cup with a steady hand, but she did not put down the pot. "This is quite the tale," she said. "You have quite the imagination, Ms. Serra."

"I assume the intention was to retire quite soon," Inara said. "Move on. Leave the Guild to someone else. If the fraud was uncovered—because it is fraud, Ms. Becker, and the Guild frowns upon it—then you would be long gone. Using yet another name. Probably not your real name. The Guild knows that one. Knows that you were expelled ten years ago."

Hilde was smiling. Zoë readied herself.

"Your mistake was aligning yourself with Jacob Roberts. He's under arrest, by the way. They have people willing to testify against him. What happened? Did he find out about you? Or did you come to him with the idea?"

Hilde's retaliation, when it came, was very sudden, but Zoë was way ahead of her. She grabbed the other woman's wrist, and the teapot, which Hilde was getting ready to throw at Inara, went crashing down onto the table. Finest of porcelain, shattered everywhere. Hot water, everywhere. *She'd've done it too*, thought Zoë, in disgust, *she'd have thrown that in Inara's lovely face…*

Suddenly, Zoë found herself pushed back, hard. "*Tā mā de!*" Inara had told her, once, that companions were trained in self-defense. Hilde, having broken free, was heading for the door, which opened—to reveal Anna Liu, pistol drawn, with two lawmen from the sheriff's office behind her. "No way out this way," she said. And then her face convulsed. "They were *girls*," said Anna. "Young girls! Not an *opportunity*!"

The lawmen made their arrest, and Hilde was taken away. The three women looked at each other. "Well," said Inara. "That's finished." She looked at the broken teapot and the water drip-dripping. "Thank you, Zoë. I believe that might have done some damage."

She knows, thought Zoë. *She knows what Hilde was tryin' to do.*

Inara sat, almost inelegantly, back in her seat, and took a sip of tea. Zoë, coming back round to sit beside her, squeezed Inara's shoulder on the way past. "You know," she said, looking round the plush room, "we done some good work here the past couple of days."

"Yes," said Inara. "I think so." She drank a little more of her tea. "Am I right that this is your first time inside a Guild House, Zoë?"

"One so big."

"I've lived in spaces like this my entire life," said Inara. "It's hard to imagine how they might look through outside eyes." She looked at the broken pieces on the table. "You've never said, Zoë, whether or not you disapprove of my profession."

"You've never said whether or not you disapprove of mine." Zoë shrugged. "I've killed a lot of people, Inara. Maybe lovin' 'em is the better way."

"I'm glad to know you think that way." Inara gave a sigh of relief. "It's restful, isn't it, when the men aren't around?"

"Ain't sayin' they don't have their uses," said Zoë. "But it surely is."

Anna came back into the room. "She's gone," she said. "Off to the sheriff's office. I can't quite believe she's gone..." She looked round the room. "What happens now?"

"The Guild have sent someone," said Inara. "They're due to arrive in a couple of days, when they'll begin their own investigation as to how this place was set up, how it's been operating. They've asked me to act as their representative until their people arrive." She glanced at Zoë. "I assume Mal can be persuaded to delay departure until then."

"Reckon so," said Zoë. She watched as Anna sat down in what had been Hilde's seat and nodded at her. *Nice work. Professional.*

"Their main task will be to restore the Guild's reputation here on Bethel. Make clear that Hilde Becker was rogue, and not representative." She sighed. "They'll have to find out which companions here knew what was happening, which ones were entirely innocent... I don't envy them their task." She looked around. "All of these preparations—such a shame it's going to go to waste."

"What do you mean?" said Anna.

"Tonight's event can hardly go ahead—"

"But it has to!" said Anna.

"I'm not sure that would be appropriate," said Inara.

"I mean it," said Anna. "Listen, Inara, this is important. People here like a show. They like to be seen in the right places and they like to have money spent on them while they're there. The truth is that most people won't care who's running this place—whether it's Hilde, you, or someone brought in from outside. All they know is they're expecting to be spoiled tonight, and the quickest way to put the Guild out of favor will be to cancel the biggest party on Bethel on the last night of Carnival."

"Sounds convincing to me," said Zoë. "Trust her to know her people."

"All right," said Inara. She sighed. "Someone will have to host—"

Zoë stretched out her legs and, crossing her feet at the ankles, put her boots up on the pretty little table. "Done my job," she said. "Time for you to do yours."

Perhaps it was a mark of how low his expectations were these days, thought Simon, that he was so happy to wake up in his own bed, in this little cabin, feeling properly rested for the first time in days. Perhaps it was a mark that he was coming to terms with the decisions he made, learning to live with them, starting to move on. He looked round the tiny space and thought fleetingly of his apartment back in Capital City. Brand new block of apartments, chic part of town, very desirable. His place had been on the eighth story of the building, with the most incredible view of downtown, and bought outright with the bonuses he made at the end of his first year at the hospital. Quickly, as soon as the line of thinking started, Simon shut it down. He was never going to see the place again—seized along with the rest of his assets, no doubt—and it was no use dwelling on what was lost. He'd made his choices. He'd swapped it all—the money, the outward trappings of success, the reputation, the parental approval—all given up for a living, breathing sister.

The ship was quiet, almost uncannily so. No sound or sight of River, and he tried not to worry. He'd hear right away if she needed him. He made himself tea and went to the infirmary. There were two boxes piled up on the bed. He opened one and realized that someone had been shopping and picked up the supplies he'd asked for. Mal? He guessed so. Simon began to sift through the contents of the open box. Mal, or whoever he'd deputized to perform this job for him, had done a good job. Not missed anything he'd asked for, and not always gone for the cheapest alternative. Simon had complained about that on several occasions. So did Kaylee, for that matter. You got what you paid for, after all. He was putting away the bandages in a cabinet (surely Jayne couldn't snack his way through all these before they next made planetfall), when Book came by.

"Hello son," said the Shepherd. "You get some shuteye?"

"I certainly did," said Simon.

"Good," said Book. He tapped his cheek. "And how's the…?"

"Oh," said Simon, gently touching the affected area. "I'll live, I guess." Just another black eye. Maybe Mal was right and he had one of those faces that asked to be punched.

"Can't ask for much more than that," said Book. "If you're wondering where River is, I left her sitting quietly in the cargo bay. She was drawing."

Simon smiled. "What is it this time?"

"Hot air balloons, of all things," said Book. "I think she saw some in the sky above the city earlier. Beautiful patterns. That girl has real gifts."

"Yes," said Simon. "I know." More—the girl *was* a gift. And drawing meant she was calm. That she was happy. Simon felt his shoulders ease down, ever so slightly.

"So with River peaceful," said Book, "and me here to keep an eye on her, maybe you could join the others at the Guild House?"

"The Guild House?"

"You know," said Book. "Inara's party. You were thinking of joining them, weren't you?" He looked round the infirmary. "Can't spend the rest of Carnival hiding away in here."

"Oh… I'm not sure… I don't really like to leave River, not if I can avoid it…" Simon gave a short laugh. "Last time I left her alone she somehow ended up breaking a casino."

"Hand on heart, son," said Book, "I can promise you that me and that little girl will not be hitting the casinos tonight. I've seen more than enough of Neapolis. And Mal's here too."

"He didn't want to go to Inara's party?" said Simon. And what exactly was going on there? Everyone on this ship seemed to have an opinion on him and Kaylee but nobody seemed to want to talk about Mal and Inara and their weird whatever-the-hell-that-was.

"Hard as this might be to credit, but Mal does not want to go to a party at the Guild House," said Book. "But you really should go." He gave Simon a meaningful look. "Kaylee would be glad to see you there."

"I know…" Simon closed the door of the cabinet and started to empty the second box. He thought about Kaylee and River and where his life was now.

"Something troubling you, son?" The preacher's voice. The man of God. Someone wise, with good ideas about how to conduct yourself. How to live your life.

"Sometimes," said Simon, "I think I make some very bad choices."

"Son," said the Shepherd, quietly, "you don't know what it *means* to make bad choices." A little warmth came into his voice. "You know, while the rest of us were running around causing mayhem, breaking casinos and, well, all the rest of it… While we busy making all kinds of trouble, you were busy saving a young man's life."

"Oh…" So someone else *had* noticed. Someone else had cared. "I… That's nothing, really, I was just doin' my job—"

"Saving a life is never nothing," said Book.

"I… I suppose not."

"Not only is that young man going to be testifying against Jacob Roberts, but I think that when he gets a mite older and looks back on his life and when it all changed, he'll remember the doctor that saved his life. Gave him the chance to turn things around. You made a real difference there, son."

"River's money made the real difference," said Simon, with a smile. Which was fine. Being outclassed by River had been a feature of Simon's life more or less since her arrival. A familiar refrain, through her childhood: *River's walking months before you did… River's talking is way ahead of yours at this age... I see River topped your grades...* Simon stopped himself thinking about his parents. Oh, another line of thought to shut down, and one of the most painful. Better not to think about that. Better to think about River's triumphs. River's happiness.

"That most certainly did not hinder," said Book. "Still, since you seem to be asking for my advice, I'd say that you should try not to be so hard on yourself, Simon. You're not doing so badly out here, you know." He turned to go. "I think I'll see how those drawings of River's are coming along. You get out now, see how Kaylee's doing. That girl deserves some fun. And maybe you might consider the possibility that so do you."

About half an hour later, Book went into the bridge, where he found Mal sitting up-front and ready for take-off.

"You got that boy off the ship?" said Mal.

"Uh-huh," confirmed Book, settling down into the other seat. "Didn't take too much persuading in the end. I told him Kaylee would want to see him."

"Kaylee's a good girl. Deserves a little fun. Not sure how exactly the doc might deliver on that, but Kaylee knows her own business there. What about his sister—she gone on off with him?"

"Nope," said Book. "Seems River's done with parties for the weekend. She's still down in the cargo bay. Though I get the feeling that River wouldn't mind so much where we're taking *Serenity* right now."

"Huh," said Mal. "'Spose that'll have to do. Shall we go?"

"Ready when you are," said Book.

Mal was no Wash, didn't have the magic touch when it came to flying, but *Serenity* was his ship, and he knew well and good how to treat her. Gently, he lifted her up from her spot at Roby Docks, and pointed her northward. The city and its pleasures quickly gave way to barren hinterlands.

"Hard country," said Book, looking out. "Makes for hard folk."

"Maybe," said Mal. "But seems to me that even the hardest know what's right and what's wrong. And if they don't, maybe they need to be told."

"Maybe," said Book, equably.

Serenity continued on her mission. She flew over several small settlements; groups of shacks huddled together set a little way from the mining works. All a long way from Carnival. The fifth of these sad towns was their destination. Mal put *Serenity* down a mile or so away, and together he and the Shepherd made their way into town. A sunset you'd see only in your dreams unfolded ahead of them: burnt orange sky; yellow blaze of the sun sinking behind the black silhouettes of the houses. These poor gorram worlds, thought Mal, they should be full of hope and wonder, and instead the wealth got sucked out and folks here ended up left with nothing but the dust.

They came to the edge of town. *Uncle Nate, Evansville, in the Croker Valley*, Ava had said. Hadn't been too hard to find his face on the Cortex. Drunk and disorderly more often than was good for him. In town, they found the bar where he spent his evenings. Waited for the bar to close and for him to stagger out. Followed him a little way, down into a quiet alley. Came out at him from the darkness.

"Well, as I live and breathe," said Mal, "if it ain't Uncle Nate."

"What?" The man looked glassily at them. Mean-looking little piece of *lè sè*, not anything that anyone would miss. "Who the hell are you two fellas?"

"We're friends of Ava," said Book.

"Ava—?" Her Uncle Nate blinked. "What the hell do you know about Ava?"

"Nice girl," said Mal. "Deserved a damn sight better than a piece of crap like you."

"What?" said Uncle Nate. He looked round, the thought, maybe, coming to him that perhaps he was in more than a little danger.

"There's a special hell," said Book, "for men like you."

"What the hell is this?" said the man. He lurched forward and took a swing at Book, who stepped nimbly out of the way. "Who the hell are you two ruttin' bastards—?"

"Justice," said Mal, and shot him dead.

The town was quiet. Nobody going to come and take a look. Nobody wanting to be next. The two men returned unhindered to their ship. When the cargo bay doors opened, they found River standing there, waiting. "He was not good," she said. Her voice was shaking, but Mal thought he heard a fair amount of approval too. "He was *bad*-bad."

"You got that right, little River," said Mal.

Her eye fell on the Shepherd. "He was not Godly."

"No, River," said Book. "He wasn't. God is just, but…" He sighed. "We live in hope of his mercy."

River turned and slipped off into the darkness. Mal watched her go and then turned to the Shepherd. "You think she knows what we just done here?"

"I can't tell what that little girl knows," Book said. "A lot more about what's going on around her than you'd think. More perhaps than makes me comfortable."

This troubling thought between them, they made their way in silence back to the front of the ship. Mal took *Serenity* up again and pointed her southward. Next to him, the Shepherd sighed, and reached for his bible. What did River call that, now? His symbol.

"Bethel ain't been so much a house of God for you, has it, preacher? More what you might call a den of vice." Mal nodded over at the bible. "How you squarin' that with your good book and your good lord?"

"I'm not sure yet, Mal," said Book, leafing through the pages, looking for… Well, for what? What exactly did he hope to find there? There weren't nothin' there, Mal could tell him that. "All I can say is, I'm trying," said Book. "That's all I can do, every day. Some days, that's all any of us can do." He sighed. "You recall, perhaps, I told you the story of Jacob's Ladder. The bridge between Heaven and Earth."

"I recall. Didn't much like the tale, but seemed no way of stoppin' you tellin' it."

"The promise that God is always present in our lives." Book put down his symbol. "Sometimes he seems a little distant. Sometimes… you got to fall back on faith."

That, to Mal's mind, was a recipe for disappointment, but he liked the Shepherd, and had no desire to kick a man when he was down. So he held his tongue, and let the silence grow between them. *Serenity* soared back over the plains, and, as they came to the edge of the city, they saw the fireworks bursting brightly against the ink of the sky.

"You know," remarked Mal, "past few days, I seen the space docks, the train depot, not a bad little diner, and the sheriff's office. "But those sparklers out there—that's all I seen of Carnival."

Book relaxed back into his seat. "Don't be too disappointed, Mal. In my experience, when you've seen one parade, you've seen 'em all."

In the Guild House, the party was now fully underway. Inara, moving through the rooms with Joseph Liu on her arm, said, "Thank you for being so accommodating about the alteration to our plans."

"Well," said Joseph, "I suppose I *was* planning to come to this party with you anyway. The only difference now is that you're the host..." He laughed. "And I'm hardly disappointed about that."

Inara smiled up at him and Joseph smiled back. No, he was not disappointed with the way that the last couple of days had turned out. Change was coming to Neapolis. Everyone here knew. Jacob Roberts under arrest; Hilde Becker too, and the word was that some fierce-looking representatives from Sihnon would be arriving soon on Bethel to speak to her … This world had been turned upside down, and the rich and powerful of Bethel were falling into line behind the new powers. The sheriff. The Liu family, fortunes on the rise again with the younger generation. Joseph wasn't entirely sure he knew the full story yet, although he had many discreet enquiries underway.

The doors to the salon opened, and two young women came in. One of these, seeing Joseph, lifted her hand to wave. "Oh," he murmured. "My sister's here… Inara, let me introduce you…"

"We've met!" Inara laughed and greeted Anna with a kiss on each cheek. "Your sister is… a remarkable young woman."

Anna smiled. "Joseph thinks I waste my days, Inara. He doesn't know about my… work."

Inara turned to Anna's guest. "Dr. Neilsen," she said. "I'm so glad you decided to come. Simon's here. I'm sure he'll want to say hello…"

She drew the doctor away, leaving Anna and Joseph together.

"You know, Anna," said Joseph, "about your work, as Inara called it…" Zhao had put him in the picture. What had the sheriff said? *Going to draw a veil over this, for your papa and your mama's sake. But maybe she might be persuaded to give up the vigilante business now that the lawmen are back on track.*

"Yes?" said Anna.

"Zhao filled me in."

"Oh," said Anna.

"And I did a little investigating…"

"Did you, Joe?"

"Tracking down investments and so on. It's… quite a decent personal fortune." It was better than that, but then she would have needed funds to be able to buy the house in the country, support the networks out in the little towns, pay the people to help her carry out more… adventurous operations.

"Thank you," said Anna.

"I'm glad to know that your time studying on Osiris wasn't completely wasted."

"I learned a huge amount at that school."

"You know," said Joseph, "you could have come to me…"

"Come to you?"

"About the work you were doing…"

"Ah," said Anna. "I guess… I wanted to keep you out of trouble. You're so *straightlaced*, you know? The acceptable face of the family business."

Joseph laughed out loud. "I'm glad to learn you've not been wasting your time after all!"

"Second children always have more fun," she said. "I'm glad that you're not upset."

"Quite the contrary," he said. "Jacob Roberts arrested on the floor of his own casino. My sister a force for good and not a drunk…"

She tipped her glass at him.

"I'm not even upset that the Wheel was nearly cleaned out last night."

"No," said Anna, with a smile. "You don't need to be upset about that either."

Well, he'd worked that one out when Inara introduced her friends and the little man in the hideous shirt nearly fainted on the spot.

Brother and sister stood together for a while, watching the people, nodding greetings, exchanging small pleasantries. The lights and the music bound them together. Joseph saw Anna's face go suddenly sad and he, in turn, felt tears prickling in his eyes. He knew what she was thinking. If only their mother and father were here… He leaned over to kiss her on the top of her head. "Next year," he said, "we'll open up the house again. We'll host the biggest party—you and me."

"Yes," she said. "Yes. You and me. We'll put on fireworks."

"Anna," he said, "I think you've done that already."

Joseph went to find Inara. As he made his way through the room, people kept stopping him to shake his hand. They all knew, didn't they, that everything had changed? That he was the power now in this town. The one to make your friend. That was a little depressing, if you thought too hard about what it meant. Would they all switch again, should his star start to lose its shine? He'd worry about that when it happened.

Emory Braxton, sporting the finest of silk waistcoats under his considerable jacket, approached and shook his hand hard. "Well, son," he said, "I'm glad to see order has been restored."

"Order, sir?" said Joseph.

Braxton sniffed. "Never did like Jacob Roberts. Cheap. Not a gentleman. As for this place…" He looked round the room. "Something never felt right. Couldn't quite put my finger on it though…" He beamed at Joseph. "That lady of yours tonight though! She'll set things straight here."

"I think she has already."

"You know," said Braxton, "Jacob Roberts was nothing compared to your late father."

"No," said Joseph. "He wasn't."

"Your daddy was always good to me. Helped me out that one time I got myself in a terrible pickle." He laughed at the memory. "I certainly wasn't going to see you lose on the wheel the other night. Not your daddy's son. Hope you don't mind. And let me say, I'm mighty glad to see this fine city of ours in such good hands again. Mighty glad."

He went on his way. Joseph, laughing, found Inara and they stepped out onto the terrace. The fireworks were about to start.

As smoothly as a ship of her provenance could manage, *Serenity* landed again at Roby Docks. River, settling down on her back in a secret place, let her mind reach out to find all the people that she loved best.

First, and most loved, she found Simon, standing on a balcony outside the Guild House, looking tired and bruised but cautiously happy. Beside him stood Kaylee, sparkling in the lamplight. They were holding glasses of champagne. As they drank, the bubbles rose up, making Kaylee laugh, which made Simon look happier. She wished he looked more like that, more often. She wished Kaylee looked more like that, more often… Not yet. They had a way to go yet…

River's mind danced around the party. Wash and Zoë were there too, wrapped around each other, trying their luck at one of the tables, laughing more when they lost than when they won. River lingered for a while. She loved to see them together like this, because nothing lasts forever—not sadness, not grief, not pain, and not joy…

She moved on. At the heart of the party, radiant as the sun, she found Inara, holding court like a new-crowned queen. On her arm was the young man from the casino, smiling with the buoyant air of the king-in-waiting.

River did not care to go in search of Jayne. Left him to his own devices. Consigned him to darkness.

Instead, she let her mind soar beyond the city. She found the girls—her girls, she thought of them, the girls like her, who had been hurt by bad people, with hate and needles and boxes, and saved by good people. She sent them love, blew them kisses. They already had half her fortune—and Book's tithe, too, although only River knew that, and Book knew nothing of her knowledge…

River drew closer to the ship, which, since it contained what she loved best, she now thought of as 'home'. There was Book, sitting alone in his cabin, studying his damaged symbol, thinking over the events of the past few days, trying once again to square the choices that he made in the moment with the ideals he was trying to live up to, humbly contemplating his failures in this respect. River could not help him here. This was a path Book had to walk by himself—in the hope, maybe, that his God would be there when the time came to carry him. Last of all, River found Mal—bad in the Latin, good-bad in the vernacular—sitting in the bridge, feet up, whisky to hand, a man content with how the day had gone, and no need to be anywhere else other than where he was right now.

River let them all go. In her hand, she held a silver coin. "Biggest win ever," she whispered. "Out of the box and off to the ball." Closing her fist around her treasure, she shut her eyes, pillowed her head on the metal grate, and let *Serenity* sing her to sleep.

ABOUT THE AUTHOR

Una McCormack is the author of *The Autobiography of Kathryn Janeway*, *The Autobiography of Mr Spock*, the Star Trek novels *The Lotus Flower* (part of *The Worlds of Star Trek: Deep Space Nine*), *Hollow Men*, *The Never-Ending Sacrifice*, *Brinkmanship*, *The Missing*, *The Fall: The Crimson Shadow*, *Enigma Tales*, and the Doctor Who novels *The King's Dragon*, *The Way Through the Woods*, and *Royal Blood*. She lives in Cambridge, England, with her partner and daughter.

ACKNOWLEDGEMENTS

Thank you to Cat Camacho for letting me achieve a life goal by writing for the 'verse and for always being so much fun. It never feels like work!

Thank you to Max Edwards, best of agents, for taking such good care of me.

My dearest love and thanks to Matthew and Verity, who with good humor and much patience have helped me work steadily throughout lockdown. I love you both so much.

firefly

GENERATIONS

TIM LEBBON

Mal wins an old map in a card game. Ancient and written in impenetrable symbols, the former owner insists it's worthless. Yet River Tam can read it, and says it leads to one of the Arks, legendary ships that brought humans from Earth-that-was to the 'Verse. The salvage potential alone is staggering. But the closer they get to the ancient ship, the more agitated River becomes. She says something is waiting inside, something powerful, and very angry…

TITANBOOKS.COM

firefly

WHAT MAKES US MIGHTY

M. K. ENGLAND

Serenity is bound for Kerry with a hold full of unidentified cargo intended for the duke who rules the planet. He's a genial man charmingly dismissive of his title: liquor flows freely in the duke's court, and there's food and entertainment to win everyone else over. Yet in the town outside the walls, soldiers enforce bloody and merciless order over the townsfolk as the duke lives in luxury. When local dissidents beg the crew for help, there's no choice but to aid them.

For more fantastic fiction, author events,
exclusive excerpts, competitions, limited editions and more

VISIT OUR WEBSITE
titanbooks.com

LIKE US ON FACEBOOK
facebook.com/titanbooks

FOLLOW US ON TWITTER AND INSTAGRAM
@TitanBooks

EMAIL US
readerfeedback@titanemail.com